A PERFECT SCAR
and Other Stories

by Trebor Healey

Lambda Literary Finalist

Foreword by Peter Dubé

ReQueered Tales
Los Angeles • Toronto
2023

A PERFECT SCAR
and Other Stories

by Trebor Healey

Praise for
A PERFECT SCAR
and Other Stories

"Trebor Healey's writing is suffused with the purest emotion, the bravest, funniest tone, and the perfect balance of poetics, daring and charm."
— Joy Nicholson, *The Tribes of Palos Verdes*

"Shows us men and women whose lives have been, or are about to be, forever altered by love ... sharp, empathic, and unforgettable."
— Bernard Cooper, *The Bill from My Father*

"The eleven selections take the reader on far journeys in space and time, from Ireland, the forests of Alaska, and the cobblestone streets of Guanajuato to the streets and saloons of California's post Gold Rush prosperity and San Francisco in the age of AIDS ... pulls the reader in immediately and offers a journey to the distant coasts of emotion."
— Robert Ridinger, *Speaking for Our Lives*

"Trebor Healey is all soul ... The way he stacks sentences vibrates on the page. There's an impressive, experimental range in this short story collection. Trebor Healey uses multiple narrators to bring voice to a variety of human experiences."
— Kirk Read, *How I Learned to Snap*

Also by Trebor Healey

SHORT STORIES

A Perfect Scar (2007)

Eros and Dust (2016)

Falling (2019)

NOVELS

Through It Came Bright Colors (2003)

Faun (2012)

A Horse Named Sorrow (2012)

A PERFECT SCAR
and Other Stories

by Trebor Healey

Table of Contents

Foreword

For over twenty years now, Trebor Healey has been publishing a rich and accomplished body of work across a broad range of genres: novels and short stories (both more realistic and more speculative) and poetry alike. His books have been finalists for, and won, some of queer publishing's most prestigious awards, among them the James Duggins Lambda Literary Award for Mid-Career Novelists, the Violet Quill award for his first novel, and the Publishing Triangle's Ferro-Grumley Award in Fiction, twice. But, however decorated and diverse the man's works may be, they achieve a unique kind of unity in a vibrating network of shared thematic and psychospiritual concerns. And, if I came to Healey's writing a little after its debut, I connected with, and plugged into, that network of meaning very quickly when I did. Moreover, I am just about certain that I am not alone in responding to it so immediately, so viscerally. In fact, I've heard similar reports from friends – readers all – during discussions of Healey's oeuvre many times.

The excitement in my friends' words and voices is part of what leads me to one of my main intuitions about, and great appreciation of, these gorgeous and touching narratives. If Trebor Healey's writing calls out to and connects so deeply with his many readers, it is surely, at least partly because his stories and poems so beautifully embody and perform their moving concerns sentence by sentence, line by line. Trebor's work knows something profound about the human condition and speaks of, and to, it eloquently. These are books that know the power of the need to belong, to feel connected ... to other people, to the world, to everything ... and they understand both the rewards of that connection, and the dangers.

In *The Perfect Scar and Other Stories*, which was first published in 2007, these concerns take on resonant form. Not only does Healey create finely-drawn characters, he creates them in context, and in relation to those contexts. This means he creates engaging, even enmeshing miniature worlds that not only feel real, but that point us back to reality itself. Which is to say, they point us back to relationality because it is such relationships, our connection – heart to heart, mind to mind, body to body – that forms the substrate of the world in these tales. In some stories those connections take the form of community, in others romantic couples or pairs of lovers, and in some it becomes the sheer, driving energy of desire as desire, whether actualized or frustrated. But always it is the longing for connection that reaches back to us as readers, when we reach out.

In the title story, "A Perfect Scar," the darker energy of eros powers the tale. In this compelling narrative, one man's obsession with, and hunger for, a deep connection to another person, reveals such intense feeling's power to shape and mark us in a powerfully concrete metaphor, one that finds echoes, though in other forms, in all of the collection's pieces.

A related iteration of the overwhelming power of the erotic animates the mythologically informed fable, "Faun," in which a boy grows up and develops into an actual satyr, lifted straight out of Greek legend and given a twist. Unsurprisingly, he is baffled by the effect his changed nature has on the networks and communities in which he lives, but is ultimately able to come to self-acceptance and a deeper understanding when he finds another person like him. (An experience almost any queer person will recognize at once.)

The open-ended narrative "Alaska" gives such longing shape in a man's memories of a not "terribly social" writer who came to his small Northern town to take up a teaching job, and with whom he had a transient encounter, only to discover how some experiences, though over, have an impact that never truly comes to an end.

In "A California Kind of Death," another piece, significantly enough, to take its title from a place name, we are reminded that our connection to one another is not only what will get us through life, with all of its tumult, and joy, and suffering, but also what will ultimately hold our hand as we arrive at the very gate of the great darkness that awaits us at its end.

"The Mercy Seat" foregrounds another widely-shared queer person's experience: that of the effects of HIV on both health and networks of intimacy and belonging: on family, and memory, and the way things, both spoken and unspoken, can – like love itself – create enduring meaning.

But whatever the specific sort of longing, the particular hunger for contact, it is some form of that most fundamental human need that is the leitmotif of this collection, so it would be possible to enumerate the manifestations in each of them, but it may be more useful in some ways to step back and consider the pattern they form for a moment. Because, by laying out the many paths taken by longing in so various a range of contexts, Healey gives his readers a kind of map here: a guide to the roads the human heart can, and inevitably does travel – and those are always winding. But the thing about a road is that it isn't just a means to get from one place to another, it is literally the thing that connects one place to another. Roads, or paths, are what join our beginnings and our destinations ... which is to say they are a kind of narrative in themselves. And all of this writer's roads are crossroads: places at which we might change directions, enjoy life-defining exchanges, or come to transformative meetings.

Thus, the return of this collection to print in its new edition is a happy event: a chance for readers everywhere to make such new encounters themselves. A great deal has changed in queer life, culture and politics since 2007, much of it good, some less so and most recently, some downright menacing, so a return to the foundational insight that we are all human, and that being human means being connected, tied together in family, in community, in the vast web of life, is a welcome event. I invite you to rediscover it now in these pages.

You are sure to find the road rewarding. Happy travels everyone, enjoy the trip!

— Peter Dubé
Montreal
May 2022

Peter Dubé is the author, co-author or editor of a dozen books of fiction, non-fiction and poetry. His most recent work, *The Headless Man*, was a finalist for both the A. M. Klein Prize and the ReLit award.

For Sera

Acknowledgements

For their assistance in reading and commenting on this manuscript, I thank Bernard Cooper, Joy Nicholson, Ernest Posey, Greg Herren, Stuart Timmons, Felice Picano and Sera Sacks.

For their generosity, I thank Isaac Cruz, Daniel Kopyc, Horehound Stillpoint, Russell Tuazon, Gerardo Perez and Tin Minh Do (who together inspired the title!), Sera Sacks, and the Morris Graves Foundation.

For their support of my work, I thank Richard Labonté, Kirk Read, Matt Bernstein Sycamore, Michael Rowe, Karl Woelz, Greg Wharton, Ian Philips, Sean Meriwether, Susie Bright, Robert Trachtenberg, Dean Kostos, Eugene Grygo, James C. Johnstone, Aldo Alvarez, Michael Luongo, Jim Eigo, Marshall Moore, Timothy Lambert, Becky Cochrane, Simon Sheppard, Jarrett Walker, Jonathan Dixon, Larry Lesperance, Jim Gladstone, Lawrence Schimel, Ted Gideonse, Rob Williams, Larry Bob Roberts, Patrick Ryan, Matteo Bianchi, Michelle Tea, Clint Catalyst, Darin Klein, Otis Fennell, Winston Leyland, Scott Brassart, Julie K. Trevelyan, Lori Selke, John Patrick, Tom Long, Jay Quinn and Bill Cohen. Special thanks to Sven Davisson for giving this collection a second life.

And, finally, a book is made of everything that's ever happened to one, so I thank all that too.

Beauty has no other origin than the deep wound, different in every case, hidden or visible, which every man has within himself, which he preserves, and into which he withdraws when he wants to escape the world for a fleeting but profound solitude.

— Jean Genet

A Perfect Scar

It always begins with cigarettes. I don't even smoke. I don't even respect smoking. I don't think it's cool. As if what I thought would ever matter with Tran. Smoking is sexy, yes. But cool, no. Sex isn't really cool, either. I found that out, courtesy of Tran. Sexy perhaps, but cool, no. Need is never cool.

It wasn't even about him, really. It rarely is. I got him like religion. Same difference. After all, what's Christianity got to do with Christ? I came up with rationalizations, like all religious types. But in the end, it was about faith. And faith can't be explained. Tran was the man, plain and simple.

What we had in common, in fact, was our religion. And that was it. Catholic Tran. Why is it that so many Catholic cultures breed gangsters like lice? Not that Vietnamese is a Catholic culture anymore than I'm a gangster, but I wasn't reared in Belfast either. Which didn't prevent me from being a drunk. But let's not blame the Irish for that. I was generations removed, and though this tale might whore itself to a handful of stereotypes, they hide as much as they reveal. Homosexuals don't need to be Irish to have drinking problems – that's for sure. But you could say I knew the territory all the same. Had a knack for it.

I could find my way to the corner liquor store blind-folded: At eight a.m. for a newspaper and a cup of coffee; at noon for a sandwich and a six-pack to get me through the afternoon and lay a foundation for an early evening nap that would prime me for club-hopping by ten, which required one more stop for the requisite pint of Gilbeys or Old Crow.

They say it begins with one drink, blah, blah, blah. Sure thing. It began with a cigarette in this case – and it sure didn't end there. Turning it over? The higher power? Tran *was* the higher power.

Tran, his pale, milk-white, hairless skin; the appendectomy scar, so pink and narrow, fine as a crack in a windshield. A perfect scar. What a mess of hair he had on his lithe shins, the only indication at all of the truly earthbound monstrosity that lay coiled at the root of his soul. But his body was all Asian-cliché innocence. I didn't create that idea of purity, but it sure turned me on in depraved criminals. There's no greater aphrodisiac than a full-blown paradox.

I should point out that I despised Tran from the moment I met him. Tran with his low-slung Acura rice-rocket, his black Armani blazers, the gelled hair, the dangling cigarette. Tran was the worse kind of cad; a crook; a ruthless, greedy racketeer who gathered and disposed of people like so much food. But Tran had charm, and more balls than anyone I've ever met, and say what you will, the world parts seas for such a one – and did. Who was I to be the exception?

Tran looked at me with his "What the fuck are you looking at?" glare that first morning in the corner store – his first impression for everyone.

"Excuse me," I softly implored, hoping to defuse his aggression as I handed my fifty cents for a newspaper over the gum rack to Yusef, the cashier.

"Yeah! Sure thing," he half-shouted, his face erupting into a smile as he gathered his newspaper, cell phone, car keys, and wallet off the counter, the cigarette bobbing amid his cackling braggadocio.

Sarcasm? Sincerity?

He walked out and I followed him with my eyes. *Asian trash,* I concluded to myself. Every ethnicity had their trash.

The white variety might be in pickups and trailers; the Mexican might be fat, poorly tattooed, and too-focused on Honda Accord rim accessories; but it was the gangsters that occupied that worst of stereotypes in the Asian community, with their trashy vamp girlfriends and their toy cars and the ever-present cigarettes – like some sorry-ass anachronism from the golden age of Hollywood.

How could I have known (how would it have occurred to me?) that he was sizing me up, and while I wallowed in my inane prejudices, he was downloading the skinny on me.

I'd in fact completely dismissed him by the time I walked out, and so no wonder I was surprised when he addressed me from ten feet up the sidewalk, leaning rakishly against his souped-up car.

"Howdee!" he barked, cigarette dangling – and that smile. I just looked at him, vexed. *What does he want?* It crossed my mind he could be cruising, but I laughed at the thought. He was far too brazen to be a closet queen. "What's your name?" he half-commanded through his manic cheer.

I kept walking, looking perfunctorily over my shoulder. "Ben," I murmured. *He must be selling something.*

He slapped his thigh, but didn't get up. "Like Franklin!" he guffawed. "C-note. Toilet paper. Ha, ha, ha." And he laughed fully and heartily. "Go for a ride?" He told me more than asked me.

"Not today." Maybe he's a Christian or, worse, one of those Cao Dai dudes who worship Victor Hugo. Time to lose the creep.

"It's a good day to die, all that shit. Come on," and he motioned to me with his head. *What the fuck,* I thought, now he's quoting Crazy Horse. *Who is this guy – who laughs at my dismissive rebuffs and then offers me a ride in the guise of a thinly veiled threat?* But by then, without being fully aware of it, I'd stopped and turned and was staring back at his wide grin. God, what a smile – weirdly irresistible, like a clowning little kid's.

He held his keys in the air with his left hand, and gesturing with his head toward the car, he dramatically pressed the key button, releasing the door locks, which clicked resoundingly – an invitation, a casual command. I found myself opening the door as the souped-up Acura engine whined to life, thinking briefly of small children who foolishly climbed into vans with beefy, bald child molesters. And I hadn't even lost a dog – or been offered candy. Not yet anyway.

I climbed in simply because of his smile and his authority and the fact that – to be completely honest – I'd have rather done just about anything than return to my apartment and my bullshit, failing-business Web design work. In a moment of uncanny clarity, somewhere between Ben Franklin and Crazy Horse, I'd intuited an odd feeling that he knew something I needed to know.

He peeled away from the curb and through the yellow that was red by the time he was in the crosswalk. Honking ensued, matched by Tran's guffaws. "Dumb motherfuckers," he said, more affably than anyone I'd ever heard use the term.

I looked at him. Tran wasn't someone I'd take a ride from, nor even talk to. What was I doing in his car? Listening now to some kind of Viet rap. "Ben Franklin!" he announced, cracking up like the joke had been a damn good one and, as he laughed, pulling in front of a BMW ten feet before a red light. How he glared into the rearview mirror.

I disliked his showmanship; I wasn't into his looks or his extortionist's charm. But I had never held my legs so wide, so fervently, before Tran. I was so fixated on watching him enter me. Watching him in general. At liquor stores, the way he charmed Arabs, Indians, blacks, Koreans, rednecks, and racists. Every gesture, every word, perfectly laid down like calligraphy: the way he reached in his pockets; the way he giggled with his head down at jokes I know he hadn't understood, nor did he care to; the way he opened his chest, his arms poised at the back of his hips like a gunslinger, completely confident and yet pistol-less, thus defusing any aggression aimed his way. In bed, it was the same, just more esoteric. The thin alabaster hips, the long blue-black wiry hairs cresting over his cock, the tight knot of his belly button, the goose-pimpled skin of his scrotum bouncing against me – and the scar, the scar that never quite touched me as his hips bounced repeatedly against me. He banged me mercilessly, holding and massaging my wrists with his big veiny hands, all the while sporting that wide grin on his face. Ben Franklin. Lightning.

"Fuck your ass," he'd say sometimes. "Fuck your white faggot ass." And he'd laugh. Laughed like a goddamn monkey – like he did in traffic when he pissed people off. Like how his cock laughed up my ass.

And he'd pay me. Though I told him not to. I didn't understand at first. I told him I wasn't a hustler and that I did it with him because I wanted to. He looked at me, with a different, more sadistic grin then, the one that said: *You dumb motherfucker, you think I don't know a hell of a lot more about what's going on than you ever will? You think this happens because you want it to?*

Then the look would just as quickly soften and he'd revert to his old high-school-chum jibing: "Fuck you, C-note, you need the money." And he'd lay another bill on top of the one he just put down, doubling my take. Then he'd laugh some more.

I worked for him the day I met him, as did we all. Tran was the kind of crook who paid you more and more if he felt you were slipping out of his grasp, or if you didn't want to be paid. He buried people with money, smothered them in it, emasculated them into drooling junkies for it. His money was like his cum: you'd take it and like it. Tran's largesse was like the weather. A simple fact.

Tran ran a gang of Cambodian and South Vietnamese chop-shoppers. Mostly they stole cars, but they weren't above stereo equipment and all number of jewelry and fur coats from the right house in Hillsborough. They only stole from Asians – Chinese mostly – and Tran was a stickler for always trying extortion first and afterward. Thievery was below Tran. A bit of a joke even. He wasn't that into "stuff." He liked to see people's fear. He liked to laugh and smile at things other people couldn't smile at.

I never even knew his name. He used the name Tran, which, in my stupid whiteboy way, I took to be friendly, diminutive – like Tim or Tad. I didn't even know it was, in fact, a last name – and not *his* either. Imagine begging "Smith" to fuck you – when his name was Miller or Ramirez, to boot. "Fuck me, Smith." No wonder he laughed.

That first morning he'd taken me to a Travel Lodge. He'd never even asked. Six blocks from the stale yellow light, Tran had said coolly, "I been watching you," and nodding his head with enthusiasm, he'd winked at me. He was chewing gum now, which made the smile more comic. I felt my cock stir and uncoil. I hadn't really expected that. In fact, I hadn't really been thinking anything, except that I'd made a strange choice. Like I say, it was all about faith.

"Room Two-O-Six," he imparted flatly, pulling suddenly and sharply, and way too quickly, into the motel parking lot. He got out of the car without heading to the office. I watched him climb the stairs, stop, and turn. He held the key chain up again, gave a couple of big car alarm clicks, and let that smile of his spread like sunrise. I got out, and as the door shut closed, I heard that familiar finality of the locks clicking into place.

By the time I pushed open the door to 206, Tran was nude and half-hard, looking casually into the mirror. He turned as I shut the door, swaggered over to me at half-mast, the smile filling the room like the overpowering scent of something musty; something that made my knees weak: dirt and wood and water. He stripped off my clothes and pushed me with one bouncy shove onto the bed. Then he hopped on me and went wild, grinding and licking me.

There was never any need for, nor option of, negotiating

sexually with Tran. It was wholly unnecessary. He took what he wanted and the world gave him change for it. Tran didn't have to ask or worry about stepping over any lines. Tran's sexual movements had the same charm as his smile, and one simply turned one's will over to him. It was odd, how it just happened, without any thought, any consideration of any kind. Tran was in sync and the world rolled with him, plain and simple.

And Tran made me realize how out of sync I was: broke, drunk, aimless, and unhappy. Which made me want him all the more. It wasn't envy so much as a kind of hero worship. A strange hero. But that's what he was in the end. He had the karma, the kryptonite, the confidence ... the *something* that I craved.

Tran put it in slow that first day, smiling, talking "yeah, yeah" as the grin grew. He must have fucked me for a good forty minutes, holding my feet up, fascinated at my "engine," as he called it, which referred to my whole middle: ass, belly, cock, balls.

He chattered about his "business" when he slowed down his long thrusts. It was like he wove me, on and on. Or, rather, I was the loom, and what he wove – I don't know what it was, but I was his tool and he was the craftsman, and all of it tied me to him somehow. And while he wove, he told me things he shouldn't have told strangers.

"Motherfucker told the cops about one of my shops. I broke his nose." And he giggled triumphantly.

"How'd you break his nose?"

"Brass knuckle, martial arts pop. None of these sorry-ass people know how to fight like Asians," he said with disgust. Then the smile filled his face again. "Then I went by his house and played in the yard with his kids."

"And you smiled, right?"

"The whole time. Ha, ha." And he gave me a knowing look, and thrust harder into me a couple of strokes.

"Fuck, Tran, that did it, huh?"

"Fuck yeah. He never did anything after that, but I still

had to pay the cop off. Then he had to work for me for awhile."

"Doing what?" I watched his cock while we conversed. We both watched his cock moving in and out of me.

"Dismantle."

"Cars?"

"Yeah, cars. Dumb-ass motherfucker. He was a mechanic. I should have whipped it out at him. No one doubts my jack!" And he laughed.

That's what he called it. He was proud of it. It was good-sized, a fat seven-and-a-half inches, and uncut, well-marbled with veins that clung to it like vines on a column. Considering he was five-foot, seven, his cock cut quite a figure. Maybe that's what the world recognized in him, unknowingly, subconsciously. The superior, fine-ass cock. And men bought it more than women did. The straight ones especially. They knew who the boss was.

"We're gonna cum now," he finally said, and momentarily we increased our rhythm before long strings of arcing cum shot out of me as he filled me, groaning gutturally. It wasn't until then that I felt the dread of it all. I'd been lost in the fantasy, but once I'd shot I was in that old familiar place of maneuvering an extrication. Lovey-dovey boys who wanted to spend the night were one thing; straight boys who looked offended and startled at what they'd just done were another. But ruthless gangsters who related actionable crimes in detail seemed far more problematic and dicey.

Tran got dressed, smiling at the floor as he methodically buttoned up his white shirt. Then he picked up his coat, dropped something on the TV table, and walked out.

Not long after, I heard the whining rev, the peal. He wasn't going to be giving me a ride home.

I pulled myself together and left. *It was just one of those things,* I figured. A lark. He wasn't queer-identified (that's about the only difference left between gay guys and straight boys these days) by the looks of it, and he'd just had an experience with a stranger who knew nothing about him. Who'd given him a chance to talk, without repercussions. I'd been like an old-school prostitute, down to the C-note he'd left on the table before leaving. I'd gained a story.

I who'd collected stories for a decade. Every boy was a story. And the less you knew about him, the better the story. I should have remembered that as I strolled home. Most boys left their numbers; most boys I dispensed with after the third or fourth date when the story wound into suburban reminiscences and career skills. Most boys filled the lies I told myself with truth fast enough so that the story I was making up didn't ever get the chance to grow into a big fat dragon of projection.

Not Tran. Tran left me nothing but a sore ass and possibly the best fuck I'd ever chanced upon. Some heady seeds for any tale. He'd left a few million of those.

Then came the dreams. Dreams of Tran – Tran as a nice college boy in a V-neck sweater; Tran as an artsy graphic designer, drinking fine wine in a mod glass house on a hill; Tran as a young soldier; Tran as a grease monkey at the body shop two blocks south; Tran slinging coffee; Tran dancing with his shirt off; Tran boxing; Tran wrestling. And at the end of every dream: Tran fucking me to nocturnal emissions that woke me with a start; that made me break a sweat and take a deep long breath like you do when you're scared to death.

I took to lingering at the corner store all the same. I asked Yusef if he'd seen "that Asian dude."

"This isn't an Asian neighborhood," he answered, obtusely.

"I know, but he was here once – he'll come again."

"Lots of people pass through just once," he said. And he looked at me portentously.

I wished I had a picture of him because suddenly this strange guy I'd never look twice at had become a form of epic beauty in my dreams. Tran was suddenly beyond handsome to me. He was more beautiful than any surface could ever hope or have a right to be, because his beauty was not in one or two dimensions, not even three. He was like five dimensions of it. A sort of overpowering beauty – almost vaguely horrific – that made my breath catch. A sort of Möbius strip of lust for him came over me.

I needed a drink.

I told Lou the whole story at the Lucky Bar, lost in my cups. I'd bragged at first, bluffing. "Guy just picked me up, Lou, wanted me something fierce. I can't shake him now. I'm dreaming of him. I want to do him a few more times, get him out of my system."

Lou rolled his eyes: "Fat chance, Ben. Let it go, man. This is bullshit."

"No, no, Tran is not bullshit. I don't know, Lou, it was like the most doubtless hour of my life when I was with him. From the minute I saw that damn smile. I didn't think once for an entire hour. I just knew."

"What the fuck are you talking about – doubtless? Maybe you just need to do crystal more often."

"Ah, shit, Lou, this was real, man. Fuck crystal ..." I could have continued, but I didn't completely understand it myself, and I sure didn't want to cop to any mystical mumbo jumbo around Lou. Lou was a regular guy, a modern man, what I'd been until a week ago. I felt now like someone who'd been abducted by aliens, or met Jim Jones. There was no point in talking about it – they'd just laugh at you. But I knew. We knew. Those who know Jesus are just different.

"Do this for me, Lou. Come out to get *pho* with me."

"You're kidding, right?"

"It's the only way I stand a chance of ever seeing him again."

So Lou came with me to Clement Street, to Pho 87 in the Sunset, and a week later to Pho 99 in Daly City. By the third week, at Nam Dinh, he'd taken to relentlessly telling his prize joke about me and my "Trans-gression," as he called it. "*Pho*-get about it, Ben. We're Tran-spotting."

It wasn't funny. Not to me. Religious people can never take jokes. He was using the Lord's name in vain. The Lord, who not ten minutes later walked in. Who smiled in his huge way when he saw me. Who made my throat catch and heart jump and my whole body click, click, click to attention like the automatic door locks on his Acura. I felt tears well up even.

And he saw me first like Tran would. Tran, who took in a whole room in two seconds flat – he missed nothing. I don't know how I ended up on my feet, but I was moving toward him, though I stopped abruptly when three more wiry Asians in black suits came in on his heels. He barked at them in Vietnamese, turned toward me, re-smiling, and reached out his hand to shake mine, placing his other hand on my shoulder. He winked, said, "Two-O-Six, at ten," let go of my hand, turned his back, and proceeded to his table.

I'd be lying if I didn't admit I was somewhat frightened to meet him again, but it was like being a child entering a swimming pool or a lake: I didn't want to drown, per se, but I was a little fascinated by the danger of it. And as with a full-blown paradox, the full-blown insecurity of danger was erotic too.

Lou was glib. "You've fucking lost it," and he dropped his chopsticks. That was the last time Lou ate *pho*.

The awful things Tran told me were shared as he slid his prodigious jack in and out of me. And how meticulous and fascinated he was as he did so. He took such an interest in entering me, sliding it in this way and that, trying different angles and thrusts, consumed with the various placements of it. He'd literally go for hours, and he'd chatter, telling me things about his business as he moved it around in me. Crime was clearly erotic to Tran. He'd recount beatings and various swindles while he watched himself fuck me into driveling submission.

But he wasn't confessing. I'd been wrong to think I was his whore with the heart of gold. He bragged to me, in fact. So much so that I was never really sure what was true. He'd recount robberies, beatings with his "silver deuce," as he called it – a long stainless steel tube he wielded like jack sticks – and, of course, the endless litany of extortion schemes and threats.

I was as sickened as I was fascinated by the satisfaction he took in scaring people. And I was sickened and fascinated by the satisfaction I took in him – in the fact that he could kill me, but didn't; could abandon me, but didn't; could even love me, but didn't.

He used to just say it to me, during sex, in coffee shops. "I love my cock. You love it?" I did love it, but it wasn't a cheerful, happy kind of love you'd mention as small talk. I loved his cock like one loves one's country, a country like Israel or Bulgaria that costs you something dear for the love of it. Not like here. I loved Tran's cock like I loved Tran's scar. I loved his cock like I loved life. Life with its pain and misery and constant disappointments. Not that his cock ever disappointed. But it was all about the difficulty of allconsuming love. Like for a child. It owned me. I belonged to what I loved. Sure, I loved his cock. But being that I despised him, what did that make my love? And what did that make me?

Tran really had no ethics, no tenderness, nothing humane in him. The smile was the most elaborate charade of the whole picture. I never completely disbelieved it, but I taught myself to with whatever flickering spark of self-preservation I had left in me. I'd seen him turn it on and off. I'd seen how he smiled at V, his girlfriend, when she'd walk into the coffee shop and see us there.

He made up outrageous stories on a dime. "V, this is Ben. He's in computers, imports from Japan, knows all about customs shit." V didn't care, but as it gave me criminal-cred she could dismiss me and not get any ideas. Not that Tran would care. If Tran wanted to fuck boys, V would have to accept that. And it was likely she would. But more important, if Tran chose not to acknowledge it, then it wasn't there, unless Tran decided it was. That was fine with V too. Tran was God: he didn't have to explain the big bang or cop to dark matter unless he wanted to.

V was just like me, really. She had her faith too. I wondered if she watched him the way I did.

Tran was indisputably a good thing to have around. Tran

took care of everything. Tran kept troubles away. Tran intimidated trouble. So much so it didn't even bother with him after awhile. V had immigration troubles that ended abruptly when she met Tran. V had family troubles because her parents didn't want her dating a gangster. Tran lavished them with gifts and planted acquaintances who vouched for his legitimacy. And he smiled of course. Until they loved him. He got a home loan for her old man and found a way to halve the rent on her mother's nail manicurist shop. Tran even ended up getting me a job. A good job. I didn't have an easy time finding work, and Tran just pulled it out of a hat. I never figured it out. The place was one of those dot-com, organic-beer-Fridays, hipster places. Completely white and by the book. How the hell would Tran have an in?

Tran wouldn't tell of course. Just smile. God Tran works in mysterious ways. But he works. Every time.

Tran was charming and Tran was necessary. And Tran was a presumptuous and precocious little punk, who at twenty-nine was riding very high among the crooks of his circles. Too high in many people's opinion. I'd met his little lieutenants, whom he abused. Not a few of them were tight as springs with repressed anger. You could tell they had ideas. Like all too-powerful people, Tran would have to go. The world likes balls, until it doesn't. Steers outlive bulls, just look around.

I realized it one night, as he had my feet planted on the wall behind the bed, violently cumming inside me: *This too, this too is erotic, is what I crave.* That Tran is clearly doomed, a marked man. Like MLK, JFK, Ghandi – riding just too high. And smiling to boot. Unstoppable. It made people want to lay him low, or see him laid low. Crucify him and then make a religion out of him. He was unstoppable all right. You wanted to see him die, and then you'd cry like a baby at the loss. You wanted to be one with Tran, and since it couldn't be – who's fault was that? Not yours. It was his. He'd betrayed you in a sense. He was the hero, the law of nature. And as such, it had become his job to take on the final and most ominous foe.

Go Tran!

Tran was a superhero is what he was. A real-life one with all the compromises that required. There was no Krypton; there was just Saigon, a depraved city that had fallen to the communists and gotten his parents killed. But like Batman, Tran had prevailed, taken to sea with his brothers and the boat people. Found his way here. I don't know if Tran had it figured that way – that he could exact revenge for the ruination of his family and childhood. I doubt it. Tran would have laughed at Batman.

Tran laughed when I told him I'd like to fuck him sometime. No one fucks Tran. I developed a fantasy after that of fucking Tran and throwing him out to be gunned down in the street by Duc, his next-in-command. Go on and kill that which you love.

He got sick fast. He'd run a red light in the Richmond and plowed into a bus. The MRI revealed a tumor the size of a fist in his head. The hospital was hell, loads of people paying homage to fucking "Don Tran," as if he were some mafia kingpin. Hideous flowers and endless gifts, and way too much red and yellow Chinese and Vietnamese good-luck shit. And never a moment with him alone. And having to explain over and over again the lie of who I was. And V: V carrying on crying, helpless without Tran. Tran dies, God dies. I wanted to read her Nietzsche; she was getting on my nerves. I suppose because she reminded me so perfectly of my own sorry state. One day she just vanished. Duc told me she'd seen the writing on the wall, was looking for someone else. Tran had betrayed her, and she got with the program: Death, steps one through twelve.

As he slipped away from us, the smile stayed. A weird comatose smile. It made me doubt my earlier assessments that he was a con man through and through. I don't think Tran ever killed anybody. I don't think he even robbed anyone middle-class or poor. I began to see him as a Robin Hood of sorts. In those last few days, I realized I did love him – in a different way than I'd thought. Fiercely, with all my heart. I admired him for his power, but as it ebbed, there was a sweetness to his fragile, wounded body that was as multi-dimensional as his beauty.

I pulled back the sheet late one night, just me and Duc in the room. Duc nodding off. I didn't care if he saw. I pulled back the sheet and looked at Tran's naked prostrate body, how beautiful he was. How pure and virile. And I held his cock in my hand, felt it limp and heavy, the skin slack and smooth. I wept for how his cock had made me feel safe, and for its simplicity. For what it told of Tran. Always it had been that. His cock was innocent, completely guileless. It was the way I loved him. It was how he showed himself to me. Maybe to V. I don't know.

I kissed his scar then, before holding up my hand in benediction – Catholic to the end. I didn't kiss his cock. It was too holy now. I kissed only his scar, his perfect, ephemeral scar.

And when I went home, I marked myself with him. With a kitchen knife. To let him out, to unwind the weave.

Faun

Gilberto was a beautiful child; the handsomest boy in his preschool, the favorite on Sundays in the boy's choir at St. Agatha's, and the cat's meow wherever mothers and elderly women came upon him – in malls, parks, or outside the carnicería on Cesar Chavez Boulevard.

"Dios mío, qué guapo," they cooed. A pinch on the cheek, a nod to the mother, and off they went with their overstuffed bags and shopping caddies.

"Un ángel," Señora Escobar whispered to the ladies as she stirred the masa for the Christmas tamales.

"O un demonio," Señora Valdez threw in sardonically, before adding tiredly with a sigh, as she gobbled a piece of pork and wrapped up yet another tamale, "– the devil always hides in beauty. Que sonrisa tan bonita." And she looked to heaven.

They all nodded; then giggled and continued, until they got around to "bedroom eyes," and "He'll break hearts – dozens of them!"

"Please, he's just a child," Señora Rubio would protest then, disturbed by their sudden girlishness, and making a note to herself as well to be sure to keep him away from Father Espinoza. But her friends made light of her motherly remonstrations when they saw the furrow on her brow, not only because they felt she was overreacting, but knowing as well that if they were foolish enough to fall silent, they'd be acknowledging the burden of his birth, which would only encourage her, and in no time she'd be wailing about the boy's cursed father – that lowdown dog, Raul.

"Oh, Lupita, you are blest!" they sang out in unison.

It always ended this way in true Catholic fashion: Be grateful, even if the price paid seems a bit high and calls into question the very mercy of the creator himself, which – along with the birds and flowers and children – is really all the capital he's got.

All blessings are mixed blessings, and Gilberto was no different. Beautiful, yes, but a sorrowful reminder of her failed marriage as well; an indomitable spirit who inspired both joy and worry, he was a real handful. But still he was consolation, all things considered, with his playful twinkling eyes and ready smile. All was not lost. So what if he was prone to mischief – he was full of goodwill and, yes, utterly and charmingly beautiful, with his jet-black hair, big brown eyes, and perfect bone structure. What could Lupita do but sigh like the Madonna herself must have done from time to time under the weight of glorious fate?

Still, he worried her. She never knew what news she'd come home to. Not in the least vain, her little boy played fast and loose with his perfection and, what's more, inspired other children to do the same. By the time he was eight, he'd fallen out of four trees, broken both arms, and, more disturbingly, had accidentally set fire to the neighbor's plastic stroller one afternoon with a candle he'd misplaced behind its back wheel while serving an impromptu mass for the other children in the apartment complex. Once ignited, it had burned fast, belching huge plumes of black smoke into the air before melting into a blue plastic heap and dripping off the upper deck of the apartment building, a dozen or so children cheering it on, while the small boy, Alejandro – whom it belonged to – watched indifferently from his apartment window with his sister, Xochil, who appeared wholly unconcerned as she went on filing her long chola fingernails and chatting with her boyfriend on the phone.

It was Gilberto's sister Isabel who had come running out, alerted by the cheers as well as the thick hot gobs of molten blue plastic fouling the gladiolas in her flowerbox. "Que estas haciendo?!" she'd shouted in distress as she ran out, dodging the cascade of cobalt destruction and turning like a saint before the awe of God in some nameless Renaissance painting as she craned her neck to look up toward the top deck from below. When she saw the flames and smoke, and then Gilberto and the children at a safe distance watching and jumping about like monkeys, she muffled the scream rising in her throat so that it came out only as a little chirp, and – always the pragmatist – ran back to grab the hose coiled on the apartment house wall, knowing full well that the entranced children were useless to help her, and the disinterested neighbors were clearly not going to raise a finger, if they even noticed. You'd need more than a fire and smoke to get their attention; you'd need sirens to go with it, and flames actually moving through their bedrooms – flames tall enough to look like intruders.

She and Xochil got into it too, and it wasn't the first time.

"What are you, *stew-pid*?!" Isabel leaned forward, shouting at the Barrajas' window, after hosing down the stroller and berating the laughing children who scattered as she swung the hose about to drive them off. But Xochil only snarled, quipped something to her boyfriend over the phone, stuck out her pierced tongue, and boldly flipped Isabel off.

Isabel thrust her tongue out back at her: "Loser!" She then turned to confront Gilberto who stood dumbfounded on the walkway, waiting and watching, and grabbing his arm hard, Isabel led him down the stairs and into their apartment, sitting him down and giving him a long harangue on "gang behavior," reminding him that the neighborhood children were clearly a bad influence on him and to stay far away from those Barrajas upstairs. They were no good – everyone knew that. "That poor Alejandro – I oughtta call Child Protective

Services. I'm *so sure,* letting the poor little boy's stroller burn like that. Is this a circus? Are we living at a circus, Gilberto?"

He shook his head "no" obediently, eyes attentive – she was fierce when riled up – but considered what she'd just said for a brief moment and thought maybe her assessment was correct. And if so, where were the tigers and elephants? He looked out the window momentarily, half believing he'd see them strolling about the ruined courtyard, with its scarred nopal cacti and patchy lawn. But there was only a mangy, one-eyed tomcat with a bad attitude lurking among the big wheels and fast-food trash.

Calming herself, Isabel set to work sorting out her little brother's latest crime. "Who started the fire, Gilberto?"

His little eight-year-old shoulders and hands went up.

"Did you start the fire, Gil? Tell me." And she said it coolly and firmly. "I didn't," he whispered sheepishly, all but admitting his guilt.

"You can tell me, Gil; I know you didn't mean it." He never did; she knew that much after watching him for five years.

"I didn't start it."

"Well, then tell me how it started. You were there."

"I was saying Mass."

"What?" She raised her voice with incredulity and irritation.

"Mass," he exclaimed, cocking his head like she was stupid. "Don't you know what Mass is?"

"I know what Mass is, Gilberto," she said in her haughty fifteen-year-old know-it-allness. "But I'm not the one on trial here."

"I'm not on trial; I didn't do anything," he said defensively then.

"Well, why were you saying Mass? You're not a priest ..." And then, after a pause, with a smug expression on her face, she added for effect, "– yet," knowing it would inflame him.

"I'll never be a priest!" he exclaimed.

"Looks like you already are one, Gil."

"I only did it because they wouldn't stop bugging me! It

was Pepe – he kept tapping me on the shoulder and saying, 'Bless me, Father,' and 'Mea culpa,' and holding his heart, and going on and on like his mother about how he needed the Eucharist, blah, blah, blah. So I go, 'Fine, you want me to be a priest, I'll be a priest.'"

"Priests don't start fires."

"Yes they do."

"What are you talking about, Gil?!"

"Haven't you ever heard of a candle, Izzy?"

Calming herself, she asked, "Is that what started the fire?"

"The Holy Spirit started it," he said, crossing his arms.

She rolled her eyes. "Then it *was* you. Whose candle was it?"

He beamed.

"Why are you smiling?"

He put his arms up and pumped them. "You just said I'm the Holy Spirit!"

"Oh my god, Gilberto. That's blasphemy. You're *so* grounded."

His face changed to a frown then.

"Why?"

"You just started a fire and claimed to be God – do you know how bad that is?"

"Don't tell Mom."

"What do you mean, *don't tell Mom?* Of course I'm gonna tell Mom. Now where did you get the candle?"

"Xochil gave it to us," he said matter-of-factly. And then pleadingly, "Izzy, don't tell Mom."

"Xochil," Isabel shook her head. "Figures. Loser. I told you not to talk to her."

"She likes me," he said defiantly.

"She's bad news."

"Her boyfriend likes me too," he added smugly.

"He's a gangbanger, Gilberto. Do not talk to him! You hear me!?"

"If you don't tell Mom, I won't talk to him."

"No deals, Gil. I always tell the truth; there's no point

in trying to get me to lie for you." And she moved about the room, straightening things, finally plopping back down on the sofa and putting on her Walkman to get back to her math homework.

Gilberto was on his knees by then in supplication, but she ignored him, his voice drowned out by Selena's, as Isabel's eyes now rested on her problem set in her math book.

Gilberto stood up then, forced his shoulders down with determination, and stomped off, slamming his bedroom door (well, not really *his,* as he shared it with his teenage brother, Ernesto), the crack and whoosh of it bypassing Isabel's headphones and inserting itself noisily right into the middle of Selena's "I Could Fall in Love" like a snare drum interlude.

That was the first and last time he played at priest.

It *really* wasn't his fault as he saw it. It was his mother Lupita's, always going on and on about the priesthood so that almost everyone knew and all the children teased him about it endlessly until he couldn't stand it anymore. He'd only aimed to take arms against a sea of troubles by calling a Mass – finally giving them all what they wanted. And look what happens!

He was resolved now not only to avoid the priesthood at all costs, which he'd pretty much decided from the start, but he suddenly wanted never to set foot in a church again either. The church and all that followed in its ubiquitous wake always seemed to portend some kind of trouble. Sure he'd gazed obliviously at the stained-glass windows and how the sun came through them, making pretty kaleidoscopes and puzzles all over the worn red carpet in the aisle; and, certainly, he'd always got a thrill when the bells rang and the priest held the wafer up to the sun. It was true, as well, that he'd always yearned for his very own monstrance, since the day he'd first set eyes on one, and that Our Lady of Guadalupe, who presided over the altar in her cocoon of sunlight, looked and acted uncannily like his dear mother, Lupita. But once the congregation stood up and started talking and reading from that book – and singing those lousy songs – and standing and sitting and genuflecting, he couldn't help but squirm and crawl around, and it usually got him a well-aimed crack from Lupita, or at least a good number of dirty stares from the sanctimonious throng surrounding him.

And now this.

Lupita had had it out with him just as soon as she got home from work, relieving dutiful Isabel, who ran off to see a movie with her girl pals, Esmeralda and Donna.

"Dios mío," his mother exclaimed, moving her fork around through her beans and rice. "Do you want everyone to think you're some kind of demonio? Huh? You'll go to Mass like you've always gone to Mass; and when you grow up, you'll go to seminary."

"I will not!" And he thrust his fork like a flag into his sweet potato and crossed his arms.

Lupita was taken aback, but as Gilberto had proven more or less resistant to the faith from the start – regardless of her dreams and plans for him – she chalked it up to his little soul's wrestling with the angel. And it appeared to be quite a contest. An aficionado of dinosaurs, guns, and fire – like his brothers before him – Gilberto had never been attracted to gentle pursuits – other than his singing – and when she'd first suggested the priesthood to him as a vocation, he'd giggled and said, "No, Mama, I don't like priests. They're foolish." Precocious child, and not a day over five when he'd said it – with a big grin on his face to boot. She'd cuffed him on the back of the neck, but he'd laughed at that too.

Later, after Mass, she'd ventured to ask: "Why do you think so little of priests, Gilberto?"

"Oh, Mama, they're always acting like they know everything."

"Well, they know quite a bit."

"I don't think so, Mama; I don't think they know anything. I think they're guessing and the teacher told me not to guess the answers on exams."

"Life isn't an exam, Gilberto; it's a mystery."

He'd looked at her and stopped speaking then, giving her

one of his distant, old-soul looks which came over him from time to time, and which vaguely disturbed her. Was he listening, giving up on her, or in some odd way communicating with her in a language all his own? Hard to tell. An odd child, with his angelic looks and strange, knowing expressions. Maybe he *was* a demon. An angel. A demon. An angel. Bright, certainly. But that could go either way. A blessing or a curse – she could never quite tell.

Lupita sighed, holding her fork in midair, and wondered: *Sure it was arson, but he'd been playing at priest, even as he denied any interest in a vocation, and that had fate written all over it.* Wrestling with the angel. "Gilberto, my padrito," she said decisively.

But his brow was scrunched and firm. He'd had it. He was adamant about so little. Such a good-natured boy, well-intentioned and affectionate. Neither Lupita nor Isabel could remain angry with him for long, if at all, with that angelic face, his innate goodness and sincerity. He was her consolation, the bright little gift whose fate would redeem her own, who had greatness just glowing in him – she could feel it, she could, sometimes so strong that she blessed herself in his presence, simply overwhelmed by his vibrant little spirit – and it was her job to help him realize his destiny, for his sake as well as for her own. "Isabel is right," she resolved. "The children around here will drag you down." And so the decision was made. From then on, he would not be allowed to play with the other children in the complex. He was to stay inside and study.

"But I like the other children, Mama," he whimpered.

"Love them; don't like them. You are my priest, Gilberto. You are *in* the world not *of* it."

Gilberto was firm, if more politic, in his response this time. "I don't want to be a priest," he pouted – and then defiantly: "I want to be Cesar Chavez!" Another of his strange pronouncements. Not that Señora Rubio didn't approve of such a hero, but her parents had worked too hard and suffered too much in escaping the fields only to have their grandchild return to them.

"After the seminary," she'd answered back sternly.

"But, Mama, priests are foolish."

So much for politic. But if he wasn't, she still could be: "It is a sin, Gil, to call someone a fool. We mustn't judge others. Cesar Chavez liked priests." He was a third-grader now, and she wouldn't swat him.

He nodded his head back and forth slowly then, and something quivered through the ether, like the room was a TV screen losing focus for a brief second. He went back to eating then, and having meted out her discipline, half-hearted as it had been, she crossed herself impulsively, as if to protect them both. But, for the first time, in that moment, Lupita began to truly entertain the possibility that Gilberto really wasn't going to be a priest. Well, next best thing then, she quickly sidestepped – a lawyer. Lawyers *were* priests in a way, especially in America where they were often more necessary and could provide more consolation in the form of hard cash and a good living than any priest could ever hope to provide. Ah, but she was growing cynical. Perhaps she was falling into the sin of despair. Dangerous ground.

Or was it just lucidity?

She looked hard at him then as he began to scoop up the fiery orange innards of his sweet potato. None of her other children had so mystified her. Then again, none of the others had been conjured up to redeem anything.

Lupita and Raul had conceived their last child specifically in order to save their marriage – or Lupita had anyway. They hadn't slept together in years, and Lupita could only assume there were other women, when she'd finally made up her mind and bought the red lace dress and white pumps for her cousin Magdalena's daughter's Quinceañera. She felt fifteen again herself as she squirmed into it. *God, what a gut I've put on*, she thought as she looked at herself, alarmed. But it was nothing a girdle couldn't contain for an afternoon party in the backyard. All the more reason to push the seduction routine with the pedal to the metal. It would get her out of the straitjacket of female comeliness all the sooner.

And even if Raul's first drunken question when he saw it on the hanger the night before the party was, "Lupita, are you cheating on me? Who's gonna be at this party I don't know about?" she was not disheartened.

She didn't answer him directly, nor curtly with her head turned aside like she'd been answering most of his questions the past few years. Instead, she sashayed over to him and, with all her courage, blurted it out: "A man among men, Raul Rubio."

He'd burst out laughing and pushed her aside as her cheeks flushed with shame, red as the dress that hung on the door in all its nakedness and beauty, a metaphor for the mockery he'd made of their blessed matrimony.

She had her doubts then, certainly, and she entertained them at her leisure, as he soon fell fast asleep and began loudly snoring just moments after negotiating his way past her and flopping down on their wasteland of a marriage bed.

Father Espinoza had sounded so certain. "I've see it a thousand times. The Lord blesses a marriage through its children. You've been selfish, Lupita, denying the Lord his due, and it has caused your husband to wander. If you want to save your marriage, you know what you have to do."

"I am willing, Father; I have always been willing. I'm a good wife. He just stopped approaching me. It's he, not me, who wants no more children."

"Did you not read Genesis, my dear? Did Adam go digging about for carrots and turnips? Did he climb trees looking for mangoes and bananas? No, Lupita, he did nothing of the sort. Men are like lions. Adam did nothing at all until she brought him an apple. Bring him an apple, my dear, and save your family."

"But, Father, what Eve did was wrong ..."

"My child, we are fallen, and we have to play by the rules of the fallen. You'll be lifted up in the end. But until that time, you need to tend to what's left of your garden."

She thought of the dirt and nopales in their backyard, ruined by Francisco, their rambunctious pit bull. Father Espinoza's logic sounded a bit confused to Lupita, but, then again, wisdom often was confusing, and whether his interpretation was right or wrong, anyone knew that seducing your husband was an effective means of keeping him around the house. That part she got. And keeping him around the house was necessary for the raising of the children, for security and money, for fixing the roof – for innumerable things really.

"A child softens the heart of the cruelest man," Father Espinoza had concluded when their little chat at the rectory was done. "A child is the flower in a barren garden, mark my words."

So there she was in the fecund backyard of Magdalena's, with its banana trees spraying out of the ground like bouquets of lilies and its huge swaths of bougainvillea spilling over the fence like sweet gooey raspberries out of a tart. The little maraschino rolling about on the plate would be Lupita, dressed to the nines, all in red, and trying to keep an eye on Raul, who was putting back tequila shots and joking with his homies, completely oblivious to her charms. All the others noticed though. Lupita wasn't the kind to dress like that, and she stood out like, well, like a sore thumb – blood-red and swollen with garishness.

Halfway through the party the entire plan was more or less backfiring as rumors threaded round and round the party like a web that would eventually ensnare and paralyze them all, spinning out at warp speed and telling a whole other tale. Such are the best-laid plans of mice and men. And lonely wives. "She's finally left him; I'm sure of it," Señora Valdez jabbered to her sister, Hilda. "Well, she's been seeing Father Espinoza," Hilda responded before walking away. *Meaning what?* Señora Valdez wondered. One generally didn't worry about one's wife or daughter around Espinoza. But what was going on? Lupita hadn't looked so good in forever – come to think of it, she hadn't really looked good *at all* since she'd started having babies. She'd been a pretty girl, but pretty in a Catholic schoolgirl sort of way – sans makeup, but athletic, with good coloring: a fresh, energetic girl in her checkered blue parochial school skirt and white blouse. She was naturally beautiful, with small breasts and small hips, but by middle age that kind of subtle, youthful beauty is easily overlooked or forgotten. She'd certainly never been a seductress by any stretch, and now look at her. Come to think of it, Señora Valdez had *never* seen Lupita in red, let alone orange or pink, and certainly never in lace.

The ladies began to orbit and close in around Lupita, unsatisfied by the rumors they themselves had hatched – swearing of course to one another as they spun their fictions that theirs was the God's honest truth. Since they all behaved this way, no one believed anything the other said until the actual subject of all the extrapolations was herself cornered and made to confess. A telenovela was what it was, and my how sweet when one came to life outside the little box in your living room and began buying dresses, sleeping with priests, and throwing the whole community into a tizzy.

A most unlikely protagonist for such a tale, Lupita thus made an even more intriguing character and so drove the speculation up to a fever pitch. After all, she had always been one of those desexualized mothers. When she had had Oscar – who was already twelve, and just now bumbling his way through a not very graceful flirtation with the party's honoree, Elena – Lupita had turned to wearing skirts, which were really more like aprons, complemented by those ubiquitous and unfashionable tourist T-shirts she got from the Korean store, where they sold them three for ten dollars, with messages like "Beverly Hills," "California," "Polo," etc. She didn't care what they said; she just picked them by color to go with her skirts. Her children kept her too busy to think about or afford nice outfits, for little Ernesto followed a year after Oscar, and then came Julia, and finally Isabel, who nearly killed her, barreling out of her womb at eleven pounds and rupturing her, as well as giving her a nasty blood clot in the left leg that had required emergency surgery and a visit from the doctor while she recuperated.

"I think it would be wise not to get pregnant again, Señora Rubio; you may not survive. I can write you a prescription for birth control." She'd glared, then crossed herself. She'd have none of that.

She threw her lot in with the rhythm method after a consultation with Father Espinoza, and between that, repeated novenas, and her husband's growing alcoholism, she'd run the ovulation gauntlet for six years without incident. Raul remained the wild card in the whole setup, however, since he cared little for any method, other than reach-for-grab-hold-twist-off-the-top-and-guzzle-guzzle-belch-laugh. Ah, but the mixed blessings of booze did indeed prove merciful in their way, for Raul was easy to dodge when he came home drunk and horny – for Lupita it required little more than out-hop-scotching a hippo. On the rare occasions when she couldn't fend him off, the alcohol itself often provided birth control services, with Raul dozing off midcoitus. But he'd wake up morose and angry with her whenever she denied him, and they'd end up fighting and griping for days on end, so that within a few years, their marriage bed groaned, fell forward like a drunk, and died a pathetic death.

She wouldn't be the first woman to revive it with a red dress either, and though it didn't go quite as planned, it went, and when she walked him staggering home five hours later, after a lot of cajoling, as the ranchero music reached full decibel and the LAPD appeared – thanks to the three shots fired into the air for sweet Elena's now official and sacramental ripeness – she did finally seduce him. It took the effort of a saint (Espinoza said it wouldn't be easy) to keep him hard long enough to deliver the goods – and made her feel all the while like one of Lot's daughters (sex should not be so complicated or unpleasant) – but deliver he did, and thusly was conceived little Gilberto.

She beamed when she missed her first period, and when she began to show, she was downright sunny, nipping Raul on the drunken cheek as he leaned over his morning oatmeal, heading off for another Sunday's gambling at the track, which he'd decided was the only hope for them now that "she" was bringing another child into the house.

"*We*, Raul. Nosotros!" she proclaimed proudly, feeling the entire community of saints, the blessed mother – even the cardinals in the Vatican and all the substantial real estate holdings of the Church of Rome – backing her up. She figured he'd just need some time to come around. Men were that way. *Poor Eve*, she thought, *I wonder how long she had to badger him with that apple?*

Raul looked at her, surly, irritated, and hungover. He had always been a decent provider, a functional alcoholic who managed to hold down two jobs – as a janitor *and* a baker. Lupita had never seen him complain as much as he'd been doing during this pregnancy, but she had faith in Father Espinoza's holy prescription and counted on young Gilberto to not only save the marriage but force her husband to give up the drink and gambling – and find a third job too.

Instead he gave up the first two and moved in with a woman in PicoUnion to Lupita's dismay – "A woman," he barked, whom he'd been "seeing for several years – and who would never burden him with children!" But he did take Francisco, the pit bull, whose days were numbered anyway, having just three weeks prior tackled the mail carrier to the ground and shredded Señor Torero's latest issue of *Playboy* in the process, as it had been the postman's weapon of choice in desperately trying to fend off the canine brute.

Lupita had been too despondent to answer the notices left by Animal Control, thinking each time they knocked on the door that it was Raul, contrite.

She wept the tale to Father Espinoza, but all he could offer was, "Be patient. After that, well, sometimes a child is consolation for a bad marriage." An answer for everything. Thank God for the church.

She'd see her faith to the bitter end, though – she knew that about herself – and by the eighth month, she'd become convinced her child would be a priest, even dreamed it the night before his birth; shouted "Mi padre, mi padre, mi padrito! Gracias, Jesus Christo," as she clutched the nurse's hand during labor, and out popped her little angel.

Well, sort of.

The doctor looked horrified. He'd never seen an infant with chin whiskers – why they even curled into a little spike. But he collected himself and rationalized it really wasn't so different from other children who were born with hair on their backs, or on their arms and legs. "Lanugo hair" they called it. There were only five or six whiskers besides, and sure enough, like other cases of lanugo hair, they all fell off his chin after the first week. Lupita never thought twice about it, and the doctor never mentioned that he'd never seen such a case before. In all other aspects, the baby was perfectly healthy and normal, so the doctor didn't even bother writing it up in his chart, chalking it up to the usual anomalies of medical science.

With Raul gone, Lupita was in a major bind financially – the odd tailoring and day care work she'd previously gotten by on to supplement her husband's income and still tend to the children would no longer cut it. They lost the house, which they were only renting anyway, by the time Gilberto was a year old. They'd only held onto it because Raul's wages were being garnished at the bakery for child support. But then he suddenly vanished with "the woman" – Mexico it was rumored – and the family was forced to move into a two-bedroom unit (boys in one room; girls in the other) in one of those ubiquitous gargantuan stucco apartment houses that blight the LA landscape, while Lupita herself went to work downtown at a hotel, housekeeping, at wages so paltry that they had to be extremely frugal with food and clothes, and forego health care altogether.

Thus, Gilberto's formative, early years went by in a blaze, with Isabel – once she'd reached middle school – bearing the brunt of the day care and reporting on his shenanigans over dinner, when and if Lupita could get home at a decent enough hour to even dine with her family. And *shenanigans* was the word for it, whether it was the fiery chariots of the Barrajas, or the endless injuries courtesy of trees, parked cars, or other inanimate objects that Gilberto insisted on tangling with. Lupita took a second job as an office building janitor just to pay for all the casts and stitches.

They were hard years, but Señora Rubio counted her blessings and thanked the Lord for her other children's filial piety – they'd helped out, not only with caring for Gilberto, but with the bills. Oscar joined the Marines at seventeen and was able to send some money home, and Ernesto was a regular jack-of-all-trades, working construction, with an aptitude for plumbing, electrical work, and auto body and engine repair. Why, he'd bought three cars already that he'd refurbished, turned around, and sold. And he had the crisp 100-dollar bills all stacked up neatly as he handed them to Lupita to prove it.

Even Gilberto was making money by the time he was twelve, doing homework up at Xochil's while Jose visited and Isabel was away at soccer practice.

"Why are they paying you to do your homework in their kitchen, Gil?" Isabel asked suspiciously, when she caught him scurrying down the stairs one afternoon when practice had been cut short due to rain.

"I don't know – they like me."

"What are they doing while you're in the kitchen?"

"I don't know." And he hunched his shoulders. "Sleeping, I guess. I think I'm like the guard dog. They don't talk to me; they just go right into the bedroom the minute I arrive."

"The guard dog?" And then she was up the stairs and banging on the Barrajas' door. A cacophony of obscene calo filled the air, until it all abruptly ended with a slammed door and a "Same to you, loser!" courtesy of Isabel. And that was the end of Gilberto's paycheck.

Not long afterward, his lighthearted youth came to a

similarly screeching halt.

You could say he soured like all children do in time. He grew sullen and moody in middle school, his mischief smothered under the weight of hormones. He was dressing in black, but not the black of a clergyman. Lupita still held to her faith in his destined greatness, and watched to see what heroes he emulated. Fortunately he had no interest in the local thugs and drug dealers, but the priesthood had become something he wouldn't even discuss, and Cesar Chavez had become a boulevard, then a holiday, and finally a stamp. At least Gilberto had not gone over to Che like so many of the other teenagers. Gil, for his part, thought Che overly moralistic, like an amped-up cigar-smoking version of Isabel. There just didn't seem to be much fun to a revolutionary's brand of mischief. Che wanted to set the world right just like a priest – all that harsh communist crap was uncool to Gil even if it did empower the people and put the gringos on notice. Che, of course, would never become a boulevard or a stamp, you could say that for him; he'd just become a T-shirt.

His mother was grateful for this small bit of sense in her youngest son, if not for his wardrobe and sudden surliness. He may have disappointed her by attempting to sidestep the priesthood for Cesar Chavez, but choosing Che would have been an affront to her faith and her politics. Though she, like many Latinas, was torn of late. Oscar was in Iraq already and Ernesto was at Camp Pendleton, getting ready to ship out. She was getting a bit suspicious of George Bush's righteous war. She'd trusted the man for his Spanish and his love of Jesus, but she'd trusted her husband for those things, too, and what had come of that? What if she lost both her sons? Well, she had her daughters, Isabel and Julia, who already had two niños between them.

And she had Gilberto.

A boy so pretty should never go to war. And she'd see to it that he didn't. If he wasn't heading to the seminary, he was still undoubtedly college material. Or had been until the last semester when he came home with several Cs. Concerned, Lupita – still with her sights set on law school for her youngest son – harangued him to get serious and start paying attention to his grades. She'd resigned herself to the notion that law was good enough – for whether it was canonical law, corporate law, labor law, estate law, or even personal injury law, as an attorney, you were a high priest regardless. Not an ounce of work with your hands, just the indulgent exercise of the mind. She was getting tired – how her back ached now when she flipped the hotel mattresses and pushed the cart that grew heavier each year, loaded down with more and more junk: soaps, conditioners and – instead of mints – whole boxes of chocolates, fruit baskets – even complimentary slippers and several dozen ten-pound dumbbells for quick morning workouts by the bed. She was tired, and she wanted to sit with him in his big house in Arcadia some day, with nothing to do but knit and rock babies back and forth in their bassinettes. She'd always loved Arcadia, which, though expensive, was certainly not full of the dream houses of San Marino or Pasadena, where Gil could easily end up if he completed his law degree. But Arcadia was where she'd first met Raul; where he'd taken her to Santa Anita to bet on the horses. She'd felt glamorous and special, liberated from the mean streets of the barrio, free and running as the thoroughbreds that pounded the turf and emptied Raul's pockets. But why on earth was she suddenly thinking of Raul? Deadbeat Raul. And yet her heart was suddenly squeezed by the memories.

She'd collect herself, realizing that, nostalgia or no, Gilberto's slipping grades would derail any hopes of Arcadia, let alone Montebello. Once he'd turned thirteen that semester, everything had gone sour. Perhaps it was the bad luck of old "thirteen." Once he was fourteen, she reassured herself – just eight months away – his luck would change and he'd straighten out again. She chalked it up to puberty, which was hard on even the most good-natured of children. Her son was an angel after all – imagine how difficult it must be to be pulled down into the flesh and its desires from such a high perch.

But why then did he love Magic Mountain so much?

Ernesto and Oscar had gotten in the habit of taking him there when they were around, and no one loved freefall better than Gil. Well, hormones. For some, puberty was hellish. Whatever it takes to get through it, you can't begrudge the child his amusements.

But it just got worse and worse, and she really had not expected it to go so roughly for Gilberto. Oscar and Ernesto had sailed through, morphing into men slowly, like the seasons with their shoots and leaves – a charming process really. Not Gilberto. It came upon him fiercely, and of a sudden, like a flash flood. No grace to it at all. And she'd been wrong about fourteen. His eyes deepened as the fateful day approached; his brows grew more pronounced. One morning he woke up with a five o'clock shadow. Shocked, she rooted around for one of Ernesto's razors and had to teach Gil how to use it, embarrassing him considerably. The other boys had learned themselves hair by hair, starting with peach fuzz and learning how to navigate the upper lip, then later the chin, and finally the cheeks and neck. No such gradual learning curve for Gilberto. He woke up fully formed.

Perhaps he was ill? Of course she had no health insurance and he wasn't in pain, so she put the consideration aside for the time being, like all the other women at work did, though some lost children to viruses in the process, and babies to all manner of mysterious ailments. She worried all day as she made beds and cleaned toilets that he had some sort of glandular problem and would be dead when she got home.

But he was anything but dead. In fact, he was disturbingly alive. It was like coming home to a wild animal in the house. She approached the door nervously, confused by her feelings. She had to come to terms with the fact that he'd changed profoundly. He was no longer beautiful in that angelic way she'd grown accustomed to, even if it had been coupled with a fair amount of mischief. And it wasn't as if he'd lost his beauty either. No, it had simply shifted from angelic to worldly – animal, obscene. Señora Rubio had seen this happen to girls, their hips swelling so they could barely fit in chairs, their breasts blowing up like balloons, until there was nothing to be done about it but gain weight to stave off the lustful whistles, hands, and other more dangerous parts of men, and so save your soul, or at least your peace of mind.

Gilberto had become stunningly handsome, dangerously so. She found herself sometimes even nervous around him now, while doing dishes or serving his beans and rice for dinner. Her own son – imagine. She broke out in a sweat; she thought of her husband Raul, more and more – the good old days at the track when he had kissed her and her heart had beat to the rhythm of the horses thundering by, obliterating everything in the urgency of the animal moment. She considered dating. She felt things churning in her. Maybe she needed a hysterectomy. Another child?

She'd stop what she was doing then, excuse herself, and go to the bathroom, where she'd look in the mirror to ground herself. "My god, I'm a grown woman," she'd whisper, though she felt suddenly like she was sixteen again. Her nipples were coming alive; her tongue ran back and forth across the inside of her lips; her womb pulsed with heat. Eventually she'd get disgusted with herself and go get her rosary.

One morning she woke up full of dread and was absolutely certain he'd be getting – not one – but several girls pregnant, and by no fault of his own. *It may have already happened,* she thought with a start. And she couldn't fault whatever hapless females were involved either. For a beauty like Gilberto's, it was simply the way of the world. She had dreaded this day. Her other children were average looking and had all successfully run the gauntlet of high school romances – all they'd needed were reminders and curfews and a few well-placed threats about supporting a child. But such admonitions seemed pointless in the face of what Gilberto had become. What on earth was happening? After all, she had seen angelic children remain soft, grow tender and kindly – priestly even – as they became men. No such luck with Gilberto. He was a beautiful animal now, and it was just the way of the world that beautiful animals coupled, and that children came of it. Well, she liked children. She'd raise them even. She crossed herself. *Please, Lord, do not curse me with an entire generation of such earthly beauty. I'm an old, tired woman, and I have neither the resources nor the constitution to rear such a brood.*

But it was not only Señora Rubio who was disturbed by the changes that came over Gilberto that year, but also the boy himself. The hair that sprouted suddenly on his face; the overnight increase in size of his chocolate-brown nipples, and the hair that grew now like sparse grass atop his sternum; the way it flowered in his armpits and spilled like bougainvillea over his genitals. The sudden length and girth of his manhood astounded him – it looked like something that belonged in a butcher's shop; and his balls were now the size of plums when a month before they'd been like little kumquats. He'd been thirteen one day and then the next it was as if he were twenty-two.

He got a certain mileage from the other boys out of his facial hair and the fact that he was leading the pack in the adolescent race toward manhood, which when you're fourteen appears to be supercool, though by thirty, when you're balder than an octogenarian, it's a drag. But that's another story.

When Gilberto peed in the bushes or at the urinal, the other boys would sneak a peak and then later whisper among themselves. "It's like a man's ... it's ... *actually,* it's more like a horse's (dropped jaws) ... he's not like us."

Then there were his legs. Not a horse's at all. The hair was thick and wooly and covered them now like a black retriever's fur, so that in several places he had to look for the skin. At first he tried to shave off the hair, but the razors his mother had bought for his face (and how embarrassing to have your mother dragging you around Rite Aid in search of puberty management devices – where the hell was his father? In Nayarit, last they'd heard, with a whore named Consuela. Ah, but they called every woman who ran off with another woman's husband a whore. Who could say who she really was?) clogged and dulled with just one swipe.

He stopped wearing shorts and got barbers' shears with the money he stole from his mother's purse and began buzzing off the feral growth, sometimes twice a day, it grew so rapidly. Fortunately, he didn't have to change or shower for PE class at his school, so it was his secret for the time being.

He'd never been ashamed before. He'd always been the one everybody fawned over. No longer. Now they stared, blushed, or crossed the street. Mothers eyed him as a threat to their daughters' virginity. Girls got tongue-tied and grew red with modesty. Little children longed for his power and stared, wondering, at him. Men mostly grinned and chuckled: "Good luck, muchacho; keep it in your pants." The few womanizing cads treated him brusquely, bumped him, kept him on notice that the local pussy was theirs. In fact, they often went straight after it whenever they chanced a sighting of him. *What was that? Insecurity?* Gilberto made people horny. Not as an object, like others would, but as a sort of force of nature – like the sun inspires a walk, or the rain a cup of tea.

The local gangbangers began to notice him and vied for his attention in the way of thugs – through threats, kindnesses, comradery, and the blunt and unimaginative rationale of fate. But he was known as a student type, something of a mama's boy, and his brothers were in the military besides, which made him, if not sacred, worthy of a begrudging second thought. And of course there was Jose, Xochil's beau, who, though he'd long ago been carted off to prison for armed robbery and aggravated assault, still offered a kind of protection. One of a number of exiled "heroes," Jose still had clout that trickled like a stream slowly and obstinately back to the old neighborhood and the ugly stucco behemoth where lived his love, Xochil, and where a small boy once sat in the next room and through some odd quality made the sex with Xochil like nothing he'd ever known, certainly not the throwaway orgasmic releases he'd grown dependent on in the big house. "Something about that homey," the gangbangers would caddishly drop from their tongues, loitering on street corners malignantly. "I wouldn't fuck with him. You ever seen his legs?"

Perhaps it was the boys then of the Eastside Locos who started the rumor that he was a chupacabra, that Mexican legendary creature feared and loathed by campesinos from Nuevo Laredo to Tierra del Fuego for its livestock-killing ways. Though some claimed the chupacabra originated in Puerto Rico, the telltale signs and sightings were the same. Nothing less than the Latino bigfoot, the chupacabra was vampiric and alien-like, with big eyes and long, sharp teeth that it drove into the benign and defenseless necks of cattle, sheep, pigs – and of course goats, the brutal murder of which gave it its name. Like Gilberto, it too had coarse hair on its legs – and its ears were pointed, another similarity with Gilberto, which was why he now kept his ears well hidden under his black knit cap.

At first, he didn't mind such rumors. To be left alone by the recruiting gangsters of the barrio was no small blessing, even if you still could end up caught in their crossfire, your social life curtailed and proscribed by their terror. Such was the 'hood. But Gilberto didn't have much of a social life anyway, as between his mother's overprotectiveness and insistence on his studies and his own anxieties born of his recent physical transmutations, he preferred to stay in and surf the Web and play video games, which was more and more his primary means of social interaction. He Googled endlessly through the medical encyclopedias seeking explanations for his hirsute legs and pointed ears, but to no avail. He'd searched the chupacabra sites, of course, and had assured himself of the impossibility of that relationship. They were small creatures, reptilian really, hunched over, with huge black bat wings and long reptilian chicken-like feet. And though it was true that his own feet were causing him concern, as they were morphing as well, they weren't growing scaly or clawed. If anything, they were shriveling up into clubfeet, growing horny and calloused, a regular case study in rampant runaway bunionry. But they were causing him no pain and actually allowed him to walk faster, which seemed counterintuitive, but there it was.

At school, he'd become lonely and lurkish, hooded or with his knit cap pulled close down upon his eyes. Not that strange really, just another Columbine whackjob type, a type of which Buenaventura High School was full. Fortunately, he had a ready, disarming smile that alleviated others' suspicions generally – at least in terms of violent mayhem – but there was still something threatening about him. It was odd because people were drawn to him, until they got really close or met his gaze. Then they'd backpedal. It was the same thing Lupita had felt. He was like a tiger: beautiful – but shouldn't he be in a cage? Is it safe to pet him? Best just to smile back and steer clear. So he was likable, well-liked even, but he made no friends. He was somehow intimidating and almost untouchable, like a football quarterback or gang kingpin – people were afraid to approach him to make friends, as if they feared they weren't good enough, or would be rejected as not up to his level. But more important, what if he turned on them with that strange animal power of his?

This saddened him greatly, for while he was flattered that he brought smiles and joy to others – he'd grown keenly aware of this over the years and had witnessed endless examples of it: boys suddenly kissing their girls passionately when he walked by in the school hallway, and not just to show off either – there was the very real fact that no one ever gave him any joy back. He'd seen little kids on playgrounds stand up in unison and run in a pack to the jungle gym just because he'd walked by on the sidewalk, when before they'd been sitting enervated and gloomy, bored to tears – but, of course, they'd run the other way. Once he had watched a young man, who'd nervously been pacing outside a 99¢ store, take a deep breath the minute his eyes crossed Gilberto's path, and not a second later was marching in the door – and, sure enough, stepped right up to the girl at the register, with a line and dozens of people watching, and barked, "What are you doing Friday night, Cristina?" The whole line had broken into applause, beaming, many of them even directing their smiles at Gilberto, who was crossing the threshold of the doorway just as the magic moment blossomed. But they congratulated *the Romeo boy*, and no one offered a second look at the wraith-like young man digging through the hot chili pepper cheese puffs – God, but they were orange as flame.

"Joy to the World" he'd play ironically on his clarinet, alone in the house, burnt out on video games and stoned to the gills on Xochil's weed, which she proffered by the garbage bagful, forever a payer of tribute, even if she was broke and worn threadbare with the rearing of the triplets and the constant maintenance of the other dozen Barrajas and all their myriad antisocial demands – with no help from Jose, locked up as he was in some faraway prison.

It was no wonder then that all Gilberto's friends were online, with names like Ratbastard2 and Deadfunkwad and Lizardbro and Filthyclod. What he liked about them was that they had no idea about his charms – or his curse – depending on how he felt about it on any given day – and lately the curse part was feeling a lot more prominent.

Though last week he'd been surprised to find out from Lizardbro, who was an aficionado of auto-asphyxiation and lived somewhere in the Midwest, that not everyone had visionary three-hour orgasms of exploding Magellanic Clouds off Orion's belt that then morphed into visions of orgiastic elfin fairies gallivanting with enormous flower-like genitals, their hearts blooming out of their chests as jungles birthed from their mouths, vines rising up into the air and creating enormous fecund green clouds that as thunderheads drifted moaning over cities and parades, raining down multicolored flower petals that heaped themselves like psychedelic snow-drifts upon the sad, mundane, and sorrowful activities of humans, who were suddenly made to fall into one another's arms and weep for joy at the solace of companionship.

LIZARDBRO: "Uh, no, dude, that's like poetry or sumthin. I just get off and sorta blank out and clean up with a gym sock. Are you on acid or X or what?"

A gym sock? Often as not, Gilberto had needed a mop.

He'd signed off with a vague sense of dread. There was something very wrong with him, and he was suddenly very lonely.

After finishing his second bag of cheese puffs, and doing a little algebra – he'd gotten his grades back up to Bs – he signed back on. Thank god for the Internet. At least he could bounce around and find *someone* to talk to.

Gilberto was in a chat room called "Punkadoric-permutations" when he met Walt, who was involved in a group discussion about playing traditional orchestral instruments – such as tubas, violins, cellos, and clarinets – in a punk format with punk bands. Walt claimed to be a one-man-band punk accordionist himself, based out of Bakersfield.

"I want to play punk oboe," Gilberto interjected into the conversation.

"That's ambitious," Walt had commented.

GILZILLA: "I don't think it's been done."

CHRONICLE: "No, I don't think so. What other wind instruments do you play?"

GILZILLA: "Just clarinet, and I played flute when I was younger, and trumpet for awhile, until I drove my mother and the neighbors crazy."

CHRONICLE: "The oboe is known to shorten one's life."

GILZILLA: "Who cares."

CHRONICLE: "Somebody probably does, not sure who in your case."

GILZILLA: "Me neither."

CHRONICLE: "Music heals."

GILZILLA: "Whatever."

CHRONICLE: "*Whatever* is a beautiful answer, whether you meant it to be or not."

GILZILLA: "You must be a child molester."

CHRONICLE: "I've been called worse."

GILZILLA: "What?"

CHRONICLE: "Demon, Satan, animal, beast, monster."

GILZILLA: "Why?"

CHRONICLE: "Long story. Read your Greek mythology. Good night."

GILZILLA: "Wait."

CHRONICLE: Chronicle signed off 4:20 p.m.

Good timing too. Gilberto sparked one up and wondered about Lizardbro's paltry orgasms and what could be worse than a pedophile. Him perhaps? Who would ever want to be with him? They were scared for good reason. He was a monster, a demon, a beast. Just like Walt. His mother was right. He *was* a sort of saint, only it was all happening against his will. He filled the world with joy, lotuses blossomed from his heels, but he got nothing in return. He didn't want to be a saint. He went to the bathroom and grabbed his electric hair trimmer and dropped his jeans. Sitting down on the toilet in his boxer shorts, he mowed away at the thick hair, the electric razor repeatedly stalling out and choking on the sheer volume of fur. He was now shaving his legs twice a day in a desperate attempt to keep up appearances. Whatever was he going to do?

Weeks passed, and then that little bitch Val snapped at him in the middle of biology class when they were reading the chapter on asexual reproduction. "Why do you do that?"

"Do what?" he replied, his voice so deep that Val felt the need to brace herself, spreading her feet for fear there'd be an earthquake and the floor would cave in below them.

"That hum, whatever it is. It bugs me." She struggled to compose herself.

"Is there a problem back there?" Mr. Ramirez shouted over the class to the back row where the two antisocial, black-clad teens bickered.

"He's like ... humming, ... and I can't concentrate."

"Are you humming, Gilberto?"

"No, I'm not humming. I'm a clarinetist." The class burst out laughing.

"Mr. Rubio, a 'yes' or 'no' answer is all that's required. If you're humming, you need to stop. And if you don't stop, I'll have to ask you to leave the classroom."

"I won't hum, sir."

"Good."

But then Gilberto himself heard it, not a minute later, and it was rising out of his own chest. Not so much a hum as a purr. And then Val screamed.

"Rubio!" Mr. Ramirez shouted.

"Call 911!" someone shouted. For Val's hands were gripping the desk as she emitted wave after wave of blood-curdling screams.

Gilberto stood up and backed away as Mr. Ramirez approached. But he stopped halfway there. "Good god! She's having an orgasm." Most of the class went scrambling out of the room then, some laughing, others white with terror, while Gilberto backed off and cowered near the hamster cage up against the window.

"I didn't do anything, I swear." He raised his brows innocently when Ramirez glared at him.

"You'll cost me my job, you fucking freak!"

And then Gilberto's eyes dropped and, to his horror, witnessed the bulge in Mr. Ramirez's pants. He ran then too.

Home to the Internet, where he Googled "spontaneous orgasms," and calmed himself as he read in some nameless medical journal: "Common among adolescent males and females, spontaneous orgasms can occur just about anywhere, but usually in confined quarters amid large groups of people, such as in a school classroom, a mall, or a movie theater – or even an emergency room. An overpowering physical sensation, it is unknown what instigates the process, though it is believed to be a sudden hormonal surge, common to children between the ages of twelve and sixteen.

Apply cool towels to the forehead and try to be sensitive to the young person's need to shower or change undergarments privately." He searched for "causes of" but the same damn description kept coming up. A mystery. Life is not an exam, but a mystery. True that. He thought of his mother then.

And she was thinking of him just then too. Of what he might say when he learned he'd have a new brother or sister in six months, give or take. And could she count on him to help out with day care, or would it be better to leave the little one with Isabel or Julia? She suddenly shuddered that she'd even considered him as a babysitter. It would be like leaving a child in a bear's lair, or just exposed to the elements on some African savannah. Oh, but he was harmless, he was; his power was all contained, spring-loaded. She knew she needn't worry. What she should worry about was just how many children would be in the house if that spring sprung and peopled the apartment complex with a dozen or more Gilberto juniors. But what bugged her even more was that she couldn't shake the thought that he was somehow the father of the child that now gestated in her womb. It gave a kick at the very thought.

It was madness. She knew who the father was, and she felt horribly ashamed, and utterly shocked with herself, that it had happened. Only one time, mind you, and she'd confessed to Father Espinoza right away: "Bless me, Father, for I have committed the sin of adultery." And she'd broken down and wept, as Espinoza on the other side of the confessional grate smiled with satisfaction and coaxed the lurid details from her.

"He's one of the bellhops," she said, collecting herself. And then dabbing her eyes with her Kleenex, she related the circumstances: "Goodness, just a boy. My hope is that he's not yet married. The sin is less then, yes?"

Espinoza just shrugged, whispering, "Continue ..."

"Well, I have sinned against Raul and God all the same," she sniffled. "A wheel had broken on my cart, Father, and this young man – he was coming down the hall, having delivered some bags to one of the rooms on my floor – he offered to help." She paused, remembering what a strange day it had been, beginning with Gilberto in just his boxer shorts at the breakfast table, the stench of chestnut pollen thick as smoke – more than the usual. She'd opened a window for fear of fainting, and as she had, Señor Contreras had ambled by on his way to the rock quarry, dressed in overalls and carrying a lunch bucket, an obese and ornery man well into middle age. She'd stripped him with her eyes before she was able to reach for the sink counter to brace herself, imagining him taking her against the stair railing, and she'd whimpered too – "Raul."

"What?" Gilberto had casually asked, his eyes intent on the cereal box in front of him. But she couldn't even look at him.

"Make yourself decent, Gil! Do not come to the breakfast table without your shirt on!" She'd then grabbed her purse and stormed out without saying goodbye.

And not an hour later she was straddling a bellhop and roaring like a lioness as she conceived her sixth child.

"True, Lupita, it isn't like you. You've always been chaste, even when you didn't want to be," Father Espinoza wondered out loud.

"Oh, Father, I became disoriented – almost drunken. It was terrible, shocking." She wept now, big heaving sobs.

"How's that son of yours?"

Gilberto was growing alarmed. Not only at the little horn nubs now pushing out of his scalp, or the nub of a tail that was making it hard to sit on anything but couches, but at his ongoing and increasingly disturbing problems at school. Val had had to transfer high schools after it became clear she couldn't tolerate seeing Gilberto or even being within a couple hundred feet of that chestnut tree pollen smell he emitted which, when it overtook her, sent her reeling to the ground, overcome by vertigo and terrifying pulses that rocked her innermost organs and felt so good that she could do nothing but scream at the top of her lungs. She never admitted it felt good, of course. They'd think she was insane. Besides, she feared the fits would kill her eventually. She was examined and diagnosed with epilepsy for a time, until the doctor changed his mind and called it an environmental illness. Her family ended up suing the school for toxins in the drinking water, and a pretty penny they made. But Gilberto knew the real cause; he knew who and what the real toxin in her environment was. When he heard the news that a number of boys in his math class were suffering from painful and spontaneous erections that erupted through no effort on their part at the most inopportune of moments, leaving them lurching over their desks during exams, he gulped hard and began to wonder if the administration might put two and two together and finger him. Wrestling practice was suddenly cancelled. Then a rash of pregnancies swept through the school – an increase of 400 percent in one semester – and Gilberto became a truant.

Waddling like a penguin, Lupita followed him around the apartment mornings, scolding him and threatening to send him to a military academy if he didn't return to school. But he knew her threats were idle. Those things cost money. Truly, it broke his heart to see her so beside herself with frustration, but he just didn't know how to explain.

"Okay, I'll become a priest," he wailed, breaking into tears, which silenced her.

She went to him then and gave him a hug. My, but the baby kicked then. And she fell into him, screeching, fearing the baby might kick itself right out of the womb.

"Mom, what is it?" Gilberto steadied her and led her to the couch, where she momentarily passed out. "Oh my god, I've killed her," he wept. He ran out onto the patio and swiveled his head around and up: "Xochil!" But what met his gaze caused his open mouth to open further and to stay open. Xochil was leaning over the deck railing, buck naked, her breasts jiggling in front of her, while some unknown precinct walker, who'd been out canvassing for an antigay marriage protection bill, penetrated her from behind. It occurred to him, more or less irrelevantly, that Xochil had never actually married Jose, nor voted.

"What do you want, Gilberto?!" she bellowed.

He ran back inside, prepared to call 911, but Lupita was getting up. "I'm late for work," she quipped angrily. "Go to school."

"I will, Mama – look." And he began packing his book bag, grabbing his clarinet and shoving it in the bag without even putting it in the case.

Within minutes, they were closing the door amid the wails of Xochil, who had now caused the blinds in the apartments opposite to go screeching upward in response to the spectacle. Gilberto guided his mother toward the back entrance as she queried, "What on earth is all that screaming?"

"Just more drama at the Barrajas', Mom. Come on, we'll be late," he answered as casually as he could, but pushing her along before him.

"Did you do something?" She looked at him suspiciously, but he was already guiding her through the back gate. How could he even begin to answer her? Then he noticed she had on that old red dress he remembered from her closet, but that he'd never seen her actually wear. The lacy red material was stretched to bursting at her full waist.

"Come on, Mom," he said nervously, as they hurried down the avenue toward the bus stop.

But things weren't any prettier there. The Plexiglas shelter visibly pulsed as they approached, and those waiting began to fidget and move about. Gilberto tried to keep his mother distracted once the two octogenarians started making out and feeling each other up on the bench.

"Wow, look at that jacaranda tree!" he pointed, as said tree visibly blossomed and began raining its vibrant lavender flowers down on the sidewalk below it, drawing Lupita's eyes to the cyclone fence and the two copulating Chihuahuas in the yard it enclosed. Lupita appeared, as well as felt, somewhat disoriented. But then the bus, like a curtain coming across the stage, obliterated her stupefaction and jogged her mind back to the task at hand.

Gilberto guided her toward the door and pushed her up the steps. "Bye, Mom, off to school!" She looked back briefly, clearly suspicious, but she felt queasy too, a bit dizzy – what could she do? She had to find a seat before she fell over again.

Gilberto hopped up and down on the sidewalk, jolts of energy pulsing through him, as he watched his mother's bus crest the hill and disappear over the other side. Out of the corner of his eye, he saw the octogenarians now in full coitus, rolling on the grassy strip next to the sidewalk. People stared, began ogling one another, and then fell into full embrace. Gilberto ran.

He had no idea where to go, just away from people. Not easy in an enormous metropolis like Los Angeles. He'd never really left the city. He'd only been to Magic Mountain. But then he recalled, from his previous trips there, the big sloping empty grass hills of Valencia – and didn't the city sort of begin to dwindle out when you got up that way?

He ran to the onramp onto the 5 and began hitchhiking. Ten minutes went by before he began to think about how he might appear to the endless parade of commuters. *Who's gonna pick up a punk Goth Mexican teenager?* He ran into a 99¢ store where he asked for a box, and to borrow a Sharpie pen. He was back outside and onto the onramp in a flash, holding up his sign. And though it took him two hours, he got a ride finally, and as he hopped into the big tractor trailer with his book bag and clarinet, he tossed his little "not a gangbanger" sign into the bushes and bid Los Angeles farewell.

"You a runaway?"

"It's more complicated than that."

"Where you headed?"

Gilberto had to make something up, so he used the first thing that came to mind. "Bakersfield."

"What's in Bakersfield?"

"Uh, my uncle Walt?"

The truck driver didn't look like he believed him. There

was a long silence. "Why you going there?"

"Uh, well, Uncle Walt is actually my guardian."

"What are you doing here then?"

"Uh, sir, it's a long story – I was, uh, visiting my mother. I need to get home."

The driver just nodded, noticed that cars were swerving around them, lots of shocked looks on other drivers' faces. "Shit I'm horny," he stated bluntly.

What could Gilberto say to that? "Maybe you should let me off at the next exit."

"Don't worry, kid. I'm not one of those. In fact, I just haven't felt that way in a long time and I sorta was surprised. Didn't mean to offend. But goddamn, when I get home to Turlock tonight, my wife is in for a surprise. It's been years!" And he laughed fully.

Gilberto had a brief vision of Xochil, but it soon passed, as he began to wonder how and why he made all these people horny when he himself felt as if he hardly had a libido at all.

But then they hit the Grapevine.

"Uh, sir, I really need to go to the bathroom – like now."

"Diarrhea?"

"Uh, yeah," Gil answered, his face growing with concern.

But it wasn't diarrhea, and he wondered how the truck driver couldn't have noticed, even though he had his back-pack pressed hard into his lap – the problem being that his lap had risen considerably, so that his clarinet was poking his chin. He pulled it out, and as he leaned forward to place it on the floor, a fly button on his jeans went zinging into the wind-shield, where it made a knick like a stone thrown up from the pavement would do.

"Goddamn gravel trucks!" The driver shouted.

"Please, sir," Gilberto whimpered.

"Okay, okay, but goddammit, my insurance doesn't cover those and I'm out two hundred fifty bucks – at least!"

"I'm really sorry," Gilberto offered sheepishly.

"Why are you sorry? You didn't do anything."

But Gilberto was too distracted to process the misunderstanding and didn't have to answer anyway, as the driver maneuvered the truck into the Flying J at Lebec, distracting himself now with rising gas prices and deregulation, which though it loosened a lot of rules, still didn't allow for cracked windshields. "What kind of deregulation doesn't get rid of a stupid rule like that?"

Gilberto was out the door of the rig and hopping onto the pavement before they'd even come to a full stop.

"Careful there, pardner!" the driver barked, but Gilberto was now nearly sprinting on his springy hooves, making a beeline for the restroom, his book bag pressing his member against his body. Two more buttons flew off, one ricocheting off an Oldsmobile and startling the driver, while the other took off as soon as he was through the door and went zinging into the potato chips, emitting that crack which metal against a plastic Ruffles bag makes. Then he was through the restroom door and into the last stall, where he slammed the door, clicked the lock, dropped what remained of his tattered jeans, and let it rip. He bit down hard on the strap of his backpack as pint-size dollops of his seed splashed against the far wall, all over the back of the toilet, and soon began hitting the surface of the basin's water itself, cupful by cupful, making a sound like large stones dropped one after the other into a lake.

Gilberto's eyes rolled back into his head as he experienced visions of bright orange poppies blossoming and spilling down the golden baked grassy hills of the Grapevine like a flood, while long pendulous pinkishpurple tongues came twisting out of gullies to spit-shine the leaves of the scattered hallucinatory-chartreuse cottonwood trees. He saw the highway, too, as it pulsed, glowed volcanic red, and ruptured into a million geysers of white-hot steam, the entire mountain range beginning to quake and crumble while enormous rainbows arced through the air, forming gateways in the sky for huge clouds that deluged the scene in multicolored flower petals, scattering their brilliance across the whole landscape, perfuming the air, and blessing all things in their gentle rain, like tears of joy.

He came to on his haunches, his buttocks soaked by the storm, which was now running out of the stall and across the tiles. He heard a "What the fuck?" There were coughs. Then another voice: "Somebody tell the management."

He gathered himself together quickly, fastening his pants with the one remaining button, and then pulled his hood around his face. *My, how his nubs hurt today!* Then he walked out slowly, alert, counting the steps to the door, hoping he wouldn't be busted, and pushing aside his feelings of fear and confusion about what had just happened, his utter loss of control, and *what the fuck was he going to do now?* He saw the manager marching down the aisle in his direction. An idea occurred to him then: *The best defense is a good offense.* Where had he heard that? On TV?

"Dude, man, that toilet is overflowing back there – like really overflowing."

The manager bought it and brushed by him, and Gilberto hurried out, heading toward the cab. Then he remembered his pants, soaked and really putting out the blooming chestnut tree stench that had so unnerved his mother. He turned and ran, and ran, and his hooves moved quickly. Gilberto hadn't run in quite awhile and was rather amazed at the ease and speed with which he could cover terrain, and so he was far off into the hills by the time the truck driver went looking for him, wondering why the boy was taking so long – wasn't diarrhea quick?

In time Gilberto grew tired, and upon reaching a little grove of oak trees nestled along a dry creek, he settled down to rest and regroup. It was a lovely day, still early, maybe around one or two o'clock, so he stripped off his soiled clothing, and for the first time sat naked and unafraid, exploring and gazing upon his strange legs, his accentuated genitals; he touched his pointy ears and the fine scruff growing in a point off his chin; tenderly felt around the base of each horn nub pushing through his scalp. And he began to cry, big blubbery sobs, tears flowing as abundantly, and almost as overwhelming, as that other substance just had back in the restroom in Lebec.

He lay back and fell asleep until a bird's plaintive song woke him up at what he figured was about six o'clock. He could see the sun setting now over the distant peaks, the sky a smear of orange and purple, and the air still balmy. He tried to hang on to the sweet, tranquil respite. But with the approaching night, the dread came back full force. Tomorrow was another day. What then? He couldn't live out here. But how could he go back? He could no longer hide this thing in him. Even if he hid it physically, draped in all his hats and clothes – which in Southern California, was becoming just too hot to bear – he couldn't contain whatever it was that jumped from him to other people like a flame in a brushfire. That, unlike physical deformities, was totally out of his control. He was as shocked by it as everyone else was. He'd just have to commit suicide; there were no two ways about it. But, of course, someone would find him, and they'd find out what he was – and his poor mother. She'd be crushed to find out her son was a monster. A devil. A chupacabra. He couldn't kill himself until he destroyed his body. Did that make any sense? He needed to be incinerated. Burned alive. Where was the nearest volcano? You can't just hop into a furnace at a crematorium. Or can you? If he paid them? He had no money. It would cost a lot to get someone to agree to let him do that.

"Fuck!" And he grew sad again at the impossibility of his situation. "I'm just a boy!" he shouted at the sky. But he looked at himself, and he knew that wasn't true. Whatever he was, he wasn't a boy. He wasn't even human. What was he? Where had he come from? He shuddered. What help would it be to know? Whatever he was, he was stuck. What did it matter where he came from or what he was? He didn't have the luxury of such considerations. But maybe there was a cure? Were there others? Should he go to some institution for chupacabras? Was there one? They'd probably just kill him, which would explain why he'd never met anyone like himself. So why not kill himself and spare himself the agony of being hounded, hunted down, and executed?

He reached for his backpack to solace himself by playing his clarinet. But, alas, it wasn't there, and he realized he'd left it behind in the rig. He threw the pack down and buried his head in his hands, utterly defeated.

Spiraling into despondency, on his haunches, naked against a tree, Gilberto didn't see the old man until it was too late to run. Startled, he looked up when he heard footsteps in the dry, brittle grass. He immediately pulled his knees up tight to his chest and placed his head atop them, as he began to make out the approaching stranger. An old man, with long gray hair and a full gray beard, naked too, with bushy gray legs ... and hooves! And horns too! He couldn't see his ears, but so far, it was check, check, check. Then the dread hit him. He must be dreaming. He slapped his face hard. *Crack*. And he felt it. Not dreaming – check.

The old man put his hand up in a little wave. "Ho there."

Maybe it was Santa Claus. Maybe he was an elf – and that would make Gilberto an elf too, and he could go off and make toys at the North Pole, and have a life, and friends, and not cause mayhem wherever he went.

"I'm glad I found you," the old man announced.

"Were you looking for me?" Gilberto asked, disturbed.

"Oh yes."

"Do I know you?" And his expression grew more bothered.

"No – well, sort of."

"What do you mean, sort of? Is this some kind of dream? Are you God or something? Are you my father?"

"Whoa there little feller; that's a lot of questions. As for the first: Is this a dream? Well, if you're a Buddhist or an Australian Aborigine, or a serious person – spiritually speaking that is – it's certainly a dream. That sort of negates the next two, but to be completely clear – on a relative level, more or less – no, I'm neither God nor your father."

"Well, how do you know me – sort of?"

"We talked once, online." The old man had a little satchel

that hung across his back, which he pulled around and reached into, producing a set of Peruvian pipes. "I know you'd prefer an oboe, but this is really more practical, considering."

"Oh my god. Walt!"

He nodded, grinning.

"How did you find me here?" And Gilberto stood up. "What the fuck? Are you a child molester?"

Walt chuckled. "All these questions, like a press conference really." And he handed the pipes to Gilberto.

But Gilberto took a step backward. "I can't accept these. Where's your accordion? This is a little too fucked up for me," he blurted, his brow furrowed defensively.

"Okay, okay. Listen, Gilzilla, I'm not a child molester. As you can see – " and he lifted one leg and stamped with his hoof, "I'm a satyr, just like you. And I know, I know, it's strange how I found you in the middle of nowhere. I'm not a mind-reader. I found you, really, quite by accident. You caused quite a stir down at the Flying J."

"How do you know about that?"

"I was there, Gilzilla."

"Gilberto. My name is Gilberto."

"Gilberto. Nice name." He smiled. "Anyway, I'd gone in to take a pee – you must have just left. That chestnut smell is just something I recognize, you know?"

Gil looked down embarrassed, remembering the bathroom stall and thinking as he'd rushed out that it looked like the toilet had been powervomiting vanilla yogurt.

"Nothing to be embarrassed about, Gilberto. It's all quite natural. For us, that is. If you were one of them, well, we'd have a problem." And Walt gave him a quick smile. "But you're not ... one of them. And I had to tell you who you are because what happened there would never happen to one of us who knows. It was the telltale sign of a satyr in distress, with no idea how to handle himself."

"But how did you know that I was the guy from the chat room?"

"There was a truck driver there shouting your name –

'Gil, Gil, Gil!' And he had a clarinet in his hand. I put two and two together. There really aren't that many of us. I mean *really.*"

"My clarinet," Gilberto sorrowfully sighed. "But how'd you find me here?"

"I followed you." And he smiled. "But I don't run as fast."

"Yeah, I must have been long gone."

"Well, I'm good with a scent."

"That's gross."

"Well, it is what it is." He shrugged. And then reaching out with them, Walt said, "Go ahead, try the pipes."

Gilberto took them in his hands and played. And they calmed him, they did. Taking a breather, he said, while trying to hold back his smile, "They're like the wind."

"Like the wind through the trees," Walt affirmed.

"Yeah, yeah, they make sense suddenly," Gilberto enthused as he began to tell Walt where he'd first encountered them. "I used to see these guys, all decked out in that Guatemalan-looking shit, but wearing fedoras. And they really jammed on these." And he looked at the pipes lovingly. "But, but, I didn't really get it totally."

"And now you do," Walt said with satisfaction.

"Yeah, yeah." But Gilberto looked mystified.

"You know why, Gil?"

Gilberto looked at him like a confused dog, his head sideways.

Walt put his hands out and looked about. "Arcadia, Gil. You're in Arcadia." And he laughed heartily. And even though he tried, Gilberto couldn't hold it back. He guffawed. And again. And then Walt pulled out a little flute and he played, and the two of them played and played and stomped around and sang the sun down through the last purple wisps of clouds over the far hills.

A Boy and His Dog

He knew what he was before I even suspected what I now know I am. Dave was a mutt, a sort of stunted Lab. He must have been part corgi we figured. Dave's not much of a name, I know. My older brother, Keith, gave it to him. He considered it his prerogative as the oldest. My brother was a major geek, a Trekkie, a sci-fi nut. He had greasy hair and that pasty in-the-throes-of-adolescence skin back when we got Dave. I remember he was obsessed with the recent hit movie *2001: A Space Odyssey*, which we'd seen just weeks before Dave entered our lives.

Our dog was thus named for the film's hero and hapless victim of Hal, the sadistic computer who inadvertently became the agent of Dave the astronaut's enlightenment or demise, depending on your depth of understanding. I was nine, so I didn't get it. Something about a man turning into a star, and not the musical kind. Our Dave had no such destiny from what I could tell, so I didn't belabor the point.

I don't think Dave liked his name. He endured it, his head cocked to one side, confused as Keith hounded him with his verbal sadism ad infinitum, whispering, "Dave ... what's the matter, Dave? Dave? Dave ... don't you love me, Dave? ... I wouldn't do that, Dave." In that creepy voice. It drove me nuts. That and vying for Dave's love. Boys don't vie gracefully and Keith and I were no different.

We each attempted to love Dave more than the other, so as to be loved more in return. Dave, of course, didn't care. He was into food. And running around. We ended up having to chain him to a tree. And he got fat as we both fed him to gain favor. Still, he worked his way off the chain on several occasions (I think being fat actually helped him in this, as he had lots of slack fur to work with). When he ran off, we'd have to go after him with pieces of baloney to coax him home.

That's when I found out the truth about Dave. That he wasn't like other dogs, that he didn't love me best, and that he was most certainly not evolving into a star. Dave was a homosexual in love with a little, white poodle named Charlie. I bolted the slab of baloney I carried at my side and watched from the bushes as Dave humped little Charlie with abandon in the gravel drive.

Part of me wanted to cheer him on; part of me wanted to stop him, yell "Break it up!" An even bigger part felt a strange kind of recognition that made digesting that baloney problematic. I puked.

It took awhile for me to notice I was in fact jealous. Dave didn't hump me like that. Not that I wanted him to, of course – I just wanted to be his number one. Keith and I could feed him hot dogs, eggs, and red, juicy bones. But Charlie had his heart.

I betrayed Dave's secret, told my brother and his Eddie Haskell-like friend Chuck, both of whom came to look. Keith was disgusted and broke up Dave's and Charlie's fun.

Chuck just laughed. "Your dog's a fag!" he guffawed. "You're both fags, with a fag dog!" My brother wasn't a fag, but when Chuck said that to me, I ran at him. Being bigger than me and a student of tae kwon do, he made quick work of my fury, leaving me momentarily lying on my back in the gravel with Dave licking my face, Charlie all but forgotten.

"I think you need to have him put down," Chuck stated,

acting like a know-it-all, "to put him out of his misery."

"What are you talking about?!" Keith screamed.

Chuck shrugged his shoulders. "It's just one of those things, Keith."

His brows furrowed, Keith looked down at Dave, whose tail was wagging like he'd just eaten cake, which he kind of had, considering – I mean, Charlie kind of looked like one, with those trimmed little tufts of hair on his head and at the end of his tail.

"Think about poor Charlie," Chuck added.

I sat up and scrunched my own brow then. I'd seen Charlie's response. He planted his legs firmly every time and pushed his rear back into Dave. He wasn't suffering one bit.

"My Dad'll do it for you," Chuck offered innocently, like he was being helpful.

Keith was at him then, grabbing him around the neck. But Chuck's tae kwon do saved him every time, and he laughingly threw my brother down too, yipping as he ran off, "Bye, bye, girlie boys – watch your butts!"

"What do you think we should do?" I asked Keith as he rose and brushed himself off. But he didn't answer me, instead grabbing Dave's neck rolls of fat hard and smacking him on the snout with his hand, then shaking his finger: "Don't hump Charlie anymore, ya hear?!"

He then dragged Dave after Charlie, but Charlie kept running away, ten feet at a time, before turning around and barking. It looked more like courtship than discipline to me, but I figured Keith was doing what we'd done to potty-train Dave: dragging him over to his pee or crap and smacking him to let him know not to do that in the house.

Later, walking across the field that separated our cul-de-sac from Charlie's, I asked Keith, "You think you fixed him?"

"Sure I fixed him; Dave isn't a fag," Keith said. "Charlie's a poodle. Poodles look like girls. It's an honest mistake."

But Dave kept making it.

Eventually, I asked my mother about it as we did the dishes after dinner. She answered curtly, "He's a beast, dear; they do that kind of thing. But don't you worry about Dave's soul or anything; Dave's going to limbo either way." My mother had explained on several occasions when queried by Keith or me that dogs didn't go to heaven or hell, but to limbo, with aborted fetuses, goldfish, hamsters – and I think Jews.

My stomach sank and I felt a sense of dread because I was really more worried about my own prospects. She'd pretty much assured me that God was nice and as long as I kept things generally in line, I'd get into purgatory pretty easily, where I'd have to move rocks around for a few years before getting admitted to Heaven. As I understood it, purgatory was like junior college or bonehead English. My mom believed only murderers, rapists, bigtime thieves, and pedophiles went to hell – and homosexuals, of course.

"Can people go to limbo?"

"Only sweet little aborted babies, the poor dears."

It was clearly too late for me to be an abortion. "Mom, do you believe in reincarnation?"

"No, that's silly heathen talk." And she turned and looked at me, before adding, "Why?"

"I want to be a dog."

"A dog?" She turned off the faucet then, put down the big plate she was washing, and, grabbing the drying rag from out of my hands to dry her own, asked, "Why do you want to be a dog?"

"So I can go to limbo with Dave."

"Oh, you dear thing." And a tear pooled in her eye as a palpable sense of relief crossed her visage. But she'd read me wrong. She just thought I was overattached to Dave. She leaned down to my level. "I'm sure when you're in heaven you can go over to limbo and visit. God's nice, remember?"

I nodded. In a pickle.

Then it happened, and I'll never know if Chuck was involved, but I still think so.

Dave came limping home a bloody mess, with big gaping

holes in his back, courtesy of Heidi, the German shepherd up the hill. Chuck ran up, panting, out of breath, sweaty, and urgent. "It was Heidi – she was throwing him around like a rag doll. And he kept running back for more. I tried to stop him." And then Chuck began to cry. "Oh my god, look at Dave!"

Dave was whimpering, cowering at my feet, and I just froze in terror. By then, Chuck was bawling. I screamed "Mom!" over and over until she came running out.

"Good god!" she exclaimed and ran into the house to get a towel, which she then wrapped around Dave while ordering me into the car. We zoomed out the driveway as Chuck, walking away down the street now, puffy and sniffling, looked back over his shoulder at us.

On the drive down to the vet's, I kept Dave on the seat next to me. He whimpered at every bump and turn, and I didn't know what to do or say, so I just mimicked Hal: "You'll be okay, Dave ... Dave, you'll be fine." I felt like I was possessed.

The vet looked spooked when we handed him Dave, but he smiled soon enough – for my benefit, I could tell. They made us sit outside while they shaved Dave right down to the skin and sewed him up in what turned out to be seven separate places. Heidi had literally bitten holes in him. They wrapped him in thick gauze, drugged him, and placed him carefully in my outstretched arms. I carried him like that all the way home in the passenger seat, my eyes wide and expressionless, stupefied.

Keith reacted with anger. "I'll kill him." He blamed Chuck. Because everyone knew Heidi's owners kept her locked up inside the iron fence. How would Dave have gotten in there without someone putting him there?

"You're not leaving this house!" My mother shouted at him. "Killing's a sin."

"Mom," he pleaded, "Chuck's the bad guy, not me!"

"You don't know that. Besides, he brought Dave home. Maybe he saved him."

"He just felt guilty!" Keith shouted.

"Well, then, maybe he's sorry, and you'll just have to

forgive him," she said with an odd air of self-satisfaction, like she'd found the magic formula for life's chaos. "Dave is just a beast, Keith. Chuck is a real boy – you mustn't hurt him. It's different."

Keith looked appalled at his mother's logic and stormed off to his room, slamming the door behind him.

Calmly she helped me put Dave in his sleeping basket and we got him a baby bottle filled with milk.

But Dave didn't make it. He got some kind of fever and died four days later, shivering in his basket.

Keith did end up beating up Chuck, but Chuck never admitted anything, and Keith got in big trouble, detention and everything.

I was still in a daze. We decided to have a funeral for Dave in the backyard and bury him there. I told my mom I thought we should go get Charlie so he could say goodbye. My mother glared. "What are you talking about?"

"Charlie's his boyfriend," I said, wide-eyed and innocent.

"Don't be absurd; dogs don't have boyfriends."

"Mom, you said so yourself. He's a beast, and he has a boyfriend." I didn't understand why I'd become so adamant. I felt myself flush, about to cry. "I'm going to get Charlie."

"You can't just take someone's dog!" she shouted. "He's not our property." Come to think of it, we didn't even know Charlie's owners. They were old people was all we knew, who drove an Olds 98.

Keith came out of the house right then, wearing his green Star Trek shirt and holding his hand up in the Vulcan greeting, his black eye still swelling blue and red. It stopped me dead in my tracks.

My mother looked perplexed and watched him approach. He'd already dug the ditch yesterday and now all we had to do was put Dave in the ground. He was wrapped in a white blanket in his basket. Keith went and picked him up as I skulked back to the gravesite. I watched Keith place Dave carefully in the ground, stand up, puff out his chest, and proclaim, "Dave, you are now to become a star." And he looked up into the sky, where there were no stars, because it was only like noon.

He looked at me for acknowledgment. "Yeah," I said, half-heartedly.

"He's going to limbo, dear," my mother corrected him, but gingerly, aware of his grief and not wanting to provoke his temper.

"No, he's going to become a star." And he said it with finality, looking at us so strangely that my mother just had to have had a crisis of faith.

"Okay, a star, then," she allowed. "Now let's say an 'Our Father.'"

We did, and we covered Dave in dirt.

The next week I took my allowance and got Charlie a whole package of baloney, hoping he'd understand it was the only consolation I could come up with. His old man owner came out and scolded me. "What are you doing feeding my dog that human food?!"

"He's ... uh ... he's uh ..."

"He's what? He's my dog, that's what he is. What's your name?"

"I'm Sam, and my dog was Charlie's boyfriend!" I blurted.

"What?" But I was crying by then, and I could see the old man now felt bad.

"Listen, you go on home; leave my dog alone."

"Goodbye, Charlie," I blubbered and hurried off.

I loafed home across the field, my head turned toward the ground. But Keith came up behind me all smiles. "Hey, cheer up, Sam. Dave's a star now. Tonight, I'll show you. A whole new constellation called 'Dave'!" He was beaming.

I looked at him, almost angry at his inanity, but then I saw how he was doing what he could to cheer me up as well as finding some acceptable way to not go through with killing Chuck or stewing in resentment for the rest of his life.

We put our arms around each other and we walked home. We weren't homosexuals, me and Keith. We were just brothers.

Chuck and Keith didn't stay friends and Chuck always

looked hurt, like he'd been dumped; like he was the victim and not the murderer. And maybe he wasn't, and maybe Keith was too harsh on him. The more I thought about it, the more I thought, even if Chuck did do it, it's because he thought he was doing the right thing.

Goodness. I got very suspicious about what people thought of as the right thing after that.

I also started praying more to Dave than to God. But I never found a boy named Charlie myself. Though I did find a boy eventually. Not after wishing on a star either. But at a club – named Limbo.

Captain Jinx

Captain Jinx strode down Broadway like a cad, bowl-legged as a horseman, rather thin-hipped, with a cocky look on her face and a pair of piercing brown eyes just deep-set enough for her to be mistaken at a glance for a man.

But I knew what she was immediately. Me, in my corseted tent of a dress, my plaited curls, my umbrella, my high-buttoned shoes – a real lady of the era, if I don't say so myself. I gave it a go anyway. But when I saw Captain Jinx, I lost all composure and stopped in my tracks, felt a knot grow huge in my stomach. Huge and simple it spoke to me, like I'd waited all my life to hear it: *She* is the man of my dreams.

Challenged all my notions of grammar, she did. Which was something, it was, as I was just then employed in teaching the King's English to a gaggle of wee Mexican boys and girls out at the rancho. I felt lightheaded, and not just because of my sudden and overwhelming desire for this ruddy roustabout, but because it had all come to me at once: the captain's attractiveness, his presence and magnetism, his confidence and charisma – his gender.

He reached out and caught my fall, to the catcalls of the rest of the cads on Broadway – the boisterous on-the-make white men and Irish drunks, the fawning black men and native Gabrielinos who saw everything but were careful not to comment, the Mexican rancheros with their sultry Indian smiles, their whistles and glimmering eyes that knew oodles more than they'd ever show. Only the Chinamen pretended completely not to notice anything. For them, my travails were but an obstacle on the sidewalk they had to negotiate as they went about their daily business. But I knew they saw. Just as I knew I needed to go see old Chen about this business in my belly straightaway.

Shame about old Chen.

Ah, but I'm getting ahead of myself.

On that particular sunny October morning, Captain Jinx hoisted me into his arms and carried me two whole city blocks. Chivalry, I tell you. Yes, that was it. I could feel it in his strong arms. He had what few men ever achieved, but all played at. He was looking for a good deed to do, and I don't mean that in a sentimental way either. I mean that he had the good cowboy feel to him, like he'd made his choice some-where out there in Colorado or New Mexico, or maybe among the gold camps of the Sierras or the silver mines of Virginia City. He'd faced some moment of truth, some trial – and passed – and would henceforth stop at nothing to mete out justice. He was, in a word, a *man*.

He marched me right up to the Cheshire Arms Hotel and barked cheerfully at the proprietor, who was standing out front on the wooden sidewalk, on the hunt for street gossip most likely. "Lady needs a room, a bed, and a washbasin," Captain Jinx stated matter-of-factly, like a cop.

The squat hirsute proprietor jerked his head for Captain Jinx to follow him inside, but not before I overheard an angular-looking old man sitting on a crate against the wall, speaking to a boy shining his shoes: "Who's that feller, boy?"

"Thatta be Captain Jinx, sir," the little black boy answered earnestly, his greasy rag whipping back and forth across the old shoe as the old man nodded.

Indeed. Captain Jinx himself, the subject of song. Oh, I'd heard of him. I knew who he was, though I'd taken it all with a grain of salt. California was full of such stories in those days. I'd heard of Jinx like I'd heard of Joaquin Murieta, the peace-lovin' man who turned to crime when the injustices stacked up too high (or so they said); his cohort Three-Fingered Jack (but who's counting?); the brave Indian Stanislaus who jumped the mission and killed a handful of soldiers in his effort to remain free. I'd even heard of the Sasquatch. All of this in saloons mostly, from the mouths of drunken sailors and washed-up 49ers with nothing to show for their dreams but endless stories and beer guts to make any pot of gold envious.

It was on the coach down from San Francisco a year ago if I remember right. Two drunken ranchhands had been going on and on about Wild Bill Hickok, John Wesley Hardin, and Six-Toed Pete, finally getting around to our very own Captain Jinx, at which they burst out singing that old ballad that now flitted through my half-conscious mind like a lullaby in a dream.

> *He's Captain Jinx of the western prairie*
> *Once dubbed Loreen but now called Larry*
> *He's manly as whiskey – he's no faerie*
> *But he'll never join the army*
>
> *Oh, Captain Jinx of the western reaches*
> *Turned in his bodice for some riding breeches*
> *Like any feller, he's got a thing for peaches*
> *But he'll never join the army!*

Well, my peaches were pressed together in my bodice, as she hurried me scrunched up in her arms up the stairs. *What's that they say about death,* I thought – *how you're carried through a tunnel?* On my way to heaven, two steps at a time up the stairwell.

Before you know it, we're at the door, Jinx twisting the knob with one hand and kicking the door open with his foot – and I'm a bride, I am. But I was still woozy, and had to catch my breath.

The Captain sensed it and lay me down gently on the bed, brushing the hair from my brow and offering the kindliest of smiles.

"Let me get you some water, madam. You'll be okay? If I leave you for a short while?"

I nodded the best I could. "I'm fine," I managed to whisper.

And he smiled. "Well, that's an understatement, ma'am. Indeed you are." His chin went up and his chest out, like the worse kinda cad. A man alright. Full of himself.

He turned, but as he opened the door, he looked back over his shoulder for a moment to wink, before adding flirtatiously, "You were born today, madam. Mark my words: Born."

I just looked at her. Worse than a man, she was, in many ways, with her swagger and her one-liner-rife seduction routine. I wanted to correct her besides, grammarian that I was. *Born is one word – mark my "word" is what you mean, Captain.*

But the door was already closing, and then down the stairs I heard him clump, clump, clump in his cowboy boots.

Leaving me to doze off, thinking of birth and the waggery of menfolk. My lad would be going on two now, next month in fact. I knew the day: November the seventh. And Stephen on top of me the tenth ... *Stop it, Stephen, stop it, you'll hurt me.* And all his fifteen-year-old enthusiasm: *But, Constance, I dream of you, you're my best friend ... and fair!*

He'd ruptured me and I'd ended up in hospital.

"She's an Irish tart; we'll not waste a bed on her," the brute nurse quipped on the second day. "Pack her up and send her to the convent where she belongs."

"She's of the Petersons," her helper blurted out then, wide-eyed.

"Well then. Stuck with her, we are."

Stuck indeed.

And perhaps you're just now wondering how I ended up stuck here in Los Angeles, in the far reaches of America in the bad year of 1871, in love with a cowboy woman and dependent on an old Chinese fortune teller to sort out what from what. You'd be right to wonder. I never stopped wondering at it myself and about near everyone I saw in California. Whatever brought them here? And what brought me? Well, it's a long story – for me and all the others – but like all long stories it does lead somewhere. I hope. In my case, right into the arms of Captain Jinx, and the new world she promised, the ecstasy she delivered, and the trouble that seemed to follow her because she, among all the lowdown desperadoes and frontier folk, would slough no injustice off. Tragic flaw that.

"Heaven over mountain, Con-ee," Old Chen had related not a week ago, reading the yarrow sticks he'd laid out on the old wooden chopping table in the rancho's kitchen. And he raised his hand slowly as if a mountain would rise up off the floor right there in the commissary of El Rancho Santa Theresa.

"Meaning what exactly, Chen?"

"The superior man," and he grinned his usual grin – my but his teeth were black – to excuse the gender limitations of the I Ching, before adding, "retreats."

"Fat chance, not in this country, Mr. Chen. A man in this place has gotta shoot first and ask questions later."

He giggled, but then he shook his head, and waxed serious. "Bad time here; bad time coming. Don't get involved, Con-ee."

We kidded about it, sure, but I always took his advice to heart. Though I never knew quite what he was talking about, not being Chinese or poetic or any of that, he was usually right all the same. Meaning, if he said, "Lay low," I laid low. He always helped me get a sense of things before they happened, even if he was just some old Chinaman with a fish cart who visited the rancho Tuesdays and Fridays. Why, when I first made his acquaintance, he noticed my coloring and offered to take my pulse. I'd had a bad stomach for months by then, and, sure enough, he saw "fire in the lake" with his sticks, and the herbs he gave me cleared it right up. I shared all my woes with him after that, physical or otherwise, and he usually came through for me, by way of taking my pulse or laying down the yarrow sticks and telling my fortune. Even though it sounded like a whole lotta gibberish, his advice was always sound. If fire over heaven meant prosperity, who was I to doubt him? I planted squash and beans both and had a bumper crop.

Of course, he always told me to find a feller before he headed back to Chinatown, never failed. But not just any feller. "Only a prince for you, Con-ee." That wide smile, those black teeth.

"Your son?" It was our running joke, not only because of the impossibility and even illegality of mating with a Chinese fella, but because his son was a no-good gangster and womanizer who even his own father would disown. If he weren't Chinese that is. As it was, he was stuck with him. "Stuck under heaven. Together." And he'd smile and rattle the little beads he carried in his lamed left hand. And back to Chinatown he'd go.

To his sad fate. But this story isn't Chen's story, nor will he be the end of it, though he's certainly moved it along, and shall be sorely missed. Heaven over mountain indeed. He ended up ten feet up off the ground, swinging in the Santa Ana wind outside that window when it all came down. They ran him right up the lamp post they did. And I couldn't stop the tears from flowing. But this story doesn't end with Old Chen, God bless him, and curse the bastards who did him in. And if it ends with Jinx, well it's too soon to tell. He only had one bullet in him last I saw him, and though they were building makeshift gallows for a dozen Chinamen, they hadn't stooped to killing whites. Even if he was a "goddamn hermaphrodite," as I heard one of them holler when we first started taking fire. Well, it's small consolation – "and it ain't right," Jinx said – relying on the color of our skin – "but it's a Christian nation."

Indeed. And where *will it* end? In crucifixion, if the plot plays out the usual way. They've been telling themselves the same tragic tale going on two millennia now, not an ounce of imagination in a one of them. But I'm not interested in their endings.

For my part, I can only say for sure where it all began, faraway and with a lot less possibility, believe it or not, and a whole different kind of danger, on a coffin ship set sail from Kinsale, County Cork, with my mother and Da, my two little sisters, and my strapping son-of-a-bitch of a brother. Only he and I survived the passage after the fever ran through the steerage – which was unfortunate, as my brother was a mean no-good bastard, taken to raping me whenever he had the chance. He'd only had a dozen or so opportunities growing up, lucky for me, as we lived in a one-room sod hut and Da or Ma were usually there to keep him at bay, even when his eyes burned with a lust that looked to me might set the whole sorry hovel on fire, if not the whole sad, rain-soaked bog of Eire itself. Fire alright. A slow, malicious simmer in the loins.

Nothing to stop him after Ma's and Da's deaths but fear of the fever.

I mustered a retching cough.

He never even sensed my fear. My brother thought himself my protector, for Jesus' sake. Ah, but who could blame him? Poor Da was a ne'er-do-well, "settin' a fine example for his only begotten son," Ma would scold as she darned and scrubbed, for when Da had work at all, he usually quickly spent the proceeds on liquor, keeping him out of the house sometimes for weeks, "involved," he'd chortle, "in manly pursuits," which as far as we could tell involved mostly singing sad war songs and drinking at the pub, and not so much of the back-breaking work he claimed demanded the consolation of his stout. Of course, these binges would inevitably lead to Da's firing from whatever farm or mill he'd secured a position at, which meant my brother was forced to attempt to support the family (Ma had the two wee ones, one of whom was still at her breast), no small feat at ten years old, and with six mouths depending on him.

It was the peat bogs for him. And he chipped away at them for eight years before the good Lord saw fit to spring us from that blasted island. Emerald, sure, if you've got the pence to live in the dell. For the rest of us, old Eire is a rocky gray promontory of rain and dead bunch grass.

Come to think of it, my brother resembled our dear homeland in all its brutal sentimentality. Oh, he had his tender poetic side, he did, and called me his sweet Donegal parsnip when he rode me like an old cart, bumping and creaking on that old pot-holed road called "making love." What a farce. I knew it then and I learned it time and again afterward: Men, they're just cows in need of milking, no more, no less.

Imagine a young thing like myself, just fifteen when we reached the States, with nothing but *him* to protect me. No Lady Liberty back then to greet us – and so what? She wouldn't have been able to climb off her pedestal anyway. She would have just given me false hope, standing there with her bloody torch, carrying on like some drunken sot of an Irish poet: "... *Your huddled masses ... The wretched refuse ... tempest-tossed."* But who can say? A manly dame, she was – maybe she would have put down that firebrand of hers for a gal like myself and, gathering me up, gone and initiated me in the Sapphic arts, right there in New York harbor no less, thus awakening me earlier and saving me from the relentlessly ensuing series of life-threatening misfortunes they call "men."

"You'll get me pregnant," I'd screech at him when he came at me in the flophouse, not a week into New York and no luck in finding a job. He was Mick trash and he knew it, with an "O" in front of his name and the big arched elfish Irish brows to boot – the strapping Hibernian health of his ruddy, fair-skinned body; those rosy, boyish cheeks; the girth and length of his prodigious Celtic member. The English were dead set on keeping such a one down, land of the free or no. They ran the show here as they did there. That was clear from the outset.

"What did my dear, blessed Ma die for?!" He'd bellow, home from a drunk. *For you, you ungrateful bastard,* I wanted to smart-aleck back. But I held my tongue. The fact was she'd died trying, which in the final analysis amounts to nothing but an occasional sigh. The same thing that'll kill him no doubt. Ah, but I was growing mean. And determined. *I'll not die tryin',* I vowed. Which left me with what? Well, I was fifteen and vague. I had hopes of completin' something.

No, I don't blame my brother in the end. He didn't kill my siblings and my dear mother and Da. The English did. And now they'd driven him to impregnate me, or maybe even kill me. He grew more frustrated by the day; drank more. "But where are you getting your money, Bryce?" I nagged.

"Shut your trap, Constance, or I'll strike you like a bell." And he said that with an utter calm, drilling his eyes through me – it put the fear of God in me, it did.

He'd never hit me before, but it was coming, I could see it. He was aging before my very eyes. The drink was onto him like it had been onto Da. Da never hit Ma until he was well into his cups, at which point he tended to miss. Da had poor aim, unlike my brother – if his ruttin' was any indicator – and Ma was a tougher opponent besides. I'd seen her take Da down with the frying pan on a good half dozen occasions.

"Have you got a little to spare for your brother?" he whined.

And I gave it him. He wasn't one to be stingy with and I'd secured good work doing laundry for a few families up the avenue right off, and afterward was taken on as a maid by the Barney family. As for my brother, I knew he was doing something on the sly that was never really a sure-thing. It came and went, and I had to assume it involved some sort of pirating, extortion, or underhandedness. I'd long since given up offering suggestions. I "was a woman," he'd remind me, "with no knowledge of the world."

"You don't say, Bryce? Well, in the Bible it says what we've done is the knowledge that beats all."

He furrowed his brow. I did need to watch my tongue.

"What we've done? All we've done is survived, Constance, and not very well." Poor lad, playing innocent with me – he was pathetic.

I did get pregnant too. I was afraid to tell him, and, beyond that, I was also heartsick to tell him. I felt sorry for him, I did. And now this.

He was lost and he wasn't adjusting at all. His face had grown redder and bloated. Why, he suddenly looked like a man of forty and he wasn't a day over eighteen. Other than his occasional drunken outbursts in regard to life's injustice toward his dear sainted mother, neither of us had ever really talked of her or Da – or the girls, Bridgette and Eileen. What was there to say? We'd been driven into the sea by the greed and hatred of Englishmen; driven into the drink to die and no one to even check up on us to see what happened. Mother had no family to speak of, and Da – well, Da was at odds with his. He was the youngest of eight brothers, all of whom he more or less resented, and who'd written him off as worthless to boot, his folks long since dead. We never even wrote to his Aunt Mary, who'd obstinately stayed in touch over the years on account of us children, whom she was convinced weren't getting a proper catechism in the Holy Roman Church.

No, we shared our grief with no one, least of all each other. We simply buried it in the stone of New York. What city doesn't look like a graveyard? Stones all in a row. New York City took the cake.

But Bryce took my money. Garnished my wages, he did. So I had to be very crafty about hiding my money, as I'd decided not a day after missing my second moon that I best get away from him once and for all. But he'd discovered all my hiding places in the past on his drunken raves about our single room: the mouse hole, behind the running board, the loose brick outside the window that looked out over the alley; my clothing of course. I learned not to hide it there after just one such discovery. No need to tempt him. And it did take tempting. He resisted the urge to take me, he did; I could see it. It had even become more tender, though I knew that was wrong. But I felt sorry for him and it went easier on me if I was kind. He wasn't a rapist, really; he was just a horny bastard who lacked imagination or sense (not unlike most men, come to think of it). There were other girls, and I knew it because he brought home the clap or a perfume scent on occasion. But he had a habit of taking a fancy to other fellers' wives, which got him into all sorts of trouble. As his sister, he thought of me as *his*, and thus trouble-free. The nerve. He was no Catholic, that was sure, and so didn't fear the troubles the afterlife had in store for him.

Well, there was trouble right here, right now. I was with child. And I was trying to save my money to get out. I knew he wouldn't follow me, and I didn't dare imagine how he'd react to my being with child. If I could get to Philadelphia, or Baltimore – perhaps Boston would be a safer bet. Or maybe even Chicago. There were lots of Irish in all those places. I could find work in any of them, I was confident, and maybe even a little help with raising the child.

I visited the Sisters at the convent on 5th Avenue, and they sent me in to the Mother Superior, who shook her head with disgust (not such a "new" world after all). "So many Irish girls with such loose habits. A shame," she sighed, shaking her head. I never accused my brother. Sister said I was dutybound to have the child, of course, that the Lord kept a strict ledger. "Don't be getting any ideas like some of the lasses in this 'new country,'" she said derisively. "Nothing new under the sun, my dear. All is vanity. Don't forget it." I looked at the starched white of her habit, and her ignorant pride. She didn't know the half of it. Indeed, all is vanity, Sister.

I chewed my lip.

"We'll take you in at seven months, not a day before," she related, as if she were behind the counter at a butcher's shop. Extending me credit, was she?

I excused myself and bid her good day.

"Get that sullen look off your face, Constance – I can't bare it," he'd admonish me. "What is it? I'll get a job, then you can keep your damn money, find yourself a feller, be done with me." He was in his cups, no doubt, red as a beet root with the stout, full of self-pity, and clearly none the wiser about what was transpiring in my womb.

"Bryce, don't talk like that. You're my brother. I won't begrudge ya." And I'd hand him a buck or two.

The Sisters had offered to take me in, sure – but at seven months? And with my brother fifteen blocks down the street? And flat broke? I imagined him breaking into the convent some evening, drunk and naked as the night, with that big shillelagh of his, swinging it around like a mace, threatening the brides of Christ with his rambunctious seed he'd surely take no responsibility for, and which would make quick work of their vows and fill the convent to bursting with wee ones (*a mind of its own,* he'd cry on top of me, *I swear it, Constance, I mean ya no harm*). God, men were like a disease. In need of quarantine. Ah, but such was the world. I didn't have the imagination to see it any other way. I hadn't yet met Old Chen or Captain Jinx.

But I was fortunate to have an employer who had a tad bit more imagination than I did. Old Mrs. Barney had a soft spot for the Virgin Mary, even though our blessed mother had been more or less driven from her Protestant congregation. Perhaps that was why. Or maybe it was the only way she could exact some kind of justice in the world. She was a woman after all, and women understand. She was the first to notice in fact.

"Constance, may I have a word?" She'd ventured as I polished the silver. "In the study, if you will," she'd called out as she headed down the hall before me.

When I reached the study, I found her sitting behind the big mahogany desk, so I assumed it was a business matter. But she did something different this time. She smiled and stood up, and then invited me to sit with her on the settee. *What's this?* I wondered. *Is the lady going to share her troubles?* I'd heard of this before from some of the other girls. How these wealthy ladies needed someone to talk to, a little comforting, girl to girl. "It's loads of fun, Constance. Hours spent drinkin' tea and laughing. Beats scrubbing floors!" But that was Sheila. Angela had a different take on it: "Hah. I have to do both, and it makes my day twice as long. She thinks we're friends, the old sow. I'll show her friendship – and at what price!"

Old Mrs. Barney took my hands in hers, and looked me square in the face. "Now this may be none of my business, child, and I don't mean to pry. And you don't have to say ... but, I've something to ask you."

I nodded.

"Are you with child?" she ventured.

Caught me off-guard, she did. The gall of her. But without thinking, I'd pulled my hands from hers and placed them together over my womb, as if, I suppose, to protect the child. It was instinctual, it was. I was thinking she was likely to fire me next. I looked shame-faced down into my lap at the white, slightly stained apron.

She didn't have to wait for me to speak. It was clear. "I thought so. A woman knows these things." And she nodded in a self-congratulatory way before adding, "Have you told the Sisters?"

"I've told them," I whimpered.

"And? ... Will they take you in then?"

"It's not so simple, Mrs. Barney."

"But what could be more simple, dear," she cheerfully reassured, clearly assuming I was somehow unjustifiably tormented, before adding proudly, "I'm a Protestant, but I commend the Church of Rome for respecting the sanctity of motherhood."

"I can't go there, Mrs. Barney."

"But why not, Constance? It's clearly the thing. Why ever not?"

I shook my head.

"Why not, Constance? Tell me." And her hand kindly pleading on me knee.

"The father, Mrs. Barney! It's about the father!" I nearly shouted through my tears.

"O'Shaughnessy? Does he run the convent too? Is he unsympathetic?"

"No, Mrs. Barney, the *father* of the child!"

"Well, what of the father? Not a Catholic? Has he no work?

Does he drink? We'll make short work of him," she said right-eously.

I was already frustrated with her assumptions that I was exaggerating my predicament, but now I grew angry listening to her vent her prejudices about Irish fellas, all the more so because she'd in fact described my brother to a tee. Certainly, there were good Irish lads, who'd be in the right to chafe at such cruel assumptions about their vices, but my brother wasn't one of them.

The heat left my cheeks then and I began to weep. "It can't be helped, Mrs. Barney; now let me get back to my work," I protested through my tears.

"You're upset, Constance. Something's not right." She looked at me mystified. "Are you or are you not married to the man?"

"Oh, it's more than that."

"More? I don't understand. How can you be more than married?" But my tears had dried, and she sensed I'd given something away. I nearly laughed. More indeed. I'd never say it, but I thought to; it's what was in my mind then: *Have you ever taken a roll with your own blood, Mrs. Barney? You want more, do ya?*

"Constance, please. I know you live with your brother. What – did you go and marry a man who can't even lodge you? Are he and your brother at odds?"

I screeched – roared really. The grief and shame pushed that hard, from deep down in my guts, right up through my breast, kicking my little heart out of the way and bursting like a man's grunting on top of a woman, right out from my squeezed-tight lungs and quivering vocal chords. "There is no man!"

Her jaw dropped just a tad, like some Englishwoman's would, and it dawned on her right then, I think. Since she was no Catholic, I was quite sure a virgin birth wouldn't have crossed her mind. And there was only one Joseph to point a finger at. She hid her shock well though, even if her cheeks went rosy with embarrassment.

But in the end, I think Mrs. Barney got a great deal of satisfaction out of my troubles. She'd waited forever for such a wrong to right; an easy mark. I'd given her a noble cause, I had.

The next day she gave me a card for a Dr. Smith, who had a clinic on the Lower East Side, catering to "women's troubles," or so Mrs. Barney called them. But staring at the card, half-paralyzed in the street on my walk home, all I could keep repeating over and over in my mind was "troubles" – *and why make it plural unless there were twins?*

Ah, but what troubles would await me in the afterlife? That was on my mind too. I wasn't a religious woman, but if there was a God, I aimed to cross the street and go about my business. I didn't need any of his meddling.

My brother gave me an awful look the day I came home from the clinic. He'd chanced upon Dr. Smith's little packet of herbs while rifling through my purse. "You'll burn in hell, Constance."

"There won't be enough fuel for us both, Bryce," I said blithely, snatching the bag from his calloused hands – calloused from holding a pint glass to be sure, or the neck of some scallion; not from honest work, that was certain. I was tired. I'd no patience for a boy just then – so tired that I let myself run at the mouth, and I shouldn't have. Punch-drunk they call it. What a fine pair. Me punch-drunk and him gin-drunk. What a pair! But I went on with it. "Not enough fuel. Our wee ones alone will use up the lion's share of the peat."

He'd have none of that lip and he slapped me across the face and called me the devil's whore. Which made him what? "Such things cost money, you no-good bastard!" I snapped, throwing the herbs down. "There's the sin. You can't even clean up after yourself!"

But that only goaded him on, and we had a terrible row. And he was on me bareback within the hour, even as I pleaded with him. "Do me good, you wretched bastard! Maybe you'll take care of the child after all!" I screeched through my tears. "Go ahead, clean up your mess, bruise the wee fellow! Pummel him!" I bawled. And I fucked him like I never had before.

And life went on, if you could call it that.

The Mother Superior turned her nose up at me next time I saw her on the street. Well, she knew a thing or two. She'd read me like a book.

But I didn't take those herbs. Couldn't muster the courage. Nor did I really want to. I knew I'd never keep the wee one myself, but I didn't want to begrudge him this sweet, sad life either. So, other than the battering ram of my brother that night, a few feeble socks with my fist is all I offered by way of an effort. Let the wee one come then.

Mrs. Barney was shaking her head soon enough, watching me struggling with a bucket up the stairs. "You're three months if you're a day, Constance. Why didn't you go to the doctor?" But she was kindly, she was. She didn't press me. She took the bucket from my hand and put it aside, guiding me down the hall to her office. She went to her desk, sat down, and very methodically pulled out her stationery and pen and wrote a nice note, she did. And what penmanship. Oh, for a moment there I dreamed what it must be like to be a wealthy American Protestant lady, sitting about practicing your writing, playing bridge with your friends, and taking trips to the country every summer. I could stand that, I could.

"Now, Constance," she said, nervously moving her head about – a tad put out, she was – "I don't understand you Catholic girls." She sighed then. But she was chin-up in no time. "Well, it can't be helped. Take this note and cash down to Grand Central Station." My jaw dropped, but I didn't take it right off. So she poked me with it again and again. "I won't have no for an answer, Constance. You don't have to take the doctor's advice, but you can't stay here. I've arranged everything. Been working at it a good two weeks. I've known for some time you've got a full larder there. I'm not stupid."

"Of course not, Mrs. Barney," I interjected, incredulously.

She wasn't listening. "A ticket is already waiting for you and, at the other end of the line, a job in San Francisco. Thank God for the new railroad, my dear. Otherwise I'd have to send you 'round the horn, and I couldn't do that to a girl with child. No. You'd be months at sea, and lose yourself and the child both. That's no way to have an abortion." She stood up and held my chin in her hand then, a tear poised in her eye – "I'd drag you down to Dr. Smith myself if you were my own daughter, but this is America, a free country, and you can do what you please. Fact is, I need a maid, and I'd have to let you go. And I won't do it. I won't put you out. I know it's a shock, dear, for me to up and exile you, but you need to get out of New York, make a new start, with new people. Far, far away from here." And she went dreamy. Now she was envying me, she was. Oh, I suppose any woman's life is a trap. Hers and mine both. She thought she was setting me free, she did, and what could give her more satisfaction really? But you can't give anyone freedom. I learned that the hard way. They've got to take it for themselves. Or surrender to it. But it took Captain Jinx to teach me that. So, I was a slow study – *sue me*, as they say here in the States.

My dolt of a brother, he hadn't laid a hand on me in a month and we hadn't so much as talked, not even about the weather. Just came and went, we did, slept with our backs to each other. But I wanted to say goodbye to him, I did. I didn't hate the boy, no. I was sixteen now and he was all I had in the world. I even grew a tad maudlin as I packed up the two suitcases that held all my possessions. He was the only other thing that was mine. So I went down among the pubs inquiring after him, but to no avail. Just a lot of raised eyebrows. "O'Melveny, eh? He popped O'Keefe's bride, didn't he, Paddy?" And the men, joking among themselves and ignoring me right off, guffawing and swilling their stout, having their fun with my dear brother, showing neither me nor him any respect at all.

Curse the whole lot of them then.

I went home and grabbed my gear, crossed myself for luck, and hobbled down the stairs never to see him again. Poor thing. God, but whatever would become of him? Him and his only begotten son.

The train ride from New York to San Francisco was grand, though it went by like a dream. I'd a lot on my mind and stared out the window mostly. Ah, but the things I saw. The vastness of the country – just farms and forests, with a town now and again, its little church steeples and charming houses. And mountains too – and lakes and rivers rushing – enough to drown all the stars. I even saw wild Indians chasing buffalo and soldiers riding about, and steamboats on the Mississippi River after we left Chicago. And there were folks in wagon trains out in the distance as we approached the high peaks with their snowy summits, reminding me that it was only the rich that traveled like I did – by train. Rich indeed. Lucky in the largesse of the Barneys, I was. There but for the grace of God. Well, it was high time the good Lord aimed a bit of it my way.

There were fellers on the train, of course, many with an eye for a girl. The further west I went, the fewer females I saw in fact, and I could feel my stock rising like – well, like whatever they had in their drawers was likely doing as they ogled my womanly charms.

I had to shoo three of them out of my sleeping car in the course of the trip, and I grew profoundly tired of dining with one or another huckster going on and on about his "business plans" to make it rich out West. I hadn't the nerve to mutter "balderdash" at the lot of them, but I thought it, I did. What fools men are. And to think they aim to impress the ladies with such sorry bilge.

Old before my time, I was. Well, good thing.

I did let one sweet feller take me in the men's room though. He barred the door with a mop and nearly lost himself in my petticoats, his tongue waggin' about like a spaniel on the moor. I liked his enthusiasm, I did, and the fact that he settled for my bum when I mentioned I had the wee one at work upfront. What can I say? I was lonely; he had an elfin grin – a young buck of eighteen or thereabouts, out to see the world. He told me no lies and kept saying over and over again, during dinner, in his endearing Ohio twang, "I just like lookin' at ya. And goddarn, I'd love to see more. That'd be the end-all for me." He charmed me, he did. And happy to be the end-all – if not the end – of any man, I gave him my rear end.

Ah, but lovemaking with Captain Jinx. Now that, that was the end-all for a woman like me. The *what's what*. No more of that silly Priapin prodding. A woman, and a woman alone, knew how to satisfy a woman. But Captain Jinx was no woman, even though she made love like one. Oh, for a man who loves like a woman. Now that's something. Now *that's* a new world. Indeed. If the Mother Superior could see me now. But I've got a tale to catch you up on before my fainting spell on Broadway in Los Angeles and the Sapphic ecstasies that followed. A long, long way to go and far too many men. The worst of which was once again living in the same house as I was. I can still hear old Mrs. Barney's voice, going on and on about the wealthy family on San Francisco's fashionable Rincon Hill that I'd soon be in the employ of. "Oh, the Petersons – they're in need of a good maid." And I *was* a good maid ... *and fair ...* or that's what Stephen said anyway – the mischievous young fifteen-year-old son of Henry and Ada Peterson – as he took me on the dining room table six months later, not a week after I'd had my dear brother's child.

And that set some things in motion, it did. The last man for me, Stephen was. I'd had it.

There'd been others, of course, in San Francisco before that fateful day. I'd made good use of the second trimester, hoping I suppose to find a husband in time for the birth, holding out against hope that I wouldn't have to give the wee one up for adoption.

I met the local Irish gals and went to their parties and picnics, a show on weekends, met their beaus and the droves of lonely men who passed through that bawdy, windy fairy tale of a city. From grizzled miners and their rough charms to hard-working stove makers and flirtatious sailors, I gave it a go and tried to limit myself to hand jobs and the like. I never let on that I was with child, of course, and I could hide it if I dressed proper. Like any girl, I had my dreams of a home and a hearth, a babe at the breast, and a man who brought me flowers and chocolates and treated me nice. So, for a husband, I tried to find nice Irish fellas who went to church and combed their hair; who cleaned up before a date and avoided the saloons. The price, in time, was that old ride in the ox cart, or at least my hand to the pump. Not so bad really. Some were gentle; some were quick. And none of them were endowed like my brother, Bryce, thank God, when they did insist on the in-and-out. I'd no idea until I was sampling the fellas of San Francisco that men weren't all bedecked like an Italian deli with its prodigious salamis hung like a gallows.

Of course, I fell for a sailor. Bad idea that. Oh, but for a man he was good; he knew how to move it about and taught me a thing or two about how to really satisfy a bloke. Why, he rode my bum right through the eighth month. Sailors were just that way, and they say they learn it far out at sea, far from the world of women. I shuddered to think of a world where you'd have to depend on men for tenderness. Men were beasts, insects, diseases, cows in need of milking; like any animal, they needed domestication that only a woman could provide. Otherwise they'd return to the wild. I thought of Bryce at sea for six months, with not a girl on the horizon. And men had no choice but the bum. Who'd take a man of his endowment and what would become of the dear lad? I dare not think of it.

Ah, but the sailor left our enchanted city, and not long after, so did I. Not six months after delivering my wee one Liam to boot. I was a mother, but I'd never known love. I'd only thought I loved the sailor. A queer one, he was. All smiles all the time, and out to satisfy me, the devil take the hindmost – and he whatever was left after that. But what I loved,

I suppose, was his good cheer.

Something the Petersons were a bit short of. When I sat down in the study and told Mr. Peterson about his son's transgressions, his retort was pragmatic at best, callous at worst: "He should have waited at least a few weeks."

"Mr. Peterson, with all due respect, he should have never laid a hand on me. Not three months ago, not last week, not ever again." And my voice rose with the last of those.

Mr. Peterson's eyebrows were arched when I gathered myself and looked up from my lap. Shocked at my display, no doubt. I'd toughened considerably since Mrs. Barney and New York. "Is this or is this not a Christian home?" I demanded. Scrambling for the moral high ground, I was, a dubious effort at best.

"It is," he stated flatly, as if to say, "and your point?"

I knew I was stepping out of line for a girl of my position, but I couldn't help myself. The boy had nearly killed me. "And where is the child? What have you done with him?"

"Constance, calm yourself."

"I will not. Where did you send him?"

"Constance," he admonished me, acting put out, as if my question was inappropriate.

I swallowed and sat up straight.

"Your son – and I'd refer to him by name, but I don't know it – "

"Liam," I enunciated, interrupting him. "His name is Liam."

"Well, that may be, Constance, but it's really up to his parents to give him a name, and that name I do not know."

"It's up to his mother."

"I'm not going to continue this conversation with you, Constance. I am sorry for my son's behavior and can assure you it will not happen again."

"It will not." And I burst out crying.

He sat and waited, handing me his kerchief perfunctorily, but his sympathy was short-lived, and it dried up along with my tears.

"We've done you a favor taking you in, Constance. Now get a hold of yourself. And," his voice rose, "I don't think we need to discuss any of this with Mrs. Peterson. Understood? Now, let's consider the matter resolved, shall we?"

I must have looked at him with hate in my eyes, for he bodily retreated at my glare, sitting back in his chair and furrowing his brow.

"I'd like you to find me another assignment, Mr. Peterson."

"You would, would you?"

"I would."

"And what if I like you right here?"

"It's a free country, Mr. Peterson."

"Is it?" And he laughed. "It is, Constance. Go then. We've been more than kind to you. Go have your 'freedom.'" And he said it mockingly, and then frowned in disgust, opening his desk drawer, his signal for returning to his business.

"I shall then."

"We'll have the uniform." He didn't even look up as he said it.

"Bastard," I muttered, with my chin down.

"What's that?" He snapped. He was looking at me now. But I didn't repeat it.

He stood up as I stood up, but he didn't offer his hand. I'd humiliated him. "Good day, Miss O'Melveny."

"I wouldn't know what one was, sir." And I threw out my woman's breasts, which had swollen with the wee one's need. "You can keep your good day, Mr. Peterson. I've no use for it," I said proudly. And marching out, I added, without turning, "Send your son for the uniform; he's got a knack for getting it off me."

Mr. Peterson's comments on freedom notwithstanding, things didn't go well for me once I was sprung from the clutches of his employ. I became fixated on dear Liam, having no idea where he was and pining for the wee lad, for no better reason than I had no one, and perhaps for spite of that damn Mr. Peterson, his spawn and his callousness. I'd show him, I would – he'd done me no favors.

I became downright tragic, I did – even considered throwing myself at the mercy of the church. They'd placed the child after all. But that was the kind of "in" that did you more harm than good. It was like knowing the DA because he'd prosecuted you. Some connection that was.

I'd been a fool to walk out, I had. No one and not a farthing saved. They didn't pay you enough truly. Especially when you lived in. They were the company store, people like the Petersons.

So I went straight to Sylvia's. Oh, but her mother was a hag. She gave me the once-over – had evicted me before I even set foot in the place.

"What'll I do, Sylvia?"

"You'll go back and apologize."

"I shan't."

"You'll go back and you'll make amends and you'll suck it up while you look for another position." She was getting hysterical.

"Sylvia, I called Mr. Peterson a bastard. And what his son did? The whole thing's unseemly. I won't go back."

"Oh, Constance, girls put up with worse." But she saw my resolve then.

"I won't. I'm through. I'll not set foot in that house." Folded my arms and sat down, I did.

She did her utmost to help me; had a terrible row with her mother while I sat on the front stoop asking the virgin for a wee bit of assistance. Fortunately, Sylvia's mother relented with the condition that I pay rent and scrub the floors. But I was never welcome there really.

Eventually I found a position in a sailor's boarding house through a friend, but the missus didn't have a room for me, so I was stuck at Sylvia's for the foreseeable future. And to stay clear of the hovel and its ornery landlady as much as possible, I hit the shows. Penny operas, vaudeville, you know the drill. If life won't work for ya, they say, go to the shows. You can sample it all there, the trouble and happiness both, minus the consequences of course. A kind of death. What a show.

I got to know more folks that way though, and I inquired about new babes among the Irish maids. But generally to no avail. I went to after-hours saloons, of course, and within a month, though I was no closer to finding Liam, I'd taken to mimicking him, I had, reaching continually for the bottle. Oh, the breast of Mother Ireland. Mother Church. Mother Liam.

God knows what depths I'd have sunk to if I'd kept at it. I was heading for a life of drink – I could feel it, I could. Taste it even, right on my lips, first thing in the morning: whiskeys and stouts mostly. I'd wake up to the sound of ice jangling about in my head like my brains were coming apart.

And then Don Jose . He'd had his eye on me for weeks, he told me, when I finally agreed to a ride home in his coach. But it wasn't a roll in the hay he was looking for, no. And thank goodness for that. I'd have kicked him hard in the bullocks if he'd made a play for me. No, he was heartbroken – as all the beautiful Mexican men out West seemed to be. Not the ugly ones, mind you. They were forever spoiling for a roll with a man, woman, or child and "Una otra cerveza, por favor!" But Don Jose was no lowdown hard-luck ranchero. Genteel chap, he was, in the high Spanish style. Heartbroken for some actress, whom he'd scoured the theaters in search of, but with no success. He wanted me to help him find her.

"Well, do ya, Mr. Jose?" The audacity of their sex. "You can pay me then," I asserted myself.

"Gladly, madam," he nodded calmly. "I have every intention to. And, begging your pardon, Jose is my Christian name, madam. My family name is Francisco Alarcon Padilla de Villaraigosa, of the Rancho Santa Theresa de Avila." Oh, the suave nonsense of him, like some continental, he was.

But it wasn't really until I heard all those syllables that it dawned on me that I was in the presence of not just a gentleman, but a real aristocrat. No mere merchant class Peterson or Barney was Don Jose Francisco Alarcon Padilla de Villaraigosa. But still, I was having none of it.

"It'll cost you dearly, sir. More than a ride home in your coach." And I said it with some disdain. Sure thing, he had the stink of the landowner about him, just as I had the stink of the drink. I'd seen his type in Eire with the English, and I knew what sort of misery lay at the foundation of these landed gentry. I'd take him for all I could get.

"Name your price," he said, with the smug smile and refined accent of a man of extraordinary means.

I shot high. "Five hundred dollars."

He considered and nodded, the smile disappearing as he closed with, "Half now, and half upon finding her." As he said it, it dawned on me that I'd never considered even looking for her. I was shocked in that moment at my own hardness. Where would it end?

He dropped me off, handing me a stack of crisp bills and tipping his hat with a "Buenas noches, señorita."

Next day, I set to work looking for her. I was no slouch when it came to the hunt either. It sharpened my faculties, it did, and though I gained no leads on his long-lost love, within a month I'd found Liam. All of it by asking the right questions of the right folks. My wee fella was living up on Russian Hill with some railroad baron, going by the name of Lawrence Timmons St. John. I'd taken a real wallop of a swat from the hard Irish lass who was pushing him about in the pram. Drunk I'd been, and hot on the trail of the lad after a night boozing with the St. Johns' butler, Sean McGreevey. I'd swatted him just as hard when I'd awoken in some pub that night with him fiddling about in my petticoats. But he'd spilled for me. I'd asked about his work, and like any fool of a man, he'd gone on and on at the invitation, telling me more about the family he worked for than he should have. A kiss or two and an inquiry about any new wee ones about, and he'd shared the gossip that old Madam St. John was dry as mustard and couldn't bring forth a child. "You don't say? And what'll they do? Who'll they pass the fortune on to?" I inquired as nonchalantly as I could muster.

"I'm not a thief, madam, nor a conspirator, nor a man of machinations." The boob thought me a lowly criminal.

"That's a good lad," I said as I poured him another whiskey. "I'm not lookin' to deceive anyone. I just feel for the poor souls who can't have a child. Wish I could help somehow. It's a tragic thing, a barren womb." He was smiling at my charity in no time flat and telling me how I had no need to worry myself, that the St. Johns had secured a child through an adoption from none other than a business associate of Mr. St. John's over on Rincon Hill.

"Ah, you don't say. Why I know a girl, works with the Petersons, had a child out of wedlock," I goaded him on.

His eyes bugged out. "Why, it's the very child!"

I put back my last shot and marched out of that bar, surprised to find it was already well into morning. All the better for me to be calling. I huffed and puffed straight up Nob Hill from Market Street, while the cable cars rattled by. I hadn't a farthing for a lift. But I gained the summit, I did, and then I was out across the saddle and on up to Russian Hill. Winded and sweat-drenched, I was, and drunker than May. I vomited into a beautiful pot of pansies, wiped away last night's cabbage with the backside of my hand, and swallowed the burning acid that filled my throat before soldiering on up the hill. And wouldn't you know it, when I got to the address, there was the bitch, Mary Pat, pushing the pram out the big oak door.

I stormed at her to get a look, and she had the fear of death in her eyes at my approach. I must have looked like a woman crazed, and being that she had no idea who I was, I guess I can't blame her for clocking me with her umbrella. But she didn't have to keep swinging. Lord, she went at me like I was a bug. I could see she wouldn't let up till I was good and squashed. A mother's instinct. And to think she was beating back the *real* mother. A veil of tears, indeed. Truer words have never been spoken. But I was drunker than a Roman and I stumbled away. And I hadn't the nerve to ever go back. But that address was always in the back of my mind, it was.

And I knew his name at least. Lawrence Timmons St. John. One day, I'd find him.

After that, I stuck to looking for Rosa Garcia. She didn't go by that name of course. The Anglos would have none of it. She was Rose Stanton on stage and dyed her hair a ghostly blonde.

I gave it my all, and Don Jose, he did too – he gave me an expense account, paid for all the shows, and never laid a hand on me neither. And I tell you, affection grew in me for him. I, who trusted no man but a sailor with a preference for sodomy, found myself having thoughts for Don Jose. Oh, but of course he had a wife back in Los Angeles. And besides, he had other plans for me.

I never did run across Rosa, though I thought I was onto her once. Seems she'd broken a score of hearts besides just Don Jose's, and was rumored to constantly re-create herself to escape the clutches of her many suitors. There was a raven-haired beauty named Poppy who came through town once that some said was her, and there were rumors that a hugely obese seamstress down at Mission San Jose was none other than our Rosa, victim to some glandular illness. But none of those leads ever went anywhere. The woman was either dead or had stolen away somewhere. I was pretty sure she no longer graced the stage. Just another Joaquin Murieta, she was, a Six-Beaued Pete, pardon the pun. There were always folks with a tale to tell – how she'd headed north to Alaska; and one barmaid swore up and down that she'd set sail for Japan and was living with some shogun in a palace. Suffice it to say, Don Jose gave up on finding her in the end, and he returned to Los Angeles.

I hated to see him go. We'd been in the habit of having lunch at the New World Coffee Saloon downtown, with all the captains of business and back-slapping politicians. I felt out of place in my threadbare housedress, and I had to conceal my desire to scowl now and again at some of those arrogant chaps and their bellicose behavior. But what girl doesn't like a bit of glamour? I'd order oysters on the half-shell and share whatever leads I'd found, while he doled out the cash. With that quiet, distant smile of his. Like the kindly older brother I'd never had.

I missed Don Jose, I did.

And then, not a month later, I received a letter from him asking if I'd consider coming south to tutor his and his numerous sisters' and brothers' children on the big land grant they raised cattle on east of LA, El Rancho Santa Theresa de Avila. "Madam Constance, we speak exclusively Spanish on the rancho, but California is decidedly a part of Los Estados Unidos now, and the children need an English tutor."

The dear man. Well, it was high time for that bit of grace the good Lord owed me. I booked passage on a coach with the money he had sent up, which was waiting for me at the bank office downtown. What did I have to lose? When you're offered a door out of the labyrinth of San Francisco and its cryptic misty nights, you don't ask questions or get cold feet. You offer your gratitude and pack.

Heard that song then, right there on the coach ...

> *He's Captain Jinx of the western prairie*
> *Once dubbed Loreen but now called Larry*
> *He's manly as whiskey – he's no faerie*
> *But he'll never join the army*
>
> *Oh, Captain Jinx of the western reaches*
> *Turned in his bodice for some riding breeches*
> *Like any feller, he's got a thing for peaches*
> *But he'll never join the army!*

I heard Jinx returning then, in the same fashion he'd departed – clump, clump, clump, and coming through the door with a pitcher of water and a crystal goblet that looked like the Holy Grail itself. The sun was setting through the window, and the glass sparkled like a multicolored jewel as he tipped it to my lips. "There you are, miss; take a few sips."

His dark kindly eyes, and heavy brow. A unibrow, that's

what they called it – and it made my womb quicken, it did.

The Captain stepped back then and leaned himself on the window ledge caddishly, grinning seductively, the sun setting brilliantly behind him through the glass. Right there, in the Cheshire Arms Hotel, Captain Jinx just glowin' in the orange light, like our dear Savior himself, who I thought just then must have been a woman. What man would ever hang on a cross? What woman never had?

He asked me then if I believed in love at first sight, and he said it with a fair amount of braggadocio, so that I knew I wasn't the first to hear that line.

"I don't believe in love at all – not the kind you're talking about, Captain," I blurted out defensively, as I struggled to raise myself, blushing with the effort like some cheap red wine. "I need to be going."

"Now, now, miss, don't be exertin' yourself," he warned, gently pushing me back down by the shoulder with his big, calloused hand. "You've had a shock, and the Captain here is gonna see to it that a lady gets her bearings before she runs off."

I knit my brow, but relented, and he gave me a reassuring smile, before walking back to the window where he waxed philosophic, looking down into the street, showing me his backside. "Let the menfolk run from place to place without a thought. A woman's gotta collect herself and know what's happening around her. A woman's gotta know *what's what.*" And he looked back over his shoulder at me then, squinting. "Wouldn't you agree, Miss ..."

"O'Melveny," I answered.

"A good Irish Catholic gal, eh? Always did have a weakness for 'em."

"Well, I'm not much of a Catholic, sir."

"There's hope for you yet then, ma'am," he winked. "And do you have a first name, Miss O'Melveny?"

"Constance."

"Constance, eh? As the northern star?"

"I wouldn't know about such things," I sighed, running

my hands down the front of me to keep my dress in check. "I keep my head down mostly." And I had for the most part during those last most peaceful five years of my life, which Jinx was just now interrupting. She was reviving the city girl in me, she was, with all that repartee. And there I was playing innocent. I didn't miss the city life one bit. Sure, the rancho could get painfully bucolic, wee brown ones clamoring about or no, but I had the freedom to come into town once a fortnight, though LA was decidedly not San Francisco (a real frontier backwater, it was, by comparison). I'd come in for a show, purchases of chalk and parchment, a new dress, a bag of sweets with which to bribe the children. I'd just been at the confectioner's, in fact, gorging myself on chocolate, when that day's lesson presented itself in the form of a she-male cowboy-shaped lightning bolt of knowledge from out of the dusty old pages of Los Angeles.

"Constance is no dreamer, eh?" He looked me straight in the face then, posing like a real cock of the morning. "Do you know who I am, Constance?" And then he repeated it slowly, with more emphasis: "Do you know who Captain Jinx is?"

Full of himself, he was. "I've heard of ya," I offered nonchalantly.

"Ah," he gloated and sat down, so that the bed bounced as he slapped his hands on the tops of his thighs, smiling broadly with pride in his fame. "They all know me. What have you heard?" And he looked at me eagerly. Goodness, that unibrow. I felt my nipples tighten like a well-laced shoe.

"Heard?" And I tried to collect myself, I did.

"About me?" And he pointed with his thumb, poking between where his breasts should be, boisterous as a carousel barker. "Why me! – Captain Jinx!"

But I was no girl at a fair. I had my hard-earned pride. I sat up on my elbows, and his head went back like a bird's as I boldly told him a white lie. "I've never heard of ya, except for just downstairs, when some old coot asked his shoeshine boy who you were. So stop your fussing."

"My fussing?" he answered with a half-smile, standing

up. "I just saved your life, madam."

"Let's not exaggerate, Captain Jinx. I was merely fainting. This is the nineteenth century. Women do that."

"Do they? Well, I've never fainted." And out went his chest; up went his chin; to his belt went his thumbs.

I blushed then, and he grinned.

"And you know why? Because I'm not afraid of anything, Constance. And you needn't be neither. Not now." And he winked again. He turned and walked back to the window. "I guess you're new to California if you haven't heard my name."

"On the contrary, I've been a year in San Francisco, and another five here in Los Angeles."

Jinx raised his brows then, playing at incredulous, but thought better of it, and chuckled. "You play hard to get, don't you, madam?"

"Normally, it doesn't matter what I play. I'm a working gal, and I try to dodge what I can. Had my fill of menfolk, frankly. Always seem to get on the wrong side of 'em."

"What's the right side?" Jinx interjected.

We both laughed then.

I looked at her then as she gesticulated with her hand: "Always keep 'em out in front of you, at least ten feet. And be ready to draw."

"I'm not a violent woman, Mr. Jinx," I blushed.

"No, I suppose not." She knit her brow. "But there's too many of them. Trust me. I'm a cowboy. I know what's what. You handle men like you handle bulls and you'll be okay. And you know how they handle bulls?" She huffed. "Well, most of them they kill and eat. A good thing too," she added, with emphasis, before continuing. "You only need one for a herd. The rest of them just take to fighting and causing all sorts of mayhem. What I did out in Colorado, out in Wyoming and New Mexico, was castrate bulls. Until they got wise to me. Then the work always dried up, or some cowboy got hired in my place. Not because I didn't do a good job, mind you. No, they got wise to me in the bunkhouse, or the womenfolk let on."

He shook his head. "That's secret male knowledge, it is. They protect it, Miss Constance. Why if more women were a bit more curious and forceful and knew what I've come to know, men would have a hard time making an argument of it." And he nodded. "A very hard time indeed. Someday human society will get that it's the only way. As with cattle, so with men. If you castrate nine out of ten of 'em you get a peaceful herd, and just bring in the sperm in the spring. You don't need but a weekend a year of what we put up with every day in human society. A darn waste of resources, and it leads to crime. Why, right now there's something brewing in China-town, and mark my words, Constance, someone's gonna die." Jinx was on a roll, and popped in a plug of tobacco, all the while shaking his head with disgust.

I just listened. How could I have known that what was brewing right then in Chinatown would take Old Chen with it too. Brewing wasn't the word for it though. It swept like a fire. Something was simmering; that's what it was. I've cooked enough to know the difference between a simmer and a brew. A simmer can burst into flame. But, of course, that's all hind-sight. I didn't know Chinatown from Sappho just then.

But I did know a thing or two about my heart. No, brewing wasn't it at all – and whatever simmer it was on was running a tad too hot. I blushed scarlet, and attempting a recovery, I cursorily offered, "Well, what can be done about it, Captain Jinx? It's just how men are."

"Well, I know what I know." And his eyes lit up. "And I aim to apply my knowledge."

I swallowed and looked directly at him. "What you gonna do, Jinx? Castrate 'em?"

She guffawed then. "That ain't legal!" And she laughed some more. "There's different ways of castrating men be-sides. We ain't cows and they ain't bulls. I'm talkin' figura-tively, Miss Constance." She looked at me long and hard. "And figuratively, yes, I aim to castrate as many as I can."

I broke out in a laugh then too. I'd never heard such a thing. And he laughed right along with me. We laughed and looked into each other's eyes, and then Jinx reached for my crystal goblet and, using it as a spittoon, hawked out his chewing tobacco and plopped down next to me on the bed, to the chorus of the bedsprings that made me think just then that Jinx was a stone thrown in a pond, and all that squeaking the ripples spreading out across the surface of the holy water.

And then he said, no bones about it, "I've half a mind to kiss you if I might seek your permission, madam." No need to answer that. I simply closed my eyes and stuck out my tongue like the priest had just offered me the host – *In the name of the father, the son, and ...* Well, men had nothing to do with it, and the next thing you knew, our lips were pressed together like two hands praying. Holy, it was. His mouth full of the residue of sacred tobacco, or so the Indians called it. And we took it from there, we did. A tunnel alright. I fell headfirst, just spinning around. Went faint all over again.

"Dearest Virgin," I muttered. I reconsidered the virgin birth then, I did. 'Tis true no man could be involved in God coming into this world. I understood it all completely right then. That angel was either a drag king to end all, or God was a bitch in heat for Israel. And a bitch in heat is capable of just about anything, including an immaculate conception.

Metaphysics aside, what Jinx wanted were peaches, and as God is my witness, I gave them to her, my bodice spilling its fruit like a cornucopia. And Jinx was all over them like a babe famished, taking the part of my dear lost Liam. I pushed him away then, embarrassed and shocked, and got to lacing my bodice back up in a hurry. "I need to be going now, Mr. Jinx," I muttered, trying to compose myself. "I thank you for your assistance."

"Whoa there, Constance," he protested. And he was down on one knee by my side, with my hand in his hand, and he took it and he kissed it, before adding, "Forgive me, Constance, that was mighty forward of me. But if you'll excuse me for saying so, you're in no shape to be going anywhere."

I blushed again, but recovered myself enough to ask him, "What exactly are your intentions, Mr. Jinx? I'm a schoolteacher now. I don't need your trouble. Who and what are you?" My heart was beating like all get-up.

"Just a runaway like everybody else." He raised that unibrow in a reassuring innocence. "Came from Virginia originally."

"And have you got a Christian name?" I persisted.

"Have I. Couldn't be more Christian. You remember Veronica from the Gospel?"

I was reviving, I was. "I do that. She wiped the Savior's forehead on Calgary."

"She did just that." And then Jinx stood up and hitched her thumbs in her belt loops and strutted around the room a spell. "Well, folks call me Vernon." And she turned and winked.

I remembered the song then. "What about Larry and Loreen?"

She laughed, bloating with the pride of her legend. "Vern's not so good for a rhyme, Constance. Kinda falls flat."

"If you say so, Captain. But how about your last name? It isn't really Jinx is it?"

That got him to stop his pacing. "Well, it's a tad early for that story, my northern star."

"And it's a tad late for me to be asking, I daresay." And I tried again to sit up. "I do need to go, Mr. Jinx. Enrique's waiting for me up near Chinatown."

"Okay, but I hope I wouldn't be presumin' if I were to insist I escort you up there like a proper gentleman."

"Is that what you are, Jinx?"

"'Tis. I know what's what."

I turned and looked at him, "You talk in riddles, Mr. Jinx, with your *what's what* and *who's who* and *he/she*. I'm a schoolteacher. I strive for clarity." And I pulled on my boots and readied myself to go.

He leaned back on the window ledge again, not even trying to stop me this time. "You'll die strivin' then, Miss O'Melveny. It's not clarity the world has to offer."

"There you go again." And I was up now, off the bed completely, holding my own, brushing the dust and lint from the front of my dress, resolved to put up with no more of his nonsense.

"All I'm saying is that *what's what* and clarity ain't the same thing, Constance."

I was growing impatient. "Stop your confoundment, man, and speak clearly," I blurted in frustration.

"Well, for instance. It's clear you fainted. And it's clear I saved your life."

"Huh," I chuffed. "You give yourself a wee bit too much credit, sir."

"Let me finish, Constance." And he looked at me, with just a hint of pleading in it. "As the northern star?" He paused, winking with that grin of his. "You see, Constance, I don't know anything about the stars either, but I know what's what about 'em. You can sail a ship by 'em, find your way out of the mountains, and you don't have to be an astronomer. Get my drift? Half these lowdown bastards don't know what I am, but they know what's what, and when they don't, I show 'em. Sure, they're confused, but they know what's what after that. So, excuse me for disabusin' you of the notion, madam," and he got haughty, "but I don't put much stock in clarity."

I swooned again, and into his arms I fell.

When I came to, I was full in his arms, lying we were together on the bed. And his lips once again met mine, and you could say I fainted again, too, because the pleasure I fell into next made me forget where I was, who I was – and as for pronouns and interrogatives and prepositions and all that business – well, their clarity was gone. But Jinx was right: He certainly knew what was what. He ravished me, he did. I spilled my bodice like a slop bucket to a hungry litter of piglets – and God knows his passion did have something of the porcine to it. We were naked as the moon in no time flat, and as mixed up as metaphors could be, she just lapping at me like a thirsty hound, and me like a pair of open curtains letting in a blinding sun. And then she was reaching inside me for the gift I longed to give her. And I gave and I gave. Goodness, the generosity. I didn't know I was capable of it. I thought about gold panning, silver mines – I was California itself and she was a trapper, a 49er, a conquistador, and a Franciscan friar bent on my soul – and all at the same time besides. We went at it like history itself: two steps forward, one step back. Like square dancing really, only faster and rarely taking a time-out to touch the ground. But he did it all like a woman – that's what made it something else entirely. I learned a thing or two about the gentleness of a tongue and a hand, I did. You can have Priapus. It's like churning butter with a sword. And a woman's a good wooden spoon, she is. A good wooden spoon.

The sky had gone purple by the time our passion was spent, lying there we were like something thrown up on the shore. Goodness, Jinx had taken me sailing; that's what he'd done. And not on the blasted Atlantic either. No. Jinx and me had floated on air, we had. Maybe it was more like flying actually. Not sailing at all. Or maybe a little of both. I've heard stories of flying fish out toward Catalina. Fish that fly, if you can believe that. Course I've never seen them myself, so maybe it's just a legend, like Queen Calafia and her Amazon ladies from that old Spanish story of the mythical land of California. Or like Joaquin Murieta, Six-Toed Pete, and our very own Captain Jinx.

Because Jinx took me there, she did. She took me to where the legends were true, she did. She showed me what's what. And she made me recite it back to her, she did. I moaned what it was. I howled it. I belonged to the Captain and *what* she did after that, no two ways about it. Like a sailor belongs to the sea.

Jinx was playing with my curls and ruminating on Chinatown. "Like I said, Constance, men ain't terribly necessary."

But I jumped, and shouted, "Enrique!"

Jinx looked at me, his face a casual question at best.

"I've got to be back to the rancho by nightfall," I anxiously related, pushing back the coverlet.

Jinx's eyes casually rolled toward the purple light of the window. "Nonsense, Constance, we're staying here tonight."

I looked at him sternly. "Don Jose would be worried sick. And I have to think of the children. I'm like a mother to them."

"Like a mother, Constance. But children –" and he hoisted himself onto his elbows, his beautiful breasts now free of the cloth that kept them bound, "– they know what's what."

Ignoring him, I went to the window and could see dusk had clearly won out over day while our passion spent itself. I leaned against the windowsill to keep from falling, so spent was my body. I'd not make it to the coach stop where Enrique had been instructed to pick me up.

"I can't just leave Enrique out there waiting," I panicked.

Seeing that I was upset, Jinx hopped out of bed then and pulled on his trousers and threw on his shirt, wrapping the cloth around his chest first to keep his small breasts flat. "We'll go up there together and send Enrique on his way."

I struggled into my dress and boots and cursorily combed my locks, tying them in a scarf to contain the unruliness of them after that stormy sea journey with Jinx. My knees were weak. Jinx garnered that and reached for me.

"Kiss me, Jinx," I commanded.

And that he did. "Come along, Constance." And out went his arm to take me down the stairs and onto the street like a real lady, though I was something else now, and felt a tad ridiculous, and maybe even a little nostalgic for the girl who was gone now forever.

When we got downstairs, there was a bit of a ruckus, with the pudgy little proprietor ordering some boys about, having them nail boards up across the windows.

"What's the trouble here?" Jinx blurted out.

"Haven't you heard, Jinx? There's a mob, headin' to Chinatown."

"To Chinatown? What for?"

"It's been brewin' for days. A Tong war. Everyone's talking about it."

"Well, I heard that," Jinx answered, somewhat irritated, "but what's that got to do with a mob? Those Chinese gangsters keep it to Chinatown. Never seen 'em let loose outta their own territory."

"Well, they've done it this time," the little man enthused. "They've stepped over the line, and they've brought a mob down on 'em. Chen Lu and Tang Li were fighting over a woman and some fella tried to intervene. Shot him dead."

"Well, that's Chinatown," Jinx shrugged.

But the proprietor wasn't through, and he related his final words with a gravity I'd witnessed but rarely: "The man who got shot was a white man."

The color left the Captain's face all at once, and his mouth dropped to a frown. I knew then something serious was at play, and I clung to him, I did. "Go back upstairs, Constance, and don't leave this hotel."

"I'll do no such thing!" Jinx looked surprised and put upon, but I said my piece. "Enrique's out there, and he'll be worried. And Old Chen ... my god!" I knew as well as Jinx what was happening. It had happened before. The mob. Drunken and full of vengeance, I'd seen them hunt down black men, Indians, other whites, and, of course, Chinamen. For whatever reason, it always went worse for the Chinamen. There'd be hangings tonight.

Seeing my resolve, the Captain gave me a once-over. "You'll need breeches, Con."

"I've got a pair of trousers with suspenders, and a shirt," the proprietor volunteered. "But begging your pardon, Captain, I wouldn't take a lady up there."

"That'll do," snapped Jinx. And I went and followed the fellow, hoisting the garments on in his office, while he and Jinx chattered excitedly in the lobby. He handed me a bowler hat as I emerged, under which I gathered up my curls and, slipping on a pair of beat-up old Mexican huaraches he then proffered, joined the Captain and stepped out into the street. "Best to strut," Jinx advised me. "These animals respect but one thing – brute strength." She put her hand to her pistol, and widened her walk.

Several blocks up the street, we caught up to the shouting that had drawn us on, and there was the mob, surging and barking like some sick blob of mutated, depraved humanity, a roiling boiling mudslide from the Chavez Ravine come to life, hungry and drooling for blood. I could sense right off it had precious little to do with whoever had been caught in the crossfire. I could feel the frustration of those men and each and every failure that had stored itself up in their warped, wounded hearts for just this moment. What the mob was, was permission. Permission to kill, and for the meagerest of reasons.

They were marching straight toward Chinatown lookin' for "John Chinaman," and they carried rope, shovels, pistols, clenched fists, and more obscene words for Chinamen than I could comprehend or count.

"We've got to get out ahead of them; got to get up to Chinatown before they do," Jinx shouted, grabbing me by the arm and running us both up an alleyway south of Broadway and then up Spring Street parallel to the mob, dodging in and out among the drunkest of the stragglers, who likely had no idea at all what the fuss was about, but they were armed and ready to join the feeding frenzy, no questions asked.

We ran and ran, till the huaraches tore the flesh from my feet; till we saw the red lanterns swinging quietly in what was the beginning of a Santa Ana wind, those eerie breezes from the desert that always portended disaster.

We doubled back and when we rounded the corner, we saw them coming, a slow amorphous march of guttural shouting humanity, lit up by torches and shrouded in their smoke. Chinese businessmen were boarding up their shops, women and children were hiding in the upper stories or running past us to seek shelter further up the street. It was appalling and took me back to those coffin ships. Masses of humanity, moving, and the prospects not good.

"Constance," Jinx shouted, "where does your friend Old Chen live?"

But I had no idea and just shrugged. I'd never been to Chinatown; I'd only carried on my friendship with Old Chen via the rancho.

I wiped the rouge from my cheeks best I could, but I was paralyzed with fear and stood stone still on the corner as Jinx strode like a gunslinger straight down the middle of the street, hands at his belt, chin up, unibrow furrowed to show he meant business. Shots were fired in the air. I was sure he was dead. I was torn between my admiration for his chivalry and my amazement that he was walking straight into his death.

"Captain Jinx, stop!" was all I could think to say. But she just kept on.

The men walked right up to him, shouting and warning him to get out of the way; they were dead set on John Chinaman, and they'd be damned if anyone tried to stop them.

"Gentlemen!" she shouted. "It's high time we let the law handle such matters." But they only roared, and not a minute after the words left her mouth, I saw the Captain's head turn and her eyes fell upon what she'd seen others look to: officers of the Los Angeles Police Department standing sentry on the corners and blocking the side streets where the Chinese might seek to escape.

Jinx pulled her pistol. The crowd roared, but it stopped.

And then the shouts started up again, just one or two at first, and then a crescendo. "It's Jinx!" Snippets of the song: "... *Bodice for breeches ... but he'll never join the army! ...*" Laughs and guffaws. "You damn hermaphrodite freak! Get outta the way!"; "Kill the bitch!" But even though the tide had clearly turned against her, there were men who wouldn't dare kill a woman, gender-bender or no.

I breathed a sigh of relief. But only for a moment, as I watched their faces harden, the laughter increase. Because these men were making the same conclusion I had just a few hours ago. Jinx was more of a man than any of them, and if that were so, then they had every right to kill her. And maybe even more right to do so. She'd showed them all up. And nothing riles a man more than the hardest of truths: they're all, each and every one of them, to a man, cowards.

A shot rang out and I heard Jinx's pistol clatter across the paving stones and saw blood begin to drip from his hand. I ran toward him, and as I did the mob came on like a tidal wave from the other direction, swamping Jinx and calling out for Chinese blood.

"Captain Jinx! Captain Jinx!" I yelled, kneeling down in the street and covering my head as the men jostled by, their knees knocking into me, the din of their rage like a herd. A herd of cattle. My god, if the Captain's hurt, they'll be trampling her.

As they surged by and began to thin out, I spied the Captain, curled up in fetal position, bloodied and dusted over, a heap of trampled flesh. "Jinx! Vernon! Veronica!"

That's when Old Chen appeared. "Oh, thank God, Chen! Help me!"

We got Jinx up and helped her to the sidewalk and then into Chen's shop, but not before those police sentries got a good look at the three of us and started shouting, "Chinaman! Chinaman! Seven o'clock!"

The mob reeled and turned like a great beast, and Jinx, having come to, checked his gun cartridge, and then undid the safety as Chen pushed us up the stairs, "Go, go, Con-ee, up stair, go."

I followed Jinx, who found a window and aimed as if he were going to take on the whole mob himself. "Jinx, for God's sake, they'll kill you!" I warned.

"It ain't me they're after, Constance." And he said it with an emptiness I've never seen in a man's or a woman's face before – or since. We crouched at the window, and he put his arm around me and held me to him.

Then Jinx shot his bullets into the ground on the street in front of the mob to keep them back, and that's when the bullets started flying in on us. But the bastards had already gotten inside through the back, and the next thing we saw when the shooting died down and we spied out the window was Chen and his son, both being dragged by the scruff of their necks into the street, where with cheers and hollering, and no delay at all, they strung them up the lamp post, ignoring their desperate Cantonese pleas, and let them swing and expire there right before our very eyes.

I'd never even gotten out a scream. I'd gone mute in horror, my eyes blurring with the tears that had begun to flow. Good god, they're less than animals.

"You keep right on cryin', Constance," Jinx told me. "It'll keep you from fainting." But how he winced as he tightened the cloth Chen had wrapped his bleeding hand with; how all that blood and the smoke in the air; and the way Chen moved slowly outside the window – all of it made me feel faint indeed.

But more than faint, I felt dead inside. No tears left to flow. I looked at Jinx, which revived me somewhat. What a contrast. Death out the window and the most life I'd ever witnessed right next to me. I wondered why, which led me to ask, "Where's the girl, Jinx?"

"What girl?" Jinx snapped, distracted by the mob, anger now rising in her like a blood-red sun, as they began to once again head north up the street.

Everyone had forgotten the girl by then, even my dear Jinx. I was barely in the room anymore. Certainly not in Chinatown. I heard waves lapping. The waves of the Atlantic. I heard coughing, and I knew it was the fever coursing through the steerage. I heard the mournful grunts of my pathetic brother plying the waves of my own lonely sea. A long, lonely whistle followed, and I heard buffalo hooves drumming on the plain, the high-pitched screams of Indians; mountains rose. And heaven over that. Old Chen, like fruit, huge and heavy, ripe and dead. I thought then of my breasts and peaches and young Liam.

Jinx looked at me strangely then, like I was vanishing before her eyes. "You alright, Constance? Stay with me, Constance. Keep crying." And she held me to her tighter.

"I've no more tears, Veronica. Just a question. If you were the King of Sparta, would you or would you not fight for me if it came down to that?"

"There'd never be a need for it," she answered, as if the question were ridiculous. "It's my job to keep you happy so you don't feel the need to look for attention from another man. If you leave me, that's your right. You're not my chattel. You're a woman."

"What *do* you need, Captain Jinx?"

"Peaches," she said matter-of-factly.

That got the tears flowing again. "Then you'll have 'em, Captain Jinx. As God is my witness, you'll have peaches." I broke the strings of my bodice then and out I spilled. And she put my hand to her mound of Venus, and she whispered as she did so, "There's no balls here. I'd never do anything foolish *for ya* or *to ya*." And then she buried her dear face in my breasts, and that's the last I remember of her, suckling like a lamb. Like my dear lamb, Liam.

Some said he went to Mexico; some said they came back for him, and the reason I don't remember anything is because I've either shut it out of my mind or had fainted and missed the conclusion; that they hung him like Old Chen from a lamp post. Nineteen Chinamen they killed that day, including my dear Old Chen and his son, who it turned out was the instigator of the whole thing. The Paris who'd tried to steal another man's Helen, the lovely girl they called White Lotus Flower, whom no one ever saw again.

I'm back on the rancho now, but it took me several weeks of recuperation before I could once again set my mind to teaching the wee ones about the contradictions and irregularities of the English tongue. Sometimes all I want to do now is warn them of the lies and half-truths and the inevitable betrayals of life, and to hell with grammar. Ah, but the world is what it is. Jinx was right about that. If it's clarity you're looking for, you'll look forever, and you're a liar if you think you can tell anyone else what the truth about anything is. So I teach the children in the way the Captain instructed me. I tell them the only thing worth knowing. I try to teach them *what's what.* And they get angry sometimes. "Yes, my dears, math is beautiful, but it's your understanding of books and stories; your ability to never know the answer, but to sense the mystery and to listen to it – that's what counts; now that's what'll take you far, and get you through this veil of tears. That, my dears, is *what's what.*" Their pouts turn to sighs then, they do.

The human heart knows a thing or two that the sorry mind can never comprehend.

And when I have my rest, working in the kitchen garden or cooking up a stew, I don't torment myself with what became of my Captain Jinx and if he'll ever return. I see him in my mind's eye; I dream the Irish dreamer's dream, and see him in golden light on horseback, with White Lotus Flower clinging to him as they ride, carrying with them a knowledge only women can share together, and I God bless 'em both, wish them a safe journey, and I cross myself, I do.

Because we're all crucified in the end. She was a worthy Veronica, she was. And she comforted my soul, she did. Did more than that – she unveiled it; mined it out of me like a seam of silver. And if we come to this mortal coil in search of God, well, a good lover's a saint then, for showing us it's deep inside of us already, and that *he's* a *she* besides. Or both. Or neither. I've learned that much.

Sure, I think of poor Ma and Da; dear Bridgette and Eileen. I wonder sometimes about Sylvia and my sailor, about Mrs. Barney, my poor brother, Bryce, and my wee progeny, Liam. I could go looking for them all, I could. But I'd die tryin'. And I vowed long ago not to do that. I wanted to complete something, I did. To accomplish something. And that I did, far out at sea, with a rogue named Captain Jinx. Never thought I'd find what I found there, but I *did* find it – the promised land every immigrant comes looking for. And it gets me to singing, it does:

> *He's Captain Jinx of the western prairie*
> *Once dubbed Loreen but now called Larry*

He's manly as whiskey – he's no faerie
But he'll never join the army!

Oh, Captain Jinx of the western reaches
Turned in his bodice for some riding breeches
Like any feller, he's got a thing for peaches
But he'll never join the army!

My dear Captain Jinx, who knows what's what
Who cracks the shell and shows you the nut
It brings him trouble, but he rides off free
No, he'll never join the army!

The Mercy Seat

On the third Wednesday of every month I'd visit fat Dr. Pinski, an old demoralized psychiatrist who couldn't have spotted a suicide if the malcontent's errant bullet ricocheted off his desk and grazed him with a flesh wound. And chances are it would be a flesh wound, cuz he was packing. Flesh. Lots of it too.

I liked how he didn't pay attention. And how big he was. Too big to lay chase. I didn't want him to catch me after all. I guarded my heartbreak like a dog.

But it wasn't love or trauma or none of the usual culprits. I was born hangdog. It's who I am. The ground of my being, as the Buddhists would say. "An affliction," Father Mulroney called it. "A pity," said Father Cavanaugh – and he oughtta know; he was kind of pitiful himself. When we got caught, he claimed that he was just trying to cheer me up.

I told my mother what me and the Father did made me happy.

Broke her heart. She rarely cried. I didn't want to hurt her. I just wanted to be happy, and that's all she wanted me to be. Who's to say what works? A kid's young enough to think something will and to keep trying.

But they sent Father Cavanaugh away, and I came home. To My Crazy. My sad despondency, bequeathed all these years later to pathetic Dr. Pinski. The Soup is what my mother called it. The Soup with too much salt. "It's not you. It's your Soup," and she'd point to my head: "Too much salt." God bless her for trying to explain, trying to make it not-me. It's not who then; it's just what, and sometimes it's where.

My Crazy.

It's what I return to. Home.

My dinner at the end of the day. Soup. Fold up the day and give me my Soup. To warm my bones.

"No more priests for Seamus," my mother announced. That was the end of my days as an altar boy, but we still went every Sunday, albeit to the other parish across town.

You can't take that away from me …

At the ripe age of thirteen (six months after the Father's transfer and a quart of Drano under the belt on account of the whole sorry business), I entered therapy and the realm of the dumb left-brain priests of the mental health profession. I rue the day. I've learned what works for all them other folks has nothing to do with me, and that psychology's little bag of tricks is a sorry and limited one, middle class all the way, more straight and narrow than any crap any priest ever told me. Be wary of the shrink. I'd just as soon pass through the eye of a needle.

So I wasn't intimate with Dr. Pinski. He disinterestedly would state now and again that I was one of his 375 patients besides. He said it like it should impress me. *Gee, don't know how you do it, Doc.* I only wondered why he'd ended up at the Mental Health Department in the first place. What had he done wrong? He certainly wasn't there because he had a social conscience, or because it was some kind of high-paying plum job. No sirree. In fact, he seemed profoundly bothered and put out by the whole business. I figured there'd been one too many suicides on his watch out there in the world where they'd sue you for fucking up. Certainly, no one was gonna sue him at County Mental Health.

I'd spend all of five minutes with him at my monthly appointment, usually talking about movies he thought were swell. I was careful not to comment sarcastically or he might up my dose. I knew the protocol: Don't say anything negative, don't have any problems, don't show any weakness – just get the drugs and go. Half the time I walked in there near comatose with depression or frazzled to teeth grinding with anxiety. I pulled myself together. Pulled.

The drugs were free. Prozac, Paxil, Zoloft, Wellbutrin, Serzone – like some sick pantheon of old gods who sounded anything but cheerful. Happy as a clam.

They never worked.

But there was always a new one, so I kept trying. Or not me so much as whatever part of me was a good attitude. Or was it? My so-called good attitude, when I could muster it, was all tied up with proper behavior, no fear, don't panic, choose life (and other clothing lines), security, Catholicism, defeat, Mom ("You can salvage any Soup – it's just a mixture of ingredients"). It didn't necessarily dawn on me that even my good attitude was a bad one. Nothing dawned on me, no sir. I'd thought it all out so many times, I wouldn't have recognized the dawn if, like a star, it popped up one morning and whacked me upside the head with ten trillion tons of white-hot hydrogen.

People called me jaded when I talked like that. But I never understood that term. Jade is pretty and worth something, yes? I was rusted, if I was anything. Going out in an orange blaze of muted, anonymous, common-as-dirt oxidation. Nothing pretty or valuable about it. That was me, my own style of decadence, minus drugs, sex, and the usual moral culprits. Just a whacked mind, coming apart in the rain. A stubborn whacked mind. Unwhackable. Just ask the stars.

Then Jimmy.

Jimmy had a bay window on Guerrero Street. Jimmy and me on the carpet in the empty room, making love; making our first mess. A bay window and an immigrant Chinese family next door, stinking the place up with wonderful-smelling food. And with twin six-year-old mischiefmaking serotonin reuptake inhibitor-aderos to boot!

Jimmy had a job at the blood bank, as a warehouse man. Funny Jimmy. Dark Jimmy. A vampire at the blood bank. He was the warehouse man, shipped the blood all around.

"You ever drop it, Jimmy?"

"Yeah, and it bounces." His little grin.

"Never breaks?"

"Nah, the bags are thick and rubbery."

"Do you drink it sometimes when you get thirsty?"

"I smear it all over my face when I'm angry, what do you think?" Jimmy gets tired of My Crazy too, even when it's on cheerful mode.

"Just making conversation, Jimmy."

"Do you ever shut the fuck up?" Taken aback by Jimmy. But always his harsh words were kind. Hard to explain. No dears or honey-sweets with Jimmy. When he called you a motherfucker, or told you to shut up, you knew you were in. You just waited for the grin that followed.

"I'm one crazy motherfucker, Jimmy," I told him, "– and not in an interesting way either, no sir. Flat out white-middle-class, no-good-reason-for-it, annoying crazy. Unforgivable. No excuse."

Grinning Jimmy.

"Come here," he'd say. Jimmy didn't say sorry. Jimmy pulled me. Jimmy pulled and then squeezed it out of me; crushed whatever came between us in the sincerity of his embrace; flattened it like a pancake.

Jimmy could have been a wife beater. But the fight was out of him. He relented every time.

"Fuck you, Jimmy."

"Fuck you too." And a kiss.

I never really knew how to fucking love him.

Jimmy Christ Superstar.

Crucify the bastard.

Well, there you go. They did just that. Or IT did. The goddamn mother of all acronyms, like the artist formerly known as ... I don't dignify it with a name. INRI: Here's the King of the Jews.

The nails went in, one by one. Illness after illness. Pneumocystis in June: Left hand to crossbeam; two blows with the hammer will do. In August, thrush: Right hand to crossbeam. September was shingles: Fuck it, let's just pile one foot on the other and blow through 'em both with one big nail.

Jimmy.

Salmon-in-a-stream motherfucker.

I had to go somewhere else to cry now. To blubber really. *Pull yourself to-fucking-gether,* I'd shout at myself on the street. *Pull.*

I don't know how to love anybody.

Fact was I could only pull myself together when he was with me; when he squeezed it out of me with his ruthlessly compassionate embrace.

Alone, on the street, I'd just cry all the more. Growling and barking helped. Sometimes I dragged my knuckles down brick walls until they bled. That made me smile. That worked. And Dr. Pinski. I always pulled myself together for him.

I know it doesn't make sense, considering the service he was supposedly providing. But Pinski would be the last to know how I felt or what was going on in my life. I'd bagged the meds by the time Jimmy got sick, but that only made Pinski a bigger job. It's easy, after all, to get meds and be handed them monthly for eternity. Getting off them is what's tough. That's what you really need a hard-won prescription for: to not take the fucking things. He begrudgingly offered me a trial period, but not before asking me, "What's with the gloves?"

"It's the cold, Doc; it's just the cold." I wasn't about to let him see the scabs.

I kept going to Dr. Pinski once a month to check in, to convince him I didn't need him anymore because I'd come to loathe the drugs; disdained the sinister nothingness of them – they tasted on my tongue like a moderate Republican Christian: pointless and harmless in the short term, the subject of much reassurance, but insidious over time. Just you wait. The verdict ain't in on serotonin reuptake inhibitors, no sirree. Thalidomide was a miracle drug too. When the good doctor switched me to Wellbutrin and told me I couldn't drink for fear of seizures, and then my dick went south, it was only a matter of time. Because when things got real bad, I needed booze and my boner more than anything else to ride it through. Surfing my cock on a six-pack and a smile. Fuck the shoeshine.

Pinski took a whole year of convincing. I wooed him while he glared at me suspiciously. I got more cheerful. Should I bring him flowers and chocolates? The courtship of Dr. Pinski. It wasn't that I was unconvincing; it was just the program. They told me: one year on, one year off, no exceptions.

But by then, I was on Jimmy. Well, that and disability. Me and every other bohemian in San Francisco. And for that, I had to keep seeing Pinski. I'd signed up for the mental health program and if I didn't keep going till he was good and ready to release me, I'd lose the money, and he might even commit me. Or send someone after me to inquire. I wanted to rust in peace. That's the only reason I paid my credit card bills. Sure, I'd have felt guilty and all that, not to mention what being a deadbeat would do to my wheezing, emphysemic self-esteem. But I wanted to be left alone above all else. So I paid.

Paid dearly.

The last time I saw Pinski was two days after Jimmy died.

"I'm fine, Doc, never been better." Pulling. Aiming. And Firing.

I talked to his third eye, the one that was closed shut. Like a bullet to the head I told him my lies, splattering his sorry, demoralized brains all over the cheap white latex wall behind him. Beautiful. He closed my file. He signed off on me. Once again, I'd won. Written off. A truly free agent. Me and my empty little victories. Well, I liked the glass empty. I'm free. Free to rust in peace.

Out on the street, I can fall apart. In the name of Jimmy. And if God lives at all in this sorry rusted world, he's the flow of tears, the breath in and the breath out. Oxidation. It's just a world of iron faces in the rain.

And God – God ain't nothing but chemistry.

And this motherfuckin' acronym that took Jimmy away? This here's the King of the Jews.

It's never hard to tell. Who is and who isn't.

Like the too-long look, Jimmy's face had grown longer, just like his story, spooling out fast like thread or fishing line, having hooked a big one. A big fat acronym.

My father always said timing is everything (or so my momma quoted him), and he oughtta know. He assured my mother he'd marry her just as soon as he got back from 'Nam. Whoops. Timing. I'll say. He almost made it though. He was short, my mother said. Until I was sixteen, I thought he was a dwarf. What did I know? Even when I found out he was six-four, it still didn't sink in what every salmon swimming upstream knows.

I only knew I hated acronyms: ARVN and NVA, and VC, and NCO, and PFC, and DMZ, and LZ, and KIA, and all the other jargon in that pile of papers my mother bequeathed to me on my twenty-first birthday.

And now they've come for Jimmy. I counted once. All twenty-six letters are involved. Not a one of them is guiltless. A goddamn orgy of acronyms. A PTA of them.

And Jimmy wasn't short – six-two at least. And neither is the acronym, especially when you spell it all out. And back then, in the late eighties, the acronym still had time on its side. A long time. And Jimmy too. Everything about him. Long nose, long face, long arms and legs, and a big long dick. A long story. Flat-out long. Everything but his death.

He was short alright. The day I met him he was short.

Dwarfed by IT.

* * *

"You need a priest," my mother had insisted, because that was her default for anything that was getting out of hand. I looked at her whenever she said it, waiting for the Father Cavanaugh story to catch up to her anxiety and make her think better of it.

I nodded my head slowly, and then it registered.

"Well, maybe not," she conceded.

"And he don't need one either, Momma. Jimmy's alright, spiritually speaking, even if he is dying." She'd made me Russian tea and snicker doodles. Comfort food. And for Jimmy too, all wrapped up in paper and bows.

"Momma, he can't keep this stuff down. He'll throw it across the room."

She looked unhinged. She'd never even met Jimmy; she wasn't "ready," she'd told me. And not because of the acronym, she reassured me. No. It was about him being my queer lover and throwing her cookies across the room. The ungrateful bastard.

"It's just the Soup, Mom; that's all. Queer Soup. Acronym Soup. Take your own advice. It's not who we are, just where and when and what and all the rest. Homosexuality's a place, Mom – a place and a time. A where and a when; don't get all wrapped up in the who." The quizzical look.

Thing was, Jimmy didn't have much time left. Jimmy was short. And she'd done short. She wasn't doing short again. That was the reason; I knew that was the real reason.

She's different from my father. Timing isn't everything at all. Time is a goddamn nuisance and thank God it's moving because it'll pass her by.

So my momma never met Jimmy.

And he never ate her cookies. Though he puked one up once.

"Goddamn it!" he cursed, and pushed the box onto the floor, spilling the snicker doodles among his soiled socks and dog-eared books.

I was the nurse and the janitor and the candy striper, bouncing around the room in just a jockstrap, hoping to cheer up poor Jimmy.

"I'm pullin', Jimmy. I'm pullin'!"

"You're a motherfucker." The words of love.

But Jimmy had the libido then of a Zoloft droid, so I had to come up with something other than a sexy outfit.

I read him Rumi poems and put on Tammy Faye makeup.

But Jimmy lost the very thing that gave him the strength to stick by me and stick around in general. Jimmy lost his patience.

No good attitude for Jimmy. Shitting his pants and sweating all night was not for Jimmy. Jimmy was only patient while he was moving. And he was past ready to go. Jimmy wanted morphine, and lots of it. He wanted me to go get it for him.

"No, Jimmy, I'm not getting morphine for you. No, Jimmy, I can't be a part of this."

"You motherfucker," he said flatly.

I don't know how to love him.

"You know how motherfucker."

"No, Jimmy, no can do." It wasn't cuz I loved or didn't love him. It was cuz of my mother. Or the Catholic Church. Same difference. No one ever understands how some whacked faggot who thinks gay sex is a gift from the gods can't get over his Christian upbringing. But they weren't raised by my mother. I'd been saddled with a myth. My father was a martyr and my mother the widow of Jesus.

"No sir, Jimmy, I'm only crazy in boring ways. No assisted suicides for me. No Dr. Jack, no sir, Jimmy."

"Motherfucker."

But she fucked me. And good. Save the Soup. Baby and the bathwater – all that. Suicide not an option, even after I'd tried at thirteen, broken the ice. Because suicide's like sex and heroin and Jacqueline Susann – once is just not enough. She'd wagged her finger at me: "After what I've been through?"

Sorry, Ma. "Think of your dear father. Promise me." I promised.

"No can do, Jimmy."

"Then you'll have to smother me with a pillow, Shame."

"No dice, Jimmy." Killing him would be killing me.

Jimmy got mad. And good. Jimmy was a mess of diarrhea. Jimmy was weak and unable. Jimmy got on his goddamn clothes, glaring at me, and once up and heading out the door, he said, "You fucked up." And he left the house.

I was nail-biting crazy. Annoying inane. I'm the caretaker; I'm in charge of Jimmy. I'm a heartless coward and a dumb, confused motherfucker. I can't kill Jimmy. Wouldn't know love, would run screaming ...

I got up and ran after Jimmy, brushed by the two Chinese twins playing cars on the stairs, their mouths agape at the diarrhea boy.

And onto the sidewalk and his harangues: "Don't you fuckin' touch me!" he snapped. He's wearing his slippers – those goddamn kung fu shoes – and pajama pants, and an overcoat.

I followed him, like a dumb child: "Where ya goin', Jimmy?" – stumbling Jimmy – unable to help him because I was unable to help myself. All the way down to Sycamore Alley near the BART Station, where we first came up from underneath, to get his own goddamn morphine. They gave him one of their used syringes – what did it matter now?

Back home, Jimmy had to inject his own morphine while I bit my nails in the corner watching (unforgivable, inexcusable), wincing, his hand shaking, missing. The blood. Bingo.

"Better luck next time, Seamus," he muttered bleary-eyed, and that was pretty much it for Jimmy.

I climbed into bed with him and rolled myself tighter than I ever had, making a pocket of Jimmy. Empty pockets Jimmy. Flat broke in the game of life.

"What am I gonna do now, Jimmy?" Held him all those hours while he faded, muttering and blubbering "Sorry" and "Don't go" and "I love you, Jimmy"; "Forgive me; I'm so sorry for everything."

I had to call the morgue and his family both. I couldn't call my mother. That would be like lighting a candle. There was a time for that, sure, but this wasn't it.

The Government Pages, I guess? Sure enough. I took a deep breath.

"City Morgue, County of San Francisco. May I help you?"

"Hi, ah, my boyfriend died … and, uh, … I don't know what to do about it."

"Are you his power of attorney?"

"No … I don't think so."

"Who is?"

"I don't know about that stuff."

"Hmm, I see. Are you in contact with his family?"

"No."

"Do you know how to reach them?"

"I can try."

"We'll send someone out. You work on locating his family. In the meantime, give me whatever info you have and I'll do the same. His full name?"

I had to pull: "James Damon Keane. And he's from Buffalo. And that's where his family is. And I have his credit card and all that. He doesn't have a license or anything. Just a credit card."

"And what's your name?"

Caught off-guard. "Uh, …" I wanted it to be his then; I wanted to say I'm Seamus Keane. "I sure loved Jimmy" is what I said. "I sure loved him." And I came apart right there on the phone, and she was pretty nice about it. She even ended up coming out with the guy in the dead people's carcass truck, and she sat there with me and listened. Sweet Monique, a big fat black lady who did the pulling for me, until I could get a hold of the rope of this life once again and do it myself.

Like a barge, life. Pull, pull, pull. Where we all goin'? Where we goin', Jimmy?

"You want me to deal with the family?" she entreated consolingly.

"No, that's okay; we gotta cremate Jimmy; he's gotta be here with me for awhile. I'm gonna have to talk them into it." But you can't talk a bunch of Catholics into cremating their kid – what was I thinking?

Monique looked worried. "Did you say he needs to stay here?"

"Yeah."

"He can't stay here. We gotta take him in. It's the law."

"Can I visit?"

"I don't know. I suppose. No one's ever asked me about visiting the morgue unless the police are doing it, or somebody has to identify somebody."

"You just gotta keep him there at least three days. It's like a thing with him."

She was starting to look like I'd run the limits of her compassionate largesse. She got up. "He ain't goin' anywhere, once he gets there. Not until the power of attorney decides otherwise. So, you need to talk to the family."

"Okay. Thanks, Monique." She gave me a wan smile.

Jimmy's family. What did I know about Jimmy's family? Well, plenty actually, from the poems, and his late-night, book-on-the-lap reminiscings.

Jimmy was twenty-eight when he died. But he'd left Buffalo a long time ago. He only went skulking back to Buffalo when he learned that his mother was dying of a long drawn-out illness with lung cancer. He hadn't seen her since he'd left, which was ten years or more. She chastised him when he walked into her hospital room, and he looked at the floor and he took it. She never did straighten him out, but her dying sure did.

"She said awful things to me. Called me all sorts of names. She'd always been tough and mean just like I used to be – we respected each other for that. But it wouldn't have been fair to fight back, with her there flat on her back. We were mean, but we fought fair. Which is to say we were proud." Sighing

Jimmy. "So I just endured it; tried to tell myself to just go the distance. I hadn't cried in ten years either, but after three days of her insults – and while my two born-again sisters sat by sniffling silently and with satisfaction – I broke and finally yelled back at her: "Stop it! Stop it, you bitch!' We yelled at each other back and forth for maybe ten minutes while my sisters lowly wailed in prayer from the corner. Somewhere in there I'd begun crying, bawling through my hurled words, and she had too – you have to understand, we never cried, never." He huffed a big exhale of a sigh then. "I climbed into the little bed with her then, and you know what she said? "I bore you ..." She was right, but it seemed a strange thing to say, until she finished and it made sense: "I bore you ... you are my fruit." And she fucking wailed, and I knew then we were the same and we'd end the same. She died two days later, spent, but more like horrifically resigned, not so much to death but to regret.

Jimmy didn't cry then. He came close though, I could see. He shook his head out like a wet dog. But back then, Jimmy thought to do what anyone in Buffalo would do in terms of getting a new start. He went to California.

"But I didn't just go; I couldn't just go, like I used to – I don't know. I had to go in a certain way. The railroads and airplanes and cars – they all travel in circles, and I'd end up back where I started. No sooner would I set out for St. Louis than I'd end up in New Jersey. Once I went to Texas, and by the time three months had passed, I was in Florida. I actually headed for California twice before, but never made it past Denver. And then I was in Minneapolis. It was weird; I was like attached to some kind of tether. Maybe I slept wrong, in the shape of a boomerang or something."

"A closed loop. I know all about it, Jimmy," I said with my nods of assent.

"I had to go in some final way, you know. Like committed to it. At first I thought I should walk, but I knew I'd never make it. I'd end up hitching a ride or a train, and then I'd be right back in the old pattern, looping all over the fucking continent like some fucking pinball. I thought of walking because I knew I had to make it hard. I had to earn my passage somehow. I had to like climb here. Climb out of something, you know?"

I know.

He ended up doing it by bike. A bike he named *Chief Joseph* because he wasn't gonna "fight no more forever" either.

I called information. "Keane. Jack Keane." There were three "J. Keanes" listed in Buffalo.

"Hi, I'm a friend of your son's." But the first one had no son. Or was he just saying that, since it was the common response of so many fathers of gay sons? The second number was disconnected. I breathed deep for the third, but got an answering machine. "This is Jack. Leave a message." That's when it occurred to me that Jimmy's voice was still on our machine. That seemed tacky, having a dead guy's voice taking messages from people who didn't even know he was dead yet. Tacky, macabre, funny even. And there was no way I would erase it, cuz it was Jimmy's voice. That being the case, I decided against leaving our number for the final Jack.

Instead, I started going down to the corner liquor store and calling Jimmy.

"Hi, this is Jimmy and Seamus. We're not here. Beep." Music to my ears. In a Buffalo twang. Mr. Understatement. Jimmy.

The Chinese twins started watching me, wondering, pointing. Once they came over. "You don't got any phone anymore?"

"No, listen," and I handed Michael – with the metal stainless steel tooth – the phone. At which Marcus became overexcited, so I had to dig for more quarters and dial several times so they'd both get it. They got it. Big smiles, and nods – they knew who it was. "Diarrhea boy!"

"He died," I told them. But I think they knew; they'd seen him fading for months. Their faces dropped all the same, to get the news. But then they wanted to listen some more.

They'd run over whenever they spotted me there after that. To listen to the dead.

I think they had some idea that the message would change. That he'd say something – like what it was like on the other side.

"It never changes," Michael with the tooth finally said to Marcus.

"No, it never changes," I concurred.

That was the last time they ran over. Their mother had already taken to screaming at them in Chinese, something – I guessed – to the effect that they shouldn't be bothering me or running across the street. I had no idea which. I only knew she smiled at me when I looked at her, indicating that I wasn't the problem, in her insular, nonconfrontational Chinese way.

I went to visit Jimmy, but they wouldn't let me in. I gave the flowers to the security guard who sort of held them out in front of him like a soiled diaper.

"What am I supposed to do with these?"

"They're for Jimmy, the guy in there," and I motioned with my head.

"This is a morgue, sir."

"Well, you can give them to your girlfriend if you want." Hot potato. I ain't carrying them home.

I assume he threw them in the trash. Marigolds aren't romantic enough for your girlfriend. She might think you're dumping her. "Flores para los muertos."

So all I really had was the pay phone. Other than those hourly phone calls, I just stayed in bed, staring at Jimmy's bike. Or, rather, it stared at me.

You could say I owed him one. But what exactly did I owe him? What was it? This debt. Like I say, I paid my debts. So as to be left alone. I wanted to rust in peace. But that'll never be now. Jimmy fucked me, really fucked me. One-upped my mother. Jesus Christ. And he did too. He one-upped Mary, so I shouldn't be surprised. And now I've got the Holy Ghost on my hands as well. Jesus Christ alright. Let's hope I don't run into the old man; that'll cook me good.

I wronged Jimmy. Now he's like My Crazy, hounding me, haunting me. What you gonna do about your Crazy now? What you gonna do about the boy you wouldn't kill?

Nothing from the looks of it. I stalled, stayed in bed, grief-frozen and guilt-freezer-burned. Waiting. Waiting for Jimmy.

I loved Jimmy. I wanted to give him his life back, or take his life, or something. I wasn't sure. It seemed like a good idea at the time. My answer for everything. For drinking Drano, not killing Jimmy. A good idea at the time.

I didn't kill the man I love. That's my fucking crime. Crazy bigger than I am. I owe Jimmy one thing. A life I owe him. His life and mine both. Something like that. Two lives on my hands and two deaths. I'm a goddamn serial killer is the fact of the matter, and I've never even lifted a finger.

My friends keep calling, to cheer me up. They want to take me out clubbing. Julie and Sam appear, in black, showered and beaming.

"We're taking you out to dinner and Uranus."

I manage a smile, but I'll never be able to tolerate their chatter even though I'm a chatterbox too. Not anymore.

"Jimmy's dead you guys. We're staying in" – like he's ill or something, but present. And I try to close the door.

"No," Sam's motorcycle boot holds the door open. "Come on, Shame." He pushes his way in and the two of them dig up an outfit for me and take me for Pakistani food on 16th Street.

I'm fascinated by the blood-orange color of the tandoori chicken; it's the only thing strange enough to seem interesting.

We went from bar to bar; I gave it a go. It was great sometimes that in 1990 in San Francisco you could go to queer clubs that welcomed straight people and that straight people weren't afraid of, but this wasn't one of those times. Because all I could do was scan the room for Jimmy, mesmerized by every dark-eyed gangly boy. Like some particularly torment-ing obsessive compulsion, I kept searching, even though the minute I saw one I was full of regret for having even looked. I even hated them a little for playing at Jimmy. Couldn't they save that for another day? Be someone else?

Even when I wasn't looking for Jimmy, there was like a huge empty mouth waiting outside the doors, and inside as well, if the truth be told. It was in almost every face, and every heartless electronic song. Just cuz it beats like one don't make it a heart, man. I grew disgusted with the dumb same old dance, drink, blah, blah, blah, take home some sex like a doggy bag. It wasn't even sexy, the whole tired scene. I used to do this?

Julie and Sam told me to cheer up, that I should have a better attitude. Great, my mom and Dr. Pinski are on a dou-ble date with me and Jimmy. But I felt guilty all the same and found myself involuntarily concurring with them. But not for long. Cheering someone up is like "What Not to Do for a Clini-cally Depressed Grieving Potential Suicide 1A." I knew where those clubs would take me as I started to tear up and ask Jimmy, "Why'd you leave me here?" I saw the ropes fray and break that connected me to Sam and Julie. I knew what would become of my Soup if I bucked up my so-called attitude.

All it took was one full moment of silence, one trip to the bathroom, one drug-addled stare, and the hole in the fuck-ing ozone of human existence gaped open like a speechless, screaming mouth. I knew my feelings weren't original. Edvard Munch and a few others had beat me to it, but this was 3-D and planetary. I pushed through the crowd and got out. And when I hit the sidewalk, I fucking ran. I ran block after block, all the way home. Like a little boy, scared, not know-ing what to do. I ran home to his bike and the ritual space of our love, which was just four walls and a window over an acacia tree and a corner liquor store and a rickety, rusted fire escape, and the smell of Chinese food and two little boys' too-loud screechings and TV volume. And I draped his clothes all over the bike – the battered army shorts and the Red Hot Chili Peppers shirt – surrounding it like a makeshift altar with a whole slew of Virgin de Guadalupe candles, which lit up the shelves of dog-eared books and, in so doing, conjured James Damon Keane, who whispered, as always, God bless him, "Pull, Seamus. You gotta pull."

And not a moment later, Sam and Julie and the lights and sound of an idling taxi yellowing the window, and the clump, clump, clump of his motorcycle boots and the rap, rap, rap on my door.

"You okay, Shame?"

"We're having sex. Can you come back later?"

"Come on, Shame, we were worried about you."

Then a crescendo of Chinese erupts as the twins' mother cracks open her door. I'll have to let them in.

The candles quickly tame them and they sit quietly on the floor with me. I've got a bottle of Carlo Rossi jug wine and a few jars to drink from, so I pour them each a glass. And we sit and we drink and say nothing.

Sam scoots close and I let my head fall in his lap. But I don't cry. I only cry with Jimmy or alone on the street. I just stare into the candles and the cheap wine while Julie holds my hand.

They exchange looks, and Julie, ever responsible, ruins the silence with, "I think we'll stay here with you tonight, Shame."

"No, Julie. Me and Jimmy, we want privacy."

"Shame, you gotta ..."

"No, I don't."

"Julie, it's cool," Sam chimes in.

I clasp her hand, give her what little I got. If she doesn't understand, so be it. As for Sam, he's loyal, I'll give him that. Clueless, but loyal. He digs male intimacy, in a soldier-football player kinda way. I snuggle into his crotch, purposely pressing against his dick. I don't want sex; I just want someone I can count on to not turn away. I'm testing his intimacy. He pats my shoulder, and sweet heterosexual Sam passes the test.

I look over at Julie who still thinks I gotta ... pull. Now I can. It takes two straight people, I realize, where it only took one Jimmy fagboy.

Jimmy's father never called, of course, but Monique finally did.

"Mr. Blake, I have some news for you."

"Yeah?"

"Uh, Mr. Keane – your friend Jimmy –?"

"Yeah?"

"He actually did the paperwork. You don't need to call his family. He's got it all taken care of. He filed all this six months ago." And she read: "'In the event of my death, I hereby request my body be disposed of by cremation.' And he paid the fee."

"How much?"

"Twelve hundred dollars; Neptune Society."

Where'd Jimmy get all that money? Was he dealing blood on the side, shipping it to Transylvania or something?

"When you gonna do it?"

"It's done."

"What?"

"Don't worry. Day four. I held it up for you." Sweet Monique and her sweet subterfuge of the big ugly acronyms of county government.

"Oh, thank you, thank you ..." And I kept thanking her to stave off the tears.

I hung up before she shattered me with the sweet honey of her voice.

Monday I had to go get him; the dust of him.

Jesus-Jimmy, to dust you have returned.

Death is a fucking crime. No wonder everybody loves crime movies. God's a criminal; we need to keep reminding ourselves. And he always gets away. I guess in Jesus he tried to turn himself in, but apparently he only served a small part of his sentence, and is once again at large, crazier than ever. Me, I'm the iron face in the rain, turning to rust, and Jimmy, he's the chalk marks around what was his body, gone now – even the outline of him washing away in the rain.

And we'll all end up victims of the big sky god serial killer.

In the meantime, duck and cover, and bury the dead.

Or lug them along with you.

You didn't take me with you, Jimmy, but I can still take you with me. Chattering away, My Crazy and me on the bus with Jimmy in a cardboard box on my lap, like the sweet baby Jesus.

And all my *what-do-I-do-now-Jimmy?*s quit their fretting. Jimmy's voice was clear as fire, speaking from the ashes: 'The road's the place for lost souls, Seamus. Take me back the way I came."

Sure thing, Jimmy. Jesus-Jimmy, Mary, and Chief Joseph.

Looking for some manger.

Alaska

He came to Anavik in August. He didn't know anybody here and took a room in Curtis Shandley's boarding house for the fall term. He was young and tall, rangy. He looked like the typical young man from the States who came up this way – likely a mountain climber of some sort. He'd come, ostensibly, to teach school – fifth grade – at the Anavik grade school.

He kept to himself generally, though he was friendly in an aloof sort of way. Not really standoffish, he projected a public persona that you suspected wasn't the whole story, but was all you were going to get. He related in order not to relate. He let you know he was there and was harmless – you could safely ignore him. It seemed he was in a sense asking you to ignore him with this ritual superficiality he displayed.

He ate with the other boarders at Shandley's, made the usual small talk, but never made any attachments to anyone there. They were a mixed crew as it was: stoic Eskimos working the fishing fleet, gruff loggers and truckers, pipeline workers. He was the schoolteacher – he was supposed to be the talker. But he didn't assume that role. He washed the pots, cleaned up, kept himself busy that way in the idle hours when men socialized.

But if he wasn't terribly social, he seemed to take a great interest in the trees. He was often seen standing under one – a spruce or hemlock – staring up into its branches or circling its trunk with a kind of wonder and curiosity in his gaze, almost as if he'd never seen a tree before.

He wasn't a mountain climber as it turned out. He had none of the gear for it. All he'd brought with him were a laptop and a duffle bag of clothes. Curtis Shandley told us all this one night at the Hoot Owl, where I was line cook. Shandley drank and Shandley liked to spin tales. One never trusted Shandley completely. He was a fisherman and, like most fishermen, full of stories from the vast and voiceless sea that consequently could never be verified. He'd nearly died of pneumonia more than once and had infected his wife with it one fateful winter, killing her, and in his grief putting an end to his fishing career. Since her demise, he'd sought to become both of them in a sense, keeping house – sewing even – cooking meals for his boarders, while still splitting wood, fixing cars, repairing boats, and reroofing houses. Many people thought when she died, his spirit went with her body, and that her spirit jumped into his, so that he was in a sense both of them, but really more her now than himself. The manly things he did were things his body did from memory. The things he did that were formerly hers came to him in an oddly facile manner that fed superstition and wild supernatural speculation.

Shandley told us the man was writing a book of some sort.

"On trees?" I inquired.

"I don't think so. Some kind of novel."

"About Anavik?"

"I don't think so. He seems to be nearly finished with it."

"Why is he here?"

"I don't know. To teach school I guess; finish the book."

I nodded and said nothing more.

But I wondered. *Why Anavik? Why come here?* A hard place. *Why come here to write a book?* Other than the isolation, which was something, I suppose. Something writers valued I'd heard. Whatever the case, his being a writer explained his social reticence as far as most people were concerned; allowed them to forget him; to give him his place and return their attention once more to their own lives.

One night, after closing, I saw him climbing a tree. A big spruce, next to the post office. He was about halfway up it when I spied him. It was summer and the middle of the night, so maybe he was after the sunset. It was going purple and pink and it was messed with all number of clouds that gave it yellow streaks. It would be very beautiful to a stranger. It would be worth climbing a tree for.

I stood and watched him, in my stained white uniform, my parka, in the fatigue brought on by another eight-hour day frying burgers and making soup from moose and caribou stock. I liked being a cook. In a place so difficult, so cold, that required so much hard work just to survive, making food was a sacred thing. My father didn't and wouldn't understand that. He worked with heavy equipment, was all tied up with the lumber and oil companies. He was "hooked up" to Alaska he would say. Right down to the Eskimo wife and mixed-blood son. My father was here in a certain way, and it wasn't my way. There was nothing to be done about it though, so we'd grown estranged.

I sat on the bench in front of the hardware store across the street and watched him, waiting for him to stop, turn around, come back down. But he kept going, slowly and surely, up through the cracking branches, starting and stopping, making a racket as he found footholds. It was a big tree, a hundred feet at least.

I was cold; he had to be cold too. After forty-five minutes, I was too cold to sit any longer and watch this strange spectacle. But I couldn't pull myself away. I needed to understand something about it, or if not that, I needed to watch over his work, witness it. There was something important, meaningful in his climbing that tree. But I wasn't one to fret or push things too far, so I retired, went on home, turning now and again, in the lonely street – visited at this hour only by idling lumber trucks and the occasional pickup – to look back and see the disturbance in the high branches that indicated his struggle; listened for the continual snap of the dense twigs he busily furrowed through.

The next morning when he walked into the Hoot Owl, I gave him the cursory look I do all customers until it dawned on me who he was. I didn't know his name of course, had never been formally introduced. He still had spruce needles in his hair, smears of sap on his parka. There were only three other people in there, sitting at the counter: Nana, my aunt, who was the owner, having her breakfast; Katak, the fisherman; and Griswold, the postmaster. The first two weren't big talkers, and though the other was, he respected their silence, so it was quiet. It was five o'clock, and it occurred to me that the sun rising outside, yellow and pink, looked much like it had when it went down the night before.

I brought him coffee and placed it before him. He gave me an appreciative grin, looking up from the menu, which he afterward put down. I didn't smile back because I don't smile at anyone. I don't like the way people use smiles, getting in the way of who they really are, what they really mean. His perfunctory little smile nearly put me off my curiosity about him. Of course, he's a schoolteacher. He must smile. Childhood is terrifying after all. The smile of the older ones is really all that gets you through it.

He ordered eggs and pancakes, without smiling this time. He said thank you in a flat way, a straightforward way, when I put his food down in front of him.

When he'd finished eating, Griswold turned toward him, raising his voice over the three seats between them: "Teaching school over there, eh?"

"Yes," he said.

"Where you from?"

"Down south."

"Well, I figured that much!" And he laughed as if he were

with a whole group of people in on some joke, but Katak and Nana didn't even blink. "Where south?"

"California." And he said it quickly, almost shamefully.

"Getting used to our weather?" And Griswold looked to Nana, who ignored him, and to Katak, who just looked right through him.

"I like it here," the young man said. And he beamed when he said that. "It's a good place. I like the children at the school. I'm Thane." And he reached his hand across the seats. Griswold fumbled with his napkin, wiping his face and hands, a bit put out by the sudden enthusiasm of the young man's response. He clumsily grasped Thane's outstretched arm.

"Leonard, Leonard Griswold, postmaster."

"I'll see you around then," Thane said, pulling out his wallet and looking toward me. I came and told him he owed five dollars and forty-five cents. He gave me seven dollars, said thank you, again without smiling, and departed.

This was how his friendliness worked. He'd respond to whoever talked to him monosyllabically at first. Then he'd warm up in time to introduce himself, but only just before leaving, which left the impression that he was a nice person, that perhaps you could get to know him later. But it was always this way. Standoffish at first, then warm just before leaving. From then on you were an acquaintance, someone he'd gotten out of the way and no longer needed to converse with. Just a nod or a quick hello would do.

So no one got to know Thane. I figured we were probably just characters in his book. That was his world. But I was wrong about that. That morning, when he left, having come down from the tree he'd spent the night in, something between us turned, and he became curious about me after that. I could tell. He watched me for a split second too long as I poured coffee, and later when I wiped the counter. He had noticed I did not appreciate smiles – had noticed that right away, and respected it. He was careful never to smile around me after that. He knew that about me. I knew he knew other things because of that.

* * *

"Why did you climb the tree?" I asked him one morning after pouring his coffee.

I looked at him in such a way that he would know I wanted a concise answer; I didn't want to have a conversation. I realized I was interested in his strangeness, his differentness, more than in him as a person. I'm not that interested in individuals actually. Not really. I'm only really interested in what they do, what their motivations are. What they know about things.

"I like that tree," he said. "It's a nice tree." And there you have it. I wanted to ask him if he'd climbed other trees, but that would have entailed a conversation which I didn't want to have. It wasn't necessary besides. Others spoke of his passion. Even Griswold. "I was fishing up at Clay Creek, and that teacher fella – he was in a tree. I called up to him, but he wouldn't answer or didn't hear. He was way up there. I was there a few hours and he never came down." Griswold had just shrugged his shoulders, slurped his soup. Nana told me she saw him sleeping in a tree once. It was a fir tree, leaning onto another larger tree. "Like a child leaning against its mother's hip," she'd said. "He looked sweet there, curled up like a little boy. Something lost about him, I think," she said, before changing the subject to the meat order.

I chanced upon him one day, finally, myself. I liked tracking badger, much to my father's consternation, who had tried to make me a big-game hunter like himself. I was going up a steep ravine when I heard it. That snapping sound – cacophony really. Distinctive. It wasn't graceful what he did. He wasn't like a badger. Or any animal out there really.

He was clearly not made for trees. Not of this place.

I didn't immediately investigate. It seemed a solitary thing for him. I wanted to respect it as such. Of course, he'd likely scared off any badger. So, there was nothing to do but find a place to sit and watch for awhile.

I located the rustling leaves and could see he was on

the opposite side of the tree from where I sat on a boulder. I looked around, saw some birds flitting about, a butterfly, listened to the grasshoppers click, the flies buzz, the mosquitoes drone. I heard water falling as the nearby creek quickened through the gorge. And Thane. Thane was like some new, awkward animal who hadn't found a way yet to blend in. His racket was all discord and dissonance in a scene that had found a balance over millennia, that made of it one sound.

It seemed hilarious all of a sudden, and I laughed at his clumsiness – at the clumsiness of a man up a tree. Bears made such a racket too, I remembered then, but they didn't make a habit of climbing trees generally, so I hadn't considered it. Perhaps though, he was no less a part of all this than a bear. Which made him very much a part of all this. I laughed for a while, and as I wasn't one to laugh, when it came it burst out of me like water and flowed for a good long while.

He must have heard me because the rustling in the fir suddenly quieted, then stopped. I still couldn't see him and wondered if he now saw me. Like a bear. This too made me laugh: the sudden wariness of him. Like a bear. I picked up stones and began throwing them at the tree, attempting to hit the branches near him. Then I thought to hide. If he hadn't seen me yet, he'd have no idea who I was. Who knows what he'd think? He might become afraid and shimmy down. I could track him then through the woods, follow him like a badger, full of stealth and mischief. I felt suddenly like I had as a child, teasing a cat or a dog.

But he didn't come down. Nor did he resume climbing. I was in the bushes now, under the branches of a thicket. I knew he couldn't see me, and I knew how to remain still. I wondered what he was thinking up there.

It got colder, darker, and still nothing. No snapping branches, no rustling about.

There was only waiting. That was always what it was with most things. Waiting.

I would wait.

The stream grew louder in the dusk, the crickets diminished. Shadows were the things I saw now. I began to worry a bit about bear. I had my pistol, but I really should have brought a rifle if I planned to spend the night. A pistol was pretty useless against a grizzly. I suppose I should have just left. I should have known that he'd not come down. I'd seen this before, his spending the night in a tree. And now, what was the use of my mischief ? A test of wills. Or so it seemed to me. But how could I know if he even suspected I was still there? Or had ever been there? How could I be sure it was my laughter that had stopped his climbing? How could I know if he hadn't just stopped coincidentally at the same time? It was possible.

Then again, perhaps it really was a bear, and not Thane at all. A test of wills with a bear was something.

I fell off asleep all the same, and I slept then for a long time. And I dreamed about my mother. Remembered her waving goodbye from the ferry. She was going to a funeral. The whole group of them going to the funeral of a great-aunt of mine. All of them went down with the boat, as if with the relative they'd gone to mourn. For many years afterward, I waited for her. Not in the way my father did, who looked at boats in a funny, stupefied way after that – but here, out in the forest. I understood that she would come this way when she returned.

When I awoke, the little canyon was loud again with grasshoppers and birds. The water sounded fuller. The sun was high, high enough that I knew it must be past seven, well after sunrise. I looked at the tree, but detected no movement. I went over to it and circled it and looked up into it as I'd seen him do. Eventually, I figured he was gone. He never stayed late in trees as far as I knew. He was a teacher; he'd be at the school by now.

So I headed back. I needed to work that night as well and hadn't planned on spending so much time out in the woods. I was surprised he hadn't awoken me. I didn't really believe he could get out of there quietly, or if he had, that I was so tired that I wouldn't have heard him.

And then I noticed something; something different ahead. Along the creek. The rocks looked different, the dirt was all exposed like some great beast – only a bear could do it – had fouled the bank on its way down. But when I looked down there, toward the stream, I saw Thane. Propped up against a rock, he was massaging his ankle and shivering terribly.

"Hey," I said, and scrambled down the embankment. He looked frightened and I wondered how long he'd been here like this; how long he'd been shivering. He'd fallen into the creek and his clothes were drenched. Why was he still in them? How long had he been sitting here? I knew what needed to be done and I did it quickly, dragging him out of the creek, stripping off his wet clothes, and then my own, and rubbing my hands against his chest to warm his heart; pressing my body to his in a bear hug to give him my warmth. But he kept on shaking.

I needed to get him into the sun, which was difficult as we were in a ravine and he had sprained his ankle badly. I would have to carry him back up to the clearing, to the tree he had climbed, where there was a small meadow and sunshine. He was heavy, but not very, perhaps only 150 to 160 pounds. But I was only 140 pounds myself, so it was awkward. I carried him piggyback, and thusly I plodded determinedly up the trail, huffing and puffing, while he shook. When we reached the clearing, I knelt down and rolled him off me. Still he shivered, and again I embraced him as fully as possible, in the sun now, rubbing my hands across his chest and back, moving my legs against his legs, breathing my breath into his mouth – anything to generate as much heat as possible. I hadn't brought my clothes back up with us, and perhaps I should have, as it might have served as a blanket to warm him up still faster. I thought to go back for them, but I couldn't leave him there, even for a second, shivering. It wouldn't be right and it wouldn't be wise.

Next I would need to make a fire, and something hot for him to drink. But first I had to stop his shivering. I was getting worried. There isn't much time with such things. I wouldn't have time to make a fire and tea I realized. We were fortunate only in that it was warm in the sun.

What happened next didn't come from me. It came from the sun. The sun's fire. I didn't really make a decision about it at all. It just happened. I kissed him. I kept rubbing him too, and then I gave myself over to this effort completely. Perhaps I remembered how much heat it could generate. From Kita and Anna, from Valerie. Even on cold nights, we'd sweated as we'd struggled to give ourselves to each other.

Nana had told me when I was just fifteen, "Sex is a gift you give someone." She said, "People get lonely, lost, confused, unable to remember certain things. They make horrible mistakes. They get hurt. Then you chance across each other. You are a piece of good luck for each other. Sometimes a child is born. All children are lucky. They know they are, but they forget. Maybe when they grow up and have sex, they remember." And she'd giggled then, before sighing. "So much is forgotten. Remember this much."

I thought of my pistol then because I was afraid, and it was what I'd brought for safety. It was worth nothing in this fear. I wasn't saving myself now. I didn't need good luck. I was *his* good luck; I needed to act like good luck and give him a story to tell of how the sun saved him once, when he fell out of a tree and into a river. Because the sun is what saved him, though later he'd thank *me*. But I was just chance, something that had happened along.

If there'd been a boat, my mother might be alive. My mother couldn't have lasted long out in the sea. No clearing there, not even sun that day. No warm bodies anywhere around. No boats. But if there had been, would she have thanked them? They too would have been just chance, like I was. It would have been the fire in the boat, or the blankets, or the land of it in the vastness of the sea. It would have been their own bodies and the earth that saved them.

He saved himself perhaps. He responded to my kisses, to my caresses. He came alive; his muscles, so stiff and cramped before, elongated now, moved like waves far out at sea. We were squirming together, almost wrestling, and I felt myself smile because I knew now he would live. But this realization did not stop me, nor him, and as we rubbed ourselves together I felt my gift leave me, and then his a moment after, warm and mixing against our pressed-together bellies.

We panted, laughed, caught our breath. He searched my eyes, but I simply smiled.

I knew I had to get the clothes for him now, to keep him warm.

"Wait," I said, and hurried down the trail to fetch my pants and shirt and jacket; the old construction boots, the sweaty socks.

I dressed him quickly on the ground, like a child, as he couldn't stand for the ankle. I kept the jockey shorts for myself, and the boots, so I would have something to wear, walking back down the trail.

I hoisted him again on my shoulders and told him, "You rest now."

All the way back down the trail, how my back ached, how my feet burned on the stones and pine needles, for I'd put the socks on his feet for warmth and the boots were stiff against the skin of my own feet. And it was five miles to the road, and from there another several miles to town if no trucks came along to give us a ride. But it was midday; there would be someone. I knew. A road was by nature a thing of good luck.

Sure enough, an old Eskimo trapper named Kapush came down the road almost the minute we got there. I was glad an Eskimo had come upon us and not one of my father's people, who would have wanted all the details, the facts of the story; who wouldn't understand about the sun. Kapush – he understood.

"Too cold," he said. And looking up into the sky, he smiled. "Lucky for him."

I did not run into Thane for several weeks after that. I did not see him in the trees of course, nor hear about him being seen in them. It was September now, and there was little time left to wander up the canyons for tree climbing anyway. The snows would be coming. You'd die for sure if you fell in a creek then, if it wasn't frozen, which might then save you so long as the surface of it didn't crack. You could be saved by the cold just as you could be killed by it. The same went for the sun and the earth and the air. Men even. All things really.

When next I saw Thane, nothing was different. We didn't smile at each other, as was our way. It was as if that night in the canyon was in some other world, separate from this one. A dream place of sorts. We didn't speak of it at all. This felt natural. He came and went like he had before, thanking me and paying me. Then one time, in January I think it was, he left an envelope under his money at the counter.

"You forgot this," I called to him.

"No," he said. "I didn't forget it." Then he turned and left.

I read the letter later that night in my room in Nana's house. In it, he talked too much. He thanked me first for saving his life, which would have been enough, even though I did not think it was so. But then he chose to explain. Why he had come to Anavik; why he did not like the places he was from; why he had felt it necessary to make a choice and tell people of the choice he'd made. Which wasn't really a choice he told me. It was his nature. But many did not see it that way: parents, politicians, priests. I did not understand why that was so important to him. And he talked a great deal of beginnings and endings. When he came and when he would leave; when this and when that; how this had changed him, made him new; where he would go next; and what he would write about when he got there. He wondered what I thought about all this – about his feelings, about being the kind of man he was. He wondered what kind of man I was in this way. How clumsy it all sounded. How my father's people's whole culture was that way. At the end of the letter, he said he had thought often of the clearing. Of that place we had been together.

I didn't write back; I threw the letter away.

Instead, I went up to Curtis Shandley's the next afternoon, and to his room. He looked excited to see me, and secretive, like we were partners in some crime. But I did not see it that way. I saw that he was still cold inside, had been very cold for a long time. I caressed him and kissed him again like I had in the clearing. We took off our clothes and we made love in a similar fashion to how we had before. I liked the strength of it, like two things crashing together – a river and rock, lightning and a mountain, a bear up a tree. It was different than with a woman. A different place where different things met. But there was nothing new about it. Not really. How was this thing we did, then, in his mind, a new thing, unaccustomed to the world? He seemed to me like Eskimos I knew who drank, who couldn't square their world with the world of my father's people; who wouldn't live in peace or make peace with it. Who sacrificed themselves to it instead.

Before Thane, I hadn't known that they did it to their own kind. Truly, they had a different way.

We lay together for a long time afterward, caressing, and I told him a story. It was a story that Nana had told me once about a caribou that lost its herd. For a long time, it followed a creek through a wide plain, knowing intuitively that the stream flowed downward and that they were all heading that way last time he'd noticed. But he never came upon them and began to worry that he had lost his way, and that perhaps they'd gone in another direction entirely. He got strange ideas then, and climbed over mountains and waded through lakes, no longer paying attention to the facts, but letting each thing he came across suggest itself or something to him. And so, when he saw a solitary tree in a meadow, he thought to climb it. This was a ridiculous notion for a caribou, but he had gone past such prejudices and so he approached the tree, circling it. He slept below it for two nights, hoping that a method might suggest itself. On the third day, a grizzly came along and killed the caribou. He ate a good deal of him then and there, and then dug a hole to bury him in. At some point, the bear must have forgotten about the caribou or lost interest. Winter came and snow covered the animal's remains. In the spring, a mound of grass grew there and flowers. Small animals cleaned what was left of him from his discarded bones. Birds carried pieces of his hide for their nests high into the branches of the tree, and insects carried parts of him up its trunk and across its branches. And the rest of him sunk into the ground where he was received by the roots of the tree and then carried by them up through its trunk and branches high into the sky where he'd first thought to go. High enough so that he could see far off and was able to locate his lost herd. And in this way, the caribou was not lost anymore.

In June, at the end of the school year, Thane left. He had not climbed trees that spring. I did not know why he climbed trees when he first arrived, nor why he no longer climbed them that spring. And I did not ask him.

But I found myself wishing I would find him climbing one again.

He did not say goodbye to anyone specifically, but he was civil, even friendly, to those he ran across on his way to the ferry. He came as he'd arrived, unannounced, unobtrusively. He did not say goodbye to me, and this made me smile, in the same way his not smiling had made me happy nearly a year ago. It satisfied me because it made me feel he knew things.

He did not come back. Not ever.

I did not expect him to; did not wait for him, or for a letter. I did not watch the boats. Sometimes I watched the trees, that is true. I knew if he returned how he would come.

I think about him from time to time. I'd been with only women before him, and only with women afterward. I had never met a man like him before, where that was possible – that place, that piece of luck, that way that the sun could touch the world. But I didn't think about it in the way he talked of it in his letter. I did not think about it as a nature or a choice to be made, or what anyone might think of it. It was not a beginning nor an end of anything, just as it had not begun, nor ended. I thought of it as Nana had explained it: as a gift, some luck, a way of remembering something that in any other way would be lost and forgotten.

He had brought me something. Something from high in the trees.

I had given him something as well. Nana said sometimes a baby came from that kind of luck. But it was not a baby in our case – it was a place, and a lucky place, like how children are lucky. And like a place, it was permanent that way, even if I were never to visit it again. It was there. I knew this as I knew other things. And this satisfied me and made me smile.

Housesitting

The essential thing about Samuel was that he was an anarchist. Which isn't to say that this is a story about the Spanish Civil War, Mikhail Bakunin, or the American Labor Movement at the turn of the century. No, Samuel was just an inhabitant of that most political of cities – at least as far as political identities go – and he'd picked it up among his hipster friends, who neither worked blue-collar jobs nor would ever fight in an actual war.

He ate no meat, held no credit cards, possessed no assets, had no TV. He lived by strict rules, the irony of so many anarchists. But he'd been right to do so, for it was the bourgeois good life indeed that was his undoing in the end. Anarchy was just his last bastion against chaos, which is what this story *is* about.

It began with Frederick. Just a nice man he'd met at a demonstration against the war; an aging hippie. Or so it appeared. It turned out he worked in high tech and owned an incredibly well-appointed and charming Victorian in the fashionable Duboce Triangle neighborhood of San Francisco. And he made a momentous decision. Not for him, but for Samuel. He decided to go to Greece for three weeks with his new partner, Sven, a charming Swedish post-hippie-era hippie with a penchant for oracles and other mystical and ancient means of supraliminal determination.

Frederick considered getting a housesitter, to take care of the cats and plants. He'd farmed them out in past years, but it got complicated, transferring plants around in the back of his Miata (even ex-hippies apparently have midlife sports car fantasies – oh, do they ever), and negotiating with the cats who weren't hip to leaving their domestic routine and familiar territory.

Samuel was an ideal choice. A dutiful lad, reliable, obsessively responsible, and rather cute. Like many aging gay men, Frederick shared his largesse with young attractive men on the off chance that one would be "easy," grateful, guilty, horny, troubled, or just hot for him. Samuel wasn't a promising candidate in any of these categories (more of the morose cuteboy type – reluctantly, annoyingly handsome), but you've got to be present to win, as they say in Vegas, and Frederick figured Samuel would be quite a take if he did one day let his guard down. If he had enough setbacks, one on top of the other, he could see Samuel breaking and needing to fuck like a dog with whomever happened to be in range, or whoever offered the needed drugs or alcohol in the right atmosphere. Frederick's décor, lighting, and furnishings were perfect for such a dramatic surrender. His vintages weren't bad either, and his drug connections were superlative.

If nothing else, the boy would likely masturbate in his bed and even soil his sheets, which Frederick would be sure not to launder upon his return. And he didn't necessarily figure Sven would last through the trip, let alone beyond (oh, but he did, and with impeccable timing chaos-wise). Either way, gotta keep lining up new options, Frederick would chortle to himself, shaking his weenie off after a pee.

Samuel didn't say yes right away. Frederick was dangerously bourgeois, and though a friend, Samuel would be the first to denigrate him as sell-out hippie trash to his angry anarchist buddies, who prided themselves on their Tenderloin addresses and low incomes. Samuel himself lived on

Market Street near City Hall, a boast-worthy address for an outsider, living off the grid (the philosophical and economic grid that is – he had hot water, electricity, a gas stove, and heat of course). He also had a crack dealer next door who kept late, loud hours, but Samuel was too dogmatic about his poverty or too afraid to confront the other victims of capitalism (the less-educated, less-nuanced, and less-Hamlet-esque ones) to take arms against that particular sea of troubles.

Staying at Frederick's would be a relief and a downright pleasure. But he'd have to play it cool with such a gig, not invite his friends over or even let them know he was whoring himself to the luxuries of the capitalist scum who were oppressing them all.

"Sure, Frederick, would be happy to help you out." As if.

First came dinner with the two lovebirds (Sven had lived there all of two weeks), so they could show Samuel the ropes: which plants got how much water, what to feed the cats, and other complexities of domestic maintenance.

Good food and a nice bottle of wine were exempt from judgment among all political movements in San Francisco, just so long as they weren't imbibed in fashionable restaurants, so Samuel enjoyed his evening and got rather drunk on the '98 Rappaccini chardonnay that Frederick had served with halibut steaks, wild rice, and a salad of radicchio, arugula, and baby Napa lettuce hearts. He was half stumbling when it came time to matriculate in his floral and faunal responsibilities around Frederick's enchanted little Edwardian palace. Frederick was carrying on, holding a childish, flowery watering can with a spout pornographic in scale. "And this one ... give it a full load, ha, ha, ha."

Samuel smiled cursorily, while watching Sven out of the corner of his eye as he bent over to pick up one of the cats. Samuel's Adam's apple bobbed like – well, like an apple in a barrel – as he swallowed reptilianly. He'd never met Sven until tonight and though he'd suppressed the thought through dinner, three glasses of wine, and now Sven's butt in the air above the cat, Samuel surrendered with that swallow to the insistent knocking of his libido at the door of his cerebral cortex. His libido was decidedly not looking for a cup of sugar.

"I need to fuck him," it announced in the same tone of expected compliance a cop would employ when requesting a valid driver's license. "Now!"

Sven had that stoned-too-many-times, glassy-eyed sensuality about him. Coupled with his Scandinavian masculine good looks and lithe body, he was a formidable force, slutwise. Frederick had clearly not realized his recruiting abilities. Or perhaps he had, but dwelling on such a trait would likely have led to the uncomfortable thought that the days of their coupledom were indeed numbered, if not doomed. It occurred to Samuel then that perhaps that's why they were going to Greece so suddenly, having only dated for three weeks. Did Frederick think he could squirrel him away somewhere, cement the bond, protect him from all the other men who not only would be drooling in pursuit of Sven, but whom Sven would likely be seducing, one by one, while Frederick tried to rush through the mundane activities of defecation, sleep, and showering, anxiety attacks hot on his tail, knowing Sven could likely fellate half the town in the time it took Frederick to brush his teeth? Greece? Strange place to hide a homosexual. Only someone in San Francisco would consider such a ridiculous notion. Well, it's all relative, Samuel supposed.

Sven had sat down by then, holding and stroking Frederick's Siamese cat, Tallulah, his legs spread casually, just wide enough for Samuel to spy a luscious crescent of scrotal skin in a mess of blonde hair on the poorly guarded border of his briefs. He thought how easy it would be for hundreds of Mexicans to sneak right into Sven's pants, unimpeded. Fucking Sven thus agreed with Samuel's politics.

By the time he'd returned his gaze to his host, Frederick was looking back and forth from Samuel to Sven, slackjawed. But not for long. Frederick did the math, and saw the 10 percent in it for himself. He stepped boldly toward Samuel and took his hand. Sven was up and by his side as fast as a turned page, and within seconds Samuel was lost inside his own "United Farm Workers" T-shirt as it was pulled violently over his head and tossed aside like universal health care by a Republican Congress. Frederick was on his knees momentarily, pulling open Samuel's belt while Sven furiously French-kissed the lad, whose own face was contorted with unbridled lust. Samuel's cock dropped out of his pants like a bass note as Frederick succeeded in freeing it, and it was soon in the old hippie's chardonnay-blanched mouth. In no time flat, they had the boy completely naked and on his back on the Oriental rug, kicking like an upended bug. Sven was naked too, though Frederick couldn't remember how that had happened so fast, as he struggled to catch up, pulling off his jeans and socks. (He shouldn't have been shocked. People like Sven dispense with their clothing like card tricks – a slut's sleight of hand. They're not really wearing it. It's just with them until they can find a place to put it down.)

Sven ended up inside Samuel. (Frederick had missed the mechanics of that as well, even though it had involved lubing Samuel's asshole and getting that prodigious uncut Swedish schlong into a condom. Was it possible that Sven was carrying both in his pockets? Quite.) And while Samuel worried he'd be compromised into sucking off Frederick, the addled homeowner – clearly distracted by his lover's bouncing buttocks – chose instead to fuck Sven, so that while Samuel had the substantial weight of both of them on top of him, he only had to taste Sven. Yum!

They came as fast as they'd commenced the rut, and Samuel was glad of it. He didn't want any complications with Frederick going into this gig, and figured if the sex was quick and unconscious, he could dodge whatever intimacy might come up. Only a faggot could kid himself into such nonsense, but Samuel was a faggot, and an anarchist faggot to boot, and as he rushed into his clothes and grabbed Frederick's spare keys off the entryway Victorian end table, claiming he was late for a friend's (10:15 p.m. on a Wednesday night? He hadn't mentioned it earlier), he convinced himself they'd all have more or less forgotten about it by morning. And since Frederick and Sven would now be gone for three weeks, they'd certainly have little or no recollection by the time they returned, just so long as he didn't linger. If you kept it to dick, and dick alone, you could figure your dick would get lost in the three week's worth of dick most homosexuals would accidentally indulge in or chance across, and yours would be lost in the crowd like just another common thief. Such was Samuel's logic.

Sounds kind of anarchist. Why not?

He moved in the next day, lugging his army duffle bag, stuffed to bursting with his Dickies, T-shirts, William S. Burroughs and Noam Chomsky tomes, CDs, and other sundry hipster necessities. To celebrate, he made himself a latte with Frederick's Krupps espresso machine and read the just-delivered copy of the *New York Times*.

At some point, midway through section A, he realized he hadn't even put on a CD to listen to. It must have been the silence. Back on Market Street at the Allen Hotel, Samuel had to play his music top volume, not so much because he liked it that way but as a defense of sound waves (a sort of low-level missile defense system à la Star Wars – he'd never use such an analogy, of course) against the rap bouncing through the walls from the crack dealer's next door.

He flipped through Frederick's CDs, but not being in the mood for Annie Lennox, Sade, Diana Krall, or Andrea Boccelli, he opted for the radio. He then made himself another latte and prepared himself a bagel with sliced organic yellow tomatoes and pickled red peppers. Sweet Frederick, the bourgeois pig, had left the fridge well stocked. Samuel belched and browsed through the wine rack, picking out a vintage for later.

He hadn't figured on anyone just walking by as he turned to lock the door on his way out.

"Dude, what are you doing down here?"

It was Hari, as in Om, an ex-Krishna who'd grown out his hair and eschewed nonviolence for revolution six months back when he'd deserted the commune, absconding with enough rice, curry, and tofu to get him through the two weeks it took him to get back on his feet.

"Uh ... just feeding the dude's cats. What are you doing here?"

"I just got a job at the coffee shop around the corner," Hari said cheerfully. *Too small a town,* Samuel thought, *gets you every time.* Hari was eyeing the keys as Samuel shoved them into the pocket of his tight black punk-style jeans. "Why don't you just stay here? You got the keys," Hari inquired, furrowing his brow, unable to understand how someone could fail to take advantage of ... well, pretty much anything.

"Uh, well, I think someone else is moving in, in a day or two." He was right, in fact, though he'd be the last to believe it just then, on the street talking to Hari. Especially since Hari was the very person who would be moving in. He was the first anyway.

"So, Samuel, you know we're planning something kinda big for the demonstration."

Samuel chewed his nails – no easy task, as they were chomped to the stubs, and at any given time three or four were painfully hangnailed. He winced. "Yeah, I heard. What's the plan?" It was the 512th anniversary of Columbus, and a big march was planned, but Samuel hadn't heard any specifics.

"Dude, man, they're planning to blow up a bunch of Starbucks."

Samuel felt the second latte rumbling in his stomach as the caffeine it had released zinged through his tortured skull. Why was he feeling tortured, you might ask? No reason. He always felt that way.

"Anyway, tons of people are coming down from Eugene. ELF people, all them."

"Cool," Samuel replied dryly, trying to sound appropriately casual and angry in a politically sophisticated way.

"Well, we'll talk about it later at the meeting. I wanna ask you something." And he aimed his double cappuccino pointedly at Samuel, as if to impress upon him that he really meant it. Like something specific.

The meeting he was referring to was planned for that night at the New School. Samuel planned to skip it (he thought violent rioting cool generally, but didn't want to get arrested when he had the cats and plants to watch after and all this great food in the fridge) and stay in with a bottle of wine and some Cadinot French porn, now that he had a TV and VCR to use (TV at 850 Bryant was only available to long-termers besides). After that, maybe he'd head out and spend the porn-induced hard-on up some speed-addled cute young thing's ass at the Detour. Bourgeois homosexuality was just so great, and San Francisco had it down pat, like a mall or a superstore; like one of those places with a permanent "SALE" sign out front. Samuel didn't think of it that way of course. He thought of sex as chaos, and his participation as a politically radical act. In such a universe, what he didn't consider – that Jim Bakker and Jimmy Swaggart are sooooo hip for instance – couldn't upset his tenuous political and mental stability. He truly was an anarchist, inside and out.

Truly, no one was in charge.

Rap, rap, rap! Samuel heard someone knocking way too hard on the stained-glass door windows.

"Who the fuck is that?" Samuel raised himself, midstroke, still sliding in and out of the twink's well-lubed asshole ("Fuck me, fuck me," the boy went on annoyingly), as he perked up his ears to see if he could pick up the voices he heard conversing beyond the door. They must be Frederick's friends, he figured, diving tongue-out back into the boy's hungry mouth, and pelvically slamming into him with all his might.

"Samuel! I know you're there."

Just as he came, the image of Hari's unattractive face entered his mind.

Sex could be such a drag that way.

The stained glass shattered.

"Fuck, dude, are you cut?" It was Hari's friend Femo's voice.

Meanwhile, the twink moaned with narcissistic delight as globs of his own semen splattered across his chest. He giggled. "I'm uncut," he answered, making a joke of what they'd just heard outside. *Not funny, considering,* Samuel thought. And now that he'd cum, he wasn't interested in putting up with this boy's bullshit.

"Goddammit," and he pulled his cock out with a pop.

"What's the matter?" The boy unselfconfidently queried.

"Someone just broke the window – didn't you hear?"

A sultry, self-satisfied look crossed the twink's dimwitted face. "I was cumming cuz your big cock was in me. I didn't hear anything but 'Are you cut?'" And he giggled some more like the cheap tart he was.

"You gotta get the fuck out of here, dude," Samuel not really reluctantly informed him.

"What, am I not your type?" The boy's low self-esteem reared its ugly head, which was not only gelled, but dyed a very unflattering auburn with blond highlights.

"What?" Samuel responded impatiently, peering down the hallway from the bed. "Dude, I got a situation here. Sorry. Here's my fucking phone number." And he dug one of his cards out of his jeans, his half-mast cock still shrouded in muddied latex. "We'll do it again."

A real charmer, that Samuel.

He yanked off the condom ruthlessly, tossed it into the ficus tree's pot, and, grabbing a bath towel, ran toward the door.

"Hari, you fuck, you broke the window," Samuel shouted, approaching the front door.

"That's not a window. That's a fucking crime, dude. It cut my hand. This bourgeois fuck cut my hand!" Hari had never met Frederick, but accusation by economic or class association was plenty good enough when indicting a homeowner, so no reason to sweat details.

Hari was clearly drunk. And bleeding. *God, they fall hard when they leave the cult,* Samuel thought irrelevantly. Hari's pal, Femo (as in easier to work with than traditional ceramics), was spilling excuses like one of the ten beers he'd probably just imbibed. "He insisted, man; he really needed to talk to you."

"Thanks, Femo," and he pulled Hari in and slammed the door in Femo's face in one fluid motion.

"Harsh" was heard, courtesy of Femo, while Samuel dragged stumbling Hari down the hall to the bathroom.

The twink, more or less dressed, and just then primping his gelled hair, furrowed his brow and whispered as Samuel pushed Hari past him, "Not cute."

"Bye, uh … fuck, sorry, what's your name?"

"Michael. I'm sure. It's not a hard name to remember," he offered bitchily.

"No, you're right," Samuel answered, "but since one in three people use it, it's easy to misfile."

Strike two, Samuel. If he'd only told the boy to shut up while he was fucking him, he would have scored a perfect three strikes. But gay sex wasn't baseball was it? Nor was it a crime any longer. So just what the fuck was it? Bowling? Badminton?

Hari was now crying and bleeding all over the bathroom. "Hari, sit on the fucking toilet!" Samuel commanded.

"He doesn't give a fuck about me!"

"What the fuck are you talking about?"

"Veebee."

"Who?"

"The guy I've been seeing. Samuel, I'm really hurting …"

"I know, honey, sit down." Hari dropped like a bag of groceries onto the toilet lid, and Samuel lifted the boy's arm up in the air to staunch the bleeding. He then rifled through the drawers, looking for first aid supplies, and, while doing so, his towel dropped off.

"Dude, nice cock." And it was in Hari's hand before

Samuel could defend himself. "Taste?" Hari's eyes had perked up, his tear-stained cheeks suddenly losing their flush as his lips quivered.

"Fuck off, Hari." Samuel yanked his cock away, picked up the towel, and resecured it around his waist.

"Harsh."

He then wrapped Hari's hand in gauze and sighed deeply. "Okay, now you gotta get the fuck out of here so I can clean this mess up."

"Dude, you can't throw me out; I got nowhere to go."

"What are you talking about?"

"I gave my place to some ELF guys at the meeting."

"Why'd you do that?"

"Hey man, the movement."

"Well, where the fuck are you supposed to sleep?"

"I don't know, man, but you gotta be hospitable to guests. They came all the way down from Eugene."

"Sure, but you still gotta sleep somewhere."

"Well, Veebee …" Samuel rolled his eyes, nodded. "And I just figured I could stay here."

"But, I told you I wasn't even staying here, Hari!" he retorted incredulously.

"Yeah. What's that about?"

"Well, I'm not. I was just leaving."

"You don't look like you're leaving. Come on, be a bro, Sam, let me crash on the couch."

Samuel looked at Hari and thought how pathetic he was, resolving that a drunken moron on the couch was not that big of a problem. He'd be far easier to throw out in the morning than now.

"Alright, but you're going to sleep right now."

"Cool, cool, cool," and he nodded his head repeatedly. "I'm drunk anyway. I'll just go to sleep," he nodded cheerfully. "Less you wanna do something?" he added. And a truly moronic and lecherous grin (if such a thing can manifest on the face of a twenty-three-year-old – amateurish lechery is the worst kind) animated his visage.

"I just got through fucking somebody. No thanks." Which reminded him. Where was Todd, or John, or whoever?

"Hey, ... dude, you still here?"

He heard voices. "Shit, Femo's still out there," Samuel muttered to himself.

He yanked open the front door. "Yeah, he's really cute too!" It was Michael's voice and he was chatting with four dogmatic-looking young men dressed in black. "Anarchists," Michael enthused, "aren't they cool?"

"Get the fuck out of here, you stupid queen!" Samuel barked at Michael, venting all his frustration on the poor little tramp.

Michael glared bitchily back. "You'll never fuck me again!" (Why would a boy in San Francisco think such a statement carried any weight?)

"Fine!" Samuel shouted cruelly back, shocked to see he was literally holding the door for the four anarchists, who were now loading their gear in, bag by bag, muttering "Excuse me," and "On your left, dude."

"What are you guys doing?" Samuel asked.

"Slut! Your cock sucks!" Michael was now screaming from the street.

"Wait a second, you guys. Who are you?" Samuel persisted. They didn't answer, just smiled. "Femo!" But Femo was already in hot pursuit of Michael.

"Michael, where are you going?" Femo inquired softly. Oh brother. Once inside, the four black-clad insta-boarders relaxed somewhat. "We really appreciate this, man. Where's the basement?"

"What?" But it was all falling into place. Hari had likely met them at the meeting and offered the place. Or was it Femo? He'd never know now. Femo was gone, bent on sloppy seconds with the tart.

Samuel slammed the door, sending a few more shards of expensive glass flying onto the front porch, and marched back down the hall. "Hari!' he shouted. Hari was curled up in the bathtub. Samuel thought of turning the shower on him, but realized the less conscious Hari was, the better.

He turned in time to see the Four Horsemen of the Apocalypse disappearing down the basement stairwell to the garage, and he rushed after them.

"You guys – hey, you guys, this isn't my house."

"That's actually better," one of them reassured him.

"At least tell me who you guys are and why the fuck you wanna sleep in the basement."

"Didn't Hari tell you?" They all looked at one another.

"Hari's a fucking fool. He didn't tell me anything. I'd like to help you guys out, but this isn't my house, so I can't offer it to you guys. I'm not even supposed to be here."

They continued down the stairs, and upon reaching the basement, one of them looked back at him blankly. "It's better if it's an anonymous location. Don't worry."

"Don't worry?" Samuel was exasperated. "Dude, I'm responsible for this place."

The same guy reached out a hand. "Vic." He then motioned with his thumb at the others in rapid succession: "Dean, Tree, Poison."

"What's all that stuff ?" Samuel then asked worriedly as Poison began unloading a black canvas bag full of brightly colored plastic rectangles in yellow, blue, red, and green, and placing them all over the hood of the Miata. "And, uh, could you like not do that on the car?"

Poison picked them up cautiously and carried them carefully to the workbench and gingerly placed them one next to the other.

"What is that?"

"It's for the action tomorrow," Tree informed him. "We're not telling you anything else. No offense." And he shrugged his shoulders. "We really appreciate you letting us set up here."

"I'm not letting you set up here." And Samuel looked at Tree, who looked at Dean, who looked at Poison, who looked at Vic, who looked briefly at Samuel and said:

"We're here man. Be cool."

"We thought you were an anarchist," Dean chimed in, which stabbed Samuel momentarily in the gut.

Samuel collected himself. "Of course. When are you leaving?"

"Around nine tomorrow morning. Is there a back door?"

"Yeah, but I don't think you can get out through the backyard."

"We can hop the fence."

"Whatever." Samuel was calling it a day.

He woke up to a deafening din of "Helter Skelter." For a moment, he thought he was back at the Allen Hotel. But, no, it must be Hari.

"Hari, turn it down!"

What he heard next was not Hari. It was a bullhorn informing them to "Come out with your hands up and there won't be any trouble. We have the house surrounded."

Samuel's eyes bugged out. Oh, fuck. His first urge was to run outside and turn himself in. But he had to assess the situation, and consider the implications of his actions politics-wise. As he attempted to kick the covers off, he noticed an enormous lump at the other end of the bed. He poked it with his toe and felt flesh. He grimaced. That fucking disgusting Hari. The lump stirred, and an arm threw back the cover, revealing Sven.

"Sven, what the fuck are you doing here?"

Sven flashed the same just-stoned Cheshire grin that he'd probably wear if he were on board the listing Hindenburg. Which isn't as far-fetched an analogy as it seems. Just you wait. He smiled inebriatedly. "I never even got on the plane. To hell with Greece. I couldn't get your ass out of my mind."

Samuel was not in the mood for seduction. He furrowed his brow, flabbergasted at Sven's nonchalance. "Where the fuck is Frederick?"

"Well, I lied to him and told him that I was going to meet him over there next week, that I had some sudden business come up. Actually, I don't even have a legal visa; I can't leave the country, or I won't get back in. Anyway, I told him to just get on the plane. Who knows if he did." Sven smiled.

"How long have you been here?" Samuel inquired, baffled.

"I came back last night, around three a.m. I wanted to fuck you so bad, but you were so tired, I couldn't wake you up. You kept slapping me." He chuckled and reached for Samuel.

"You have fifteen seconds!" the bullhorn roared.

"Jesus, Sven, we gotta get out of here."

"Samuel, I can't risk dealing with the police. My visa, all that. We'll have to find another way."

"Dude, we're surrounded."

Sven lunged, pinning Samuel down and ravishing him with his tongue, driving his pelvis into Samuel's crotch.

"There's no fucking other way!" Samuel heard Vic shout from downstairs.

Struggling to push the big Swede off him, Samuel exclaimed, "Let's get the fuck out of here, Sven! They've got fucking bombs downstairs!"

Oblivious, Sven cooed, "I want to plant my bomb up your ass."

There was a burst of automatic gunfire, and Samuel instinctively lunged for the floor, pulling Sven with him.

Police started shouting, "They're firing! Hold your fire; hold your fire!" The gunfire was coming from the basement.

"We're fucking dead," Samuel announced. Sweet surrender – the one Frederick had prepared for. But Frederick wasn't there for the surrender.

"Fuck me, Sven." Hurray for Samuel, true to the cause. He'd go out in a truly anarchic chaotic orgasm of cum and violence. Sven mounted him, not bothering with a condom, as they had no viral, bacterial, or any other kind of pathological future to worry about.

There was more sporadic gunfire, more announcements

from the bullhorns, mounting threats from the Feds. Samuel wondered about Frederick, where he might be, as he watched Sven's enormous marbled tool plow him like an apple corer. He felt close to cumming. Things began to shatter – a vase, a mirror; leaves tore off the ficus tree. Samuel imagined himself and Sven holed up like Bonnie and Clyde, blasting away, cum and bullets flying all around them. He had a vision of Frederick rushing past the police line, professing his love for Sven, while Samuel squeezed off a round and watched the sorry hippie trash pirouette into a rhododendron bush and collapse into a heap.

The bullets came right through Sven's back – one, two, three – splattering blood and muck across Samuel's gaping mouth and orgasming face, his own semen interrupting the path of the lead projectiles that whizzed over his head into the TV, which instantly exploded with a pop. A cat screamed. And then he felt himself lifted. Lifted, with Sven's motionless heap of a body collapsed on top of his own, rising, rising. This must be death he thought, rising, rising – but then he felt his back tearing, and an unbelievable, searing pain filled his no longer blissed-out mind. He held on to his still erect cock as the only morsel of security he had left.

Hari's dull-visaged face watched from the street, wrapped in a police blanket, his jaw dropping so precipitously that he looked stupider than ever.

"Woooowwww," he uttered slowly, "Hari fuckin' Krishna."

At first, in the initial police barrage, most of the windows had been blasted inward, and several of the cornices had been reduced to splinters and powder. Then, suddenly, all the remaining windows had come flying out in the opposite direction like they'd been punched out from the inside. After that, the house rumbled and then sort of belched and lifted off its foundation a few feet, before settling back down and then collapsing like a cake, the top floor into the bottom, and the bottom explosively outward in all directions in a gust of chalky dust and colored planks. A huge plume of white smoke ascended, and when the house finally reappeared, it was a pile of burning rubble with a siren soundtrack, and a well-insured owner on the sidewalk with his hands on his cheeks.

Samuel ended up on T-shirts (cute as Che the boy was, sans beret) and is remembered as a hero among many. He died a radical anarchist. He died for a cause. He almost died smiling.

Winter Count

It was Denny who had made me curious about tattoos. Denny who had marked his demise defiantly in word and image upon his own body. Denny who had tattooed HIV+ in big green letters on his back when he was diagnosed. Later, in an ill black humor, he'd tattooed a skull and crossbones on his forehead. Denny went more or less mad with it, but I admired his demand to be heard. His body continued to speak in those final months, even when he no longer could.

It was Denny who made me realize tattoos were news.

His certainly were, and part of that news was that "we" were over. Denny adopted that sense of urgency that many of the newly infected felt in the late 1980s. Denny knew he had very little time. Probably a few years. So Denny threw himself into ACT UP, marching, and political performance art. He changed his diet, did yoga and qi gong. He found himself a positive boyfriend who wouldn't be afraid, as he suspected I was.

For awhile I'd tried to keep up with him. I marched and got arrested, though I regretted it. I remember, just as it was happening, Karl had said to me – he had a tattoo of Munch's Scream on his Adam's apple – "Don't get arrested unless you've decided to beforehand." I'd just looked at him and thanked him as I realized I hadn't made that decision. And then the police were on us and it was too late.

In time, I succumbed to the guilt and low self-esteem of the negative, forever junior varsity to the HIV-positive varsity team. A weird hierarchy and a macabre one. But *just* somehow too. After all, what the hell did I really know about it? Easy enough to march for others when you knew you'd been spared. I felt like a fraud. But I couldn't mope about such things or, worse yet, walk away as if it had nothing to do with me.

In the end, I decided activism just wasn't my forte. I volunteered at the hospice instead, sitting with middle-aged men as they wasted away and died. That was how I served in those years – running down to the corner market to buy candy bars and ice cream; watching TV programs; cheering folks up. A sorry little do-gooder who wasn't doing much good.

But at night, I searched for news. Because I missed Denny, though I wouldn't quite admit it. I concurred with others that Denny had gone off the deep end. But I admired him for his madness. Every time I saw him, a new tattoo. After the skull and crossbones came a series of bull's-eye targets all down one arm. On the other arm, he tattooed KS lesions that got all mixed up with the real ones not six months later. An in-your-face motherfucker, Denny was. He'd always been pissy, but never political. His body politicized him, and he in turn politicized his body.

And being that I missed him, and how we hardly talked, I listened to his body and how it spoke. Each word; each picture. I searched for his voice, in a sense, on the bodies of others as well. Tattoos became like books by Denny that I wanted and sometimes found in used book shops: There one is! – that thrill of capture.

And so I found Frank at Uranus. Frank had tattooed the same numbers on his forearm that his grandmother had been forced to wear at Auschwitz. This impressed me – for its unhipness, for its respect, and for its expression of the dark side of tattooing that Denny had matriculated me in. It made sex with Frank more secretive, more taboo, and somehow more connected to the world outside the fishbowl of gay culture. Frank's tattoo made fucking a defiance against the hordes of Nazi Christian bastards who gloated as we died. I licked it as his arms, flexed, held tightly to my biceps while I fucked him.

But ultimately, it was because it was something Denny would have done. That was the clincher. If Denny were Jewish, he would have beat Frank to it. By then, I realized that I was more interested in Frank's tattoos than Frank, and we drifted apart.

I'd run into Denny in the street all the time because he was everywhere then. Denny was a public person with a public body. He was shirtless, and Denny had a new tattoo.

"Eli, how you doin'?" he said.

"Hi, Denny." I didn't have to say anything more, since he was already lifting the bandage, as "it" was clearly what my eyes were drawn to upon seeing him. Underneath, just below his left nipple, was the biohazard symbol. What could I say? Nice? I love it? I just nodded to show I understood his meaning.

"I gotta go," he quipped, and he was off. Busy Denny. We talked of nothing now. I felt like I'd been replaced by a disease and his tattoos. He was an artist of his illness and his anger. And I felt awful for feeling that. I felt awful all afternoon. So awful that I knew there was only one cure for it.

I headed straight for Buena Vista Park. And while I hiked up the dizzying cutesy San Francisco Victorian streets to reach it, I remembered a boy I'd known in high school, who'd had radiation treatments for cancer when he was fifteen. The doctors tattooed a dot on his cheek, and another on the back of his neck, which together were used to line up the beam of radiation that burned away the remnants of his cancer.

Paul's tattoos found me as much as I found them. I met him

that day in the park. He was shirtless too, and I noticed his chest was splattered with ink. We circled each other like wolves for a bit, and when he vanished into the bushes, I followed. He was ravishing me shortly after, tugging at my belt, slobbering on my chin, but I wanted to talk about his tattoos. He explained that he liked men to cum on him, and he said that the men he loved had marked him, marked him permanently, with their seed. He had three cum splashes on his chest: one in red, one in green, and one in black. On the inside of his right thigh was another, and up his spine was a beautiful more or less straight green line – to each side images of green rolling droplets where the semen had run away off his skin.

"Maybe you'll be worth remembering too," he grinned, re-routing my attention to the task at hand. I doubted it. I wanted to cum on his back too, so I tore off his jeans and got him on all fours, jacked my dick in his butt crack and splashed my cum across the long green line.

Afterward, we walked down the hill together, and he told me more about the one on his back. He explained that this particular tattoo had a special meaning, not only as the rising of his kundalini life force through his chakras, but that it was the cum shot of the man who had broken his heart, betrayed him and infected him, and thus taught him everything.

Maybe I should tattoo Denny's face on my heart, I thought, after that. Maybe I should go and get all of Denny's tattoos so that the next time I see him, he will not be able to dismiss me or ignore me. Would this be submitting to his narcissism, or would it be a romantic gesture of devotion? Or would it be both?

Because Denny was fast becoming his body in place of himself – for me, for him, for everybody. Denny's body grew increasingly profound – in illness, in word, and in symbol. Denny's body spoke to you and reminded you of things. Denny's body was not something to escape into as it had been for me before he got ill. And like so many others, I escaped into sex in my fear of the epidemic. Ironic perhaps, but, more truly, it was simply the paradox that is sex: the more harrowing sex became, the more necessary it was as a refuge.

Denny's body could never be a refuge now. Denny's body was dangerous and dead serious.

I wondered if I would be able to have sex with Denny now. With the new Denny. I loved him I believed, that was enough. But where was he? He was vacating his body, and it was as if it had become one of those abandoned buildings covered in movie posters and flyers for lost cats.

Condemned.

In my unrelenting confusion, I kept hunting tattooed boys. Sadly, most of the tattoos I came across were as common and dismissible as a tagger's graffiti. An annoyance more often than not. Not news at all, but commercials. There were the endless variations on the belly button sunburst, the band of barbed wire or Celtic weave on the bicep, zodiac signs, animals, and the commandeered images of indigenous cultures. These were so common as to have become like name brands – advertisements of "cool." *Alive with Pleasure.*

I couldn't suffer these for long. I wanted to hear something, to read something that would explicate. It had to disturb me or awaken me; it had to be a herald of something. It had to be news. It had to help me work things out with Denny.

It had to be a voice in the wilderness.

A boy I met and slept with who had attempted suicide as a teen, and who had worked his way through so much of what had driven him there, had gone out one day and had his scarred wrists tattooed with vines of jasmine flowers interwoven with barbed wire. He explained he had sealed shut the door on suicide, and opened his heart. He held me down with those wrists as he pushed his cock against my hole, whispering to me, "Open … open to me."

But suicide was not my story. Denny was. And Denny could not close the book of his body. It was open for good.

Sometimes they were simply suggestive. Peter, who smoked pot five times a day, had a tattoo on the small of his back of a listless reclining Pooh bear with heavy-lidded, glazed eyes sitting next to a honey jar, his free hand – the one not holding the bong – digging greedily into that pot of honey. I did the same to Peter's ass, all the while watching Pooh as my cock slammed into him doggie-style.

Sometimes, despite my cynicism and jadedness, I found a tattoo so beautiful it didn't need to imply anything. At the gym, a Vietnamese boy named Duc had a Chinese sentence running from his Adam's apple to below his navel. This was beautiful – and on his hairless body, profoundly masculine, as from a distance it looked like a line of hair between his pecs that ran down to his belly and beyond. I didn't want to know what it said or meant. I wouldn't let him tell me, but I came all over it and he did too.

Keith reeled me in on sheer volume of ink. He'd focused his tattoos on his ancestors. He'd "nailed down" his genealogy he told me, and so his arms were a mess of heraldic shields and Celtic knots. On his back was a map of Ireland. After twenty minutes wrestling around in his bed, I was struck with the absurdity of what he'd done. I thought the whole thing profoundly stupid. I think it was the edelweiss and shamrocks on his ass that finally did it. His body was like a cheesy scrapbook from which I wanted to tear the tattoos like pages and scrunch them up to toss across the room. Since I couldn't, I pulled my tongue out of his sphincter and buried my teeth in clover – an act which he misinterpreted in the same fashion as he had his "glorious line."

A week later, I pounced on a young boy at the Detour.

Raver Jason had Hebrew letters running down his forearm. They were beautiful in the way that languages you can't read are beautiful. You know they mean something and have meant something for a very long time. People had died for such words, you were quite sure. It inspired deference.

I dragged him out of the bar for a walk around the neighborhood. When I asked him about his tattoo and what it meant, he wasn't sure.

"It's ancient," he said, "Egyptian, I think." I offered that the letters looked Hebrew. "Yeah," he responded, "like Jerusalem, Egyptians – that's what I said." He was getting annoyed. Perhaps because I was completely appalled by his ignorance, I asked him obliquely if he knew any Egyptians. He claimed they'd all been dead for centuries. "Are you stupid, dude?" he asked, dumbfounded.

I couldn't have sex with him, but as the horse was out of the barn in a sense, I needed to find someone.

I found Vinny at the End Up. Vinny's tattoo was a blob because he kept changing it until there was nothing else to do but scribble it out completely. It remained a giant blue dot, three inches by three inches, above his left nipple, which is what first attracted me to him on the dance floor. He was a lost soul and not afraid to admit it. And so the circle his tattoos had become ultimately said more than any of the images that had preceded it.

And he wouldn't tell me about them anyway. "I erased them for a reason," he insisted.

Sucking hickeys around his blue abyss and then cumming on it felt like painting abstract art.

He was the perfect antidote to Raver Jason, who symbolized so perfectly the degradation of the whole tattooing art and tradition as it entered shopping malls and children's birthday parties. Something ancient, eh? Is that all? Sometimes I thought it all just a sociohistorical indicator, pointing to the lostness of the white race. Not that only white people had tattoos. Certainly the original Asian and Polynesian traditions were a whole other story. But for white people it seemed a function of popular culture, a culture which I always perceived had a kind of panic to it about making some kind of connection, a connection it usually – and ultimately – failed to make. Thus, a tattoo to me, more often than not, looked like a swing and a miss.

Vinny, at least, had struck out with grace.

In time, Denny became too ill for activism and yoga – and even tattooing. I joined the circle of friends who took care of him when he could no longer take care of himself. Some of his activist friends were assholes, politically correct, furious at everything, moralistic and arrogant. But they were not afraid to do what needed to be done, and this mattered more than anything I didn't like about them. At the hospice I'd meet men out on the sidewalk who were afraid to visit dying lovers. They couldn't even cross the threshold. They were mostly nice men, respectable men, friendly men – and untattooed. I liked them even, but they had failed. They were not heroes like Denny's friends were. And Denny's friends all had tattoos.

Denny didn't want to give up tattooing, so he took to writing all over himself in black felt-tip marker. He had a graph across his chest that charted his T-cell count, and when he was so far gone that he could no longer muster the energy for such scribblings, he asked me for one last thing.

"Do this for me, Eli," he strained, hoarsely. "Get a tattoo. Do it for me."

I would have preferred he ask for something else. Forgiveness maybe? A second chance while there was still a smidgen of time? But how could I be selfish at such a time? I didn't want a tattoo of course, but how could I say no?

I nodded, but didn't say yes – to buy time I suppose.

I thought long and hard about it. I hated the idea of being stuck with some image, or some word. *Well, what won't change then? What will I always believe?* I asked myself. I thought of social commentary to counter the endless bourgeois armbands and bicep bombast that threatened to deplete the world's ink supply. I considered sarcasm: I could tattoo highrises, sewage plants, and nuclear reactor cooling towers across my skin. Or perhaps actual name brands: *Nike, Tide, Coke*. Or maybe the two sides of my body could represent the duality of the world: what we had, and then what we did with it. On my left side would be trees and flowers, animals, rivers, and rock. I'd cover my right side with a city of strip malls and factories, its skies crowded with fighter jets and its streets with tanks and SUVs, while around it would be fetid, toxic pools and clear-cuts.

But that would be a desecration of my body, and it would do nothing for Denny. He'd made his body holy with ink, in my estimation. And I had to do the same out of respect for his request. *What* then?

It took me weeks to figure it out, and I saw the doubt grow on Denny's face, a doubt that tended toward betrayed. Then one day at the gym a boy walked into the showers – scrawny, a wisp of a boy. He turned on the showerhead, and when he turned his back to me to receive the water, I saw the green ink across the small of his back, and it read, "I am loved."

I filled up and nearly wept. Of course, I wanted him immediately. I looked his way, but he never turned or noticed me. He had relayed a message and that was all that was needed. I didn't need to kill the messenger. Sex with him would have been redundant, superfluous.

It would be too corny, of course, to tattoo "You are loved" for Denny. The tattoo needed to be news, and it needed to be news for Denny. It was simple. He already knew I loved him. Perhaps it could be a reminder of that? But it just wasn't Denny.

The idea sputtered along for awhile until it completely paled the day I noticed Denny's Buddha on the night table next to his bed. Denny had turned to Tibetan Buddhism in the last months of his life, and he studied with a teacher who had him meditating on what is called a "seed syllable," a Tibetan character that one envisions to enter into the meditative state, and which later morphs into a Buddha. Denny was very into this and the bardo teachings of the *Tibetan Book of the Dead,* which instructed one to focus very clearly on one's intentions and mental state at the time of death. It was important for Denny to keep this syllable in the forefront of his mind.

And so it was easy. I went and had the seed syllable *Hung* tattooed on the inside of my right palm, so all I had to do was hold it over his face and he would see it – be reminded:

Denny liked it; he held my hand hard and for a long time that day.

I am loved; you are loved.

His family came around at the end. His sister was one of those strident Christians who thought he was hellbound for his lifestyle. We all had to fight it out at the end as Denny had insisted on being kept in his bed for three days after his death in keeping with the Tibetan Buddhist view that it takes the consciousness up to three days to leave the body, and that it is important not to disturb it in any way. His family thought this was New Age crap, and they tried through legal means to wrest the body from us. But Denny had nailed the whole thing down, with a power of attorney and lawyers, and his activist friends knew how to fight such a battle.

He got his three days, though in the end he was not cremated. It had been the lawyer's idea.

"You guys have to make a goodwill gesture," he'd sighed to us. "You won this thing, but it's a death, and it's supposed to be about rest. You need to give them something, some kind of goodwill gesture. Giving them his body would be that." He looked at us with his brows raised to see if we'd accept the idea.

We did. For Denny and his rest.

* * *

Denny had told me once how the American Indian tribes of the plains had kept what were called winter counts, picture stories on buffalo hides of important things that happened in each particular year. Denny's body was his winter count; his final winter count. And it made it difficult to watch him be buried. I actually said to his mother – what politic way was there to put it? – that I thought his body was a record of something important, and as such should be preserved like a text or work of art. It was rhetorical – I think – but she was offended, and I realized too late my mistake. She was, after all, appalled by his body and what she saw as the brazenness with which he had shamed both her and himself.

She snapped at me, with disgust: "I'm sure you have pictures, lots of pictures." I let it pass, reluctant to tell her that Denny destroyed all his pictures toward the end and allowed no one to photograph him, explaining that he was the volatile center, a Tibetan sand mandala, impermanent, and thus all the more sacred. He talked about Black Elk and the tree at the center of the world. Obsessed by then with all manner of tragic figures and paraphrasing Crazy Horse, he had explained, "Why would I let you take from me my shadow?"

And so in death, Denny does not speak.

Of course I think of him often, and my tattoo makes him hard to forget even when I want to. It's on the hand that I masturbate with. Perhaps it's my guilt, but it's been disturbing me, masturbating with this symbol of enlightenment on my palm. How incongruous. Or not. In the Tantrayana, Denny had once explained, all action can lead to enlightenment if the intention is noble.

And so I too have been marked by a man I loved. San Francisco, my own private Auschwitz – which must be German or

Polish for Idaho. Marked in the end with a language I cannot read. It might as well be Vinny's Zen blob. My koan. Denny. Love is a koan then too. And Denny's tattoos like a poem I remember; like a prayer. A song, and I'm not sure of the words. But I sing it, hum Denny as I reach out with this hand, as I wave with it, eat with it, jack off with it. My intention. I'm no different from the rest. A symbol for something; a connection. No doubt I'll end up in someone else's story: a dude with a Tibetan syllable on his hand. To slap their faces with Denny's dharma, to transform their cocks into Buddha-cock as I pull upon them, to lay gently upon their hearts my hand like a blessing; to remind them they are loved, we are loved. To bring them Denny's news: the jewel is in the lotus, or the tattoo, or the body, or the cock, or this story even.

"Open ... open to me."

A California Death

His younger son lived in a dilapidated, pale blue, turn-of-the-century house on 22nd Street in the old part of Sacramento. It had a big porch with a couch on it and a few lawn chairs, and it looked out over a small rectangle of grass bisected by a cement pathway that led to the sidewalk. There was a bigger yard in back of the house with a Rottweiler in it and two lemon trees. Inside the house was Ben's band equipment – keyboards, guitars, amplifiers – lots of big black boxy things his father couldn't identify but that he recognized as things that rock 'n' roll people loaded on and off trucks for gigs. And Lisa was there, Ben's girlfriend, with the baby.

The place was a pigsty in Warren's opinion. A somewhat tense pigsty.

How could he not have asked? Didn't a man have a right to get his bearings in a new home? Of course, asking Ben questions had never been simple. Not the kind Warren asked anyway.

He sighed, inhaling deeply from his morning cigarette, the lawn chair creaking as he leaned back. This had become his morning ritual, feeling the cool air on his skin, thinking, and remembering; going over it all. Ruminating.

Well, he had his memory – that was more than some men his age had. Small consolation. He'd look about the neighborhood then – at the other houses, trees, plants, cars, telephone lines. And he'd listen too – for a train, sirens, the wind, a squirrel chattering or a bird chirping. That put a stop to the short-term memories just as it opened a door to the long. There were three fruit trees in a line next to the house on the adjacent corner, for instance – pears perhaps – which brought back his childhood visits to Uncle Hugh's. Halcyon days under a sleepy sun, the buzz of bees and the click of grasshoppers; chasing about in the sun, life as big and end-less as the sky above him. A little boy full of ideas of what to become. Now and then: short term, long term. Is it all so binary?

Too many questions. Why suddenly was he so full of nag-ging questions? Questions that he would most definitely never have the time to answer now, even if they were answerable – which was doubtful, and probably why he'd never bothered asking them before. But he had too much time on his hands now. Too much time. He was terminal and he was complain-ing of too much time. He shook his head.

Hugh. What took him? His heart for sure. He drank like a fish and ate like a king. Funny, he suddenly felt something like empathy for Hugh. Perhaps it was just nostalgia, the most fruitless of emotions. After all, as a young adult, he'd come to despise his grandfather and Hugh; been disappointed by them and their slick, heartless business cunning. Of course Warren had grown up. He didn't despise anyone after seventy-five years on this rock. Oddly, now they made his throat fill up. He put out his cigarette then. What was he going to do – cry? For chrissakes.

Was this death? Becoming a weeping, impotent old man. Was that what they'd taken from him? He wouldn't be the first to feel that after losing his prostate and the concomitant ability to get an erection. Not that he needed that anymore. Not really.

What did he need anymore, but a place to die? And, surprisingly, even if he did feel somewhat betrayed by his elder son, Scott, he liked it here: this old house, this city, with its whistling trains, its big trees and quiet streets. Sacramento. He'd only driven over it on the freeway for the past forty years, like everyone else in the Bay Area. He couldn't remember if he'd ever visited this older part of town in all those forty years. Was that possible? Had he only stopped for gas out in the sprawl all those years? Had it really not been since he was a small child? Those pear trees, and this porch, the train and elms – they'd all been waiting here, all the while holding these old memories. Or was this just death? That was death's job, to take you back full circle. He would have felt this anywhere most likely. Best not to dwell on it.

He'd lift himself up on his stiffened joints then and walk, down the lettered streets, ABCDE, among the big trees and old stately Victorians, remembering sunny Uncle Hugh in his sepia 1930s world, working for the feed and grain outfit his grandfather owned and living in gentleman farmer splendor in one of these old Victorians. What he'd loved and hated about Hugh was that ever-present smile. The man was cheerful to a fault. He welcomed you like a prince, and you were flattered, but emasculated as well. You were a prince, not a king. He was the king. His smile always broadened when he put a competitor out of business, which seemed more satisfying to him than even profit itself. By his teenage years, Warren found the man's smiles grating and clammed up in his presence.

What fools men were. Women were the consolation, sanctuaries of goodwill and reason. Dangerous ground, memory was. It always led to Judy.

His wife was from the South. She'd always disliked California – its disconnection from the past, the constant growth, the hypocritical, liberal, Yankee-style racism that spawned ghettoes. Though she spent most of her adult life in the Golden State, she'd joked she was like everyone else here: "a strange interloper with an odd sense of entitlement to its blessings." He generally agreed with her. He was fourth-generation San Franciscan, but what could that mean in California? Pretty much nothing. They'd lived all over –

Denver, Seattle, Boston, Chicago – always circling back to California and its endless opportunity. But she loved Mississippi. It was her home. Hattiesburg to be exact. She loved the pines and the sleepy towns, the slow trains, the kudzu and cicadas.

He got all that, but it wasn't his home. He always felt like he was in some novel when they were in Mississippi – *To Kill a Mockingbird* specifically – with its strange slow undercurrents of mental illness, offstage mayhem, and the weight of race. California was never like that. He hadn't lived in Steinbeck's California, and when he went there it felt like it had been erased anyway. And people didn't write novels about San Francisco because it *was* a novel. He laughed to himself then. "That's a good one," he huffed. A charming old romantic novel, unreal and unread. California, when he really thought about it, was just some place you passed through, like college – you loved it, it meant everything, but it was never yours. It belonged to no one or everybody. Like some kind of chalkboard, constantly erased and rewritten on. San Francisco he'd lost a long time ago: the hippies, drugs, and racial tension of the sixties, the highrises that marred the skyline in the seventies, the subway trains that came, the filth and the homeless masses, the crazy artsy kids and queers. He'd been displaced and had resigned himself to a different kind of homelessness than the kind he stepped over in the streets. No, California wasn't his. Mississippi, on the other hand, was always hers.

But now, wandering these streets, with his death creeping toward him, he felt almost an onslaught of that homey feeling. For the first time. In Sacramento no less. This was old California, that's what it was. There was such a thing after all: the old houses of Midtown, the economic blight that assured the past still had a foothold even if it was precarious, the big trees – his childhood. If there were any sleepy towns in California, they were these old valley towns. Of course, twenty blocks in any direction would lead you to huge parking lots and their boxy chain stores. But this place – his son's rental – with its big porch and antique stove, its cracked walkway and gnarled fruit trees, was like an old dog or threadbare sweater. It comforted him with some odd sense of immortality – or, if not quite that, a slow and poetic decay that was the antithesis of what he'd normally witnessed in the land of his birth where everything was brusquely torn down, leveled, relandscaped, and repackaged for the next generation, or the next gold rush.

Well, no gold rush here. Not in Ben's house. Ben, the good-for-nothing son. Ben and his rock bands and girlfriends. Ben, who held out to the bitter end. How strange to suddenly see Ben as the one who was more connected to the past than any of them. The rebel, the rocker, the nonconformist and contrarian. Hell, life was full of surprises.

Judy having been the biggest and best of them. And her death the worst of all. That had been a shock, had indeed taken the fight out of him, along with everything else. And now his manhood. Yes, she'd taken parts of him with her, and then left the shell of him here. She'd gone fast: breast cancer. And now prostate cancer was taking him. Were they so typical?

He'd let himself cry for Judy when she passed. And he felt angry of a sudden. He wasn't going to cry for himself or Hugh or California, or anyone or any*thing*. Not now. He was cried out. And he'd done it all alone because he was on his own then and he felt he could. There were no tears at the funeral. He'd be damned if they were going to see him break for their show. He waited. No one was taking care of him in those days, watching his every move. He had his health. He'd still been able to keep the world at bay and grieve privately. He hadn't drank much – only a few times, really, when he'd gotten sentimental, when the memories got into him like knives: that field of flowers in Greece she'd taken off through running when she was twenty-four; that night in Half Moon Bay, middle-aged, when they'd laughed deep down in their bellies about her chronic bunions; the way she'd sighed when they'd told her the cancer had metastasized, holding that wooden spoon in the kitchen, the smell of beef stew, the steam on the window above the sink.

It was then, remembering those moments, that he took the shot glasses down: one for Judy and her scotch; one for himself and his bourbon. And they drank, like two ghosts – to love and what they'd made together, and he'd blubber in his cups: "Judy. We had a good time. Why so fast?" He'd get angry then, at himself or God or whatever, and he'd slam his fist down and collapse onto the table, his hands over his crossed arms, crying and conjuring her holding him, tight, tight, so tight, obliterating his grief in her embrace.

Now he drank beer with Ben on the porch. Ben in his overalls without a shirt – God, the tattoos, up his arms and all over his chest and back. He looked like a stevedore.

"Lisa's a nice girl, Ben," Warren mustered. But Ben winced. He wanted to say, "She's a woman, Dad," but he wasn't going to do the usual routine. Not now, not with his father dying.

"You thinking of marriage, Ben?"

"No, Dad, we're fine."

"Is he your son?"

"Uh, no, he's not."

"Then why ...?"

"Can I get you anything, Dad?" He changed the subject all the time now, ever since the diagnosis, and it was driving Warren batty. Ben had always been good for a cooker before. He'd escalate to no end. How many times had he thrown Ben out of the house as a teenager? Hit him even. Twice. He knew the count on that one and he regretted them both – for Judy, if not for Ben. He'd been hard on Ben; Ben had been hard on him.

Ben went inside to get himself a Coke, and Warren overheard him talking to Lisa: "I'm not gonna fight with him. Not now."

Like a man, fight like a man. Where did that come from and why weren't they doing it? Why had they never done it? All they'd done was bickered and sniped for going on forty years. Maybe they should have had it out once and cleared the slate. A ridiculous notion. He's your son, he told himself. Yet he'd always seemed a stranger. And a hostile one at that.

He remembered how he and Judy would argue about him. "He's a normal teenager, Warren – for God's sake."

"He's not normal; he's delusional. He's not going to straighten out, mark my words."

"What a terrible thing to say, Warren." She'd glared at him. "You want him to fail, don't you?"

"At what he's doing, yes; at life, no."

"Honey, lots of boys want to be rock stars. Let him explore his world; he'll make the right decision. Our job is to love him." She'd been right of course, and he hadn't listened. He hadn't loved his son, not in the only way love is worth a damn: active support of another's dreams and well-being. Faith.

Judy had finally and resignedly concluded, when Warren had driven Ben away one Christmas over his vegetarianism, "You two fight because you're the same: stubborn and willful. Everybody wins and everybody loses." She'd just shaken her head with disgust then, a tear in her eye.

The move had been hurried, being as Scott had sold the house so abruptly. A little too abruptly, Warren thought. But Scott was efficient, take-charge – you could say that about him. And he'd handled the move, loading everything up in the SUV and driving up the day after Warren had come up with Ben.

Warren had been giving Scott the silent treatment since the decision to move him up here to Sacramento. He was waiting for an explanation. He'd wondered of late if Scott had perhaps staged the whole family meeting drama to bring him and Ben together; to enable a reconciliation, if you will. Scott was such an on-the-ball guy, always making things happen, a visionary. Warren repeated that thought in his mind as he had for years, but this time, no matter how he tried to reassure himself, he was nagged by how cavalier Scott had acted. He'd wanted to ask him – but how could he? He who'd always given Scott the benefit of the doubt. It just wasn't Scott's way to use sleight of hand with him. He was direct, just like his father. Scott had done and still did everything to plan, from football and the paper route, to college and an MBA from Stanford, to the pretty wife, the talented, precocious grandchildren, and the big house in Atherton. He'd done right by his old man. Or had he? He'd followed the plan alright – right down to suggesting a rest home or hospice, Warren thought bitterly.

He'd sat there at the "family meeting" – Scott's term – listening to the apple of his eye abandon him. He'd been speechless, shocked. *Et tu, Scott?* Judy, and now this? They talked about him as if he weren't even there. Scott and his daughter-in-law, Jill, going on and on like some damn business presentation, smiling, assuming control, asserting what was best, trying to convince Ben, who finally exploded at Scott.

"I can't believe you, Scott. He's your fucking father."

"Calm down, Ben, and don't use that kind of language around Dad."

"Oh, please," Ben said with disgust, thinking to himself what a foul mouth his father had always had. Scott was being patronizing. Ben looked at his father then, giving him a sad smile. Warren stayed stone-faced. If he had no Judy, no future, no say in how he was to die, well he had his dignity.

"You're out of your depth, Ben," Scott retorted.

"Depth? What do you know about depth? You're the shallowest person I know, Scott. Give me a fucking break."

"All I mean, Ben, was that it might have been nice if you could have grown up in time to help your parents when they needed you most, but ..."

"But what, Scott? My maturing process is some kind of thirty-year mortgage in need of refinancing – right? You've never understood anything of value, Scott. Not one fucking thing." And he glared at him hatefully.

"You guys," Jill tried to intervene. But Ben glared at her too. He made it a policy never to insult Scott's wife, but he'd be damned if she put his father in a home.

"I'm gonna take him home with me," he said resignedly, but firmly.

"Oh come on, Ben, you're hardly in a position ..."

"My girlfriend's a nurse, asshole."

"Uh, which girlfriend is this? The one with the baby?"

"No, the hunchback." And he took a deep breath in the ensuing silence. "Come on, Dad." But Warren hesitated, waiting for Scott's rebuttal.

It never came.

Instead, his number one son said, "Dad, is this what you want?"

"It's fine," he said to the far wall. They could cut him up in pieces and sort out the parcels, for all he cared. He was going to let his sons decide. What had he raised them for if not to make this decision? It was theirs to make. He was through with the whole business.

When Scott and Jill had arrived in their SUV with their two children and the paltry remains of Warren's wardrobe and personal effects, they'd grinned like Cheshire cats. Scott had condescendingly put both his hands on Warren's stooped shoulders.

"Hey, Daddy-O, how you feeling?"

"Fine," he answered in a clipped tone.

Scott then marched into Ben's house as if it were some property he was assessing the value of and would proceed to sell out from under all of them if the market were ripe.

"Would you like to come inside?" Lisa remarked to his back, rolling her eyes.

Ben gave her an admonitory look, but she just lifted her shoulders. Warren liked her frankness. Why did he like that in women, but not in men? Ben was certainly frank. But Ben had been acting cool of late, holding his cards close to his chest, hanging back.

Lisa picked up the baby when she saw Jill approaching. Jill, forever the sales executive, noted that and immediately asserted her advantage, reaching out her hand with the 300-dollar watch on it to greet Lisa. Lisa's fingers were bedecked with big rock 'n' roll rings and her arm was tattooed, all of which made Jill blanch slightly and withhold something in her handshake.

"What a cute baby," she said, smiling insincerely and effusively.

"This is Henry." Lisa feigned a smile, directing her gaze at her nine-month old son.

"Henry?" Jill seemed surprised by the name.

"The world doesn't need another Dylan or Joshua, God knows," Lisa remarked sardonically.

Jill could do nothing but blanket the following awkward moment in a big-toothed smile as she introduced her two children, Amber and Justin. Suffice it to say, Lisa didn't remark on their names as she offered everyone drinks.

And then Scott and Jill had rushed off after only two hours of carting things from the car and into the house, Scott pecking his father on the cheek with a "See you next week," and leaving Ben to finish up.

It had been a bad two years since Judy'd died. He was recalcitrantly morose and his kids had been concerned. He didn't want to bother them, but Jill and Scott were always pestering him, taking him out places – dinner, hikes with the kids, malls. When his ongoing prostate problems led to a high Gleason reading, he felt almost relieved. And maybe Scott and Jill did too. They took him to his appointments, conferred with the doctors. Ben was on the sidelines; it was Scott who was managing his affairs. But Ben was in Sacramento after all, and Atherton and the family home in Los Altos weren't that far apart.

Besides, whenever Ben came down, they argued. He'd only tried to explain the financial arrangements, his will, but Ben had rolled his eyes, expressing annoyance.

"Goddammit, Ben, you need to start paying attention to

these things. You've made nothing of yourself; you should be grateful you'll have some money. And I want you to manage it properly."

There, he'd said it. The wrong thing, he knew. Again. Judy'd been sure to point that out over and over again through Ben's adolescence. But he didn't know what else to do. He loved his son, for God's sake – why didn't the boy want what he had to give? He knew the answer to that, but even "creative types" need cash. He didn't see the point in what he saw as Ben's holier-than-thou stance and his never-ending teenage rebellion. He was pushing forty for chrissakes.

Ben would always say he "had to go" around then. Maybe the fight was out of him too.

"I better be going, Dad." He kissed his father on the cheek then. Something new. He'd never done that in the past. Was that for Judy? Was he what was left of Judy to Ben? He felt sometimes they had a bond that excluded him, and now this? He felt humiliated and pitied. Patronized in his dotage. But he felt something else too. He looked down at the blanket in his lap then, unable to meet his son's eyes.

"Goodbye, Son. Thank you for coming down."

"No prob, Dad. I'll see you next week."

Since when was Ben stoic? And why when he closed the door behind him did Warren have the sudden urge, just like from deep in his cups with Judy, to be embraced? And to hold his son tightly; cling to him; plead for him to please not go?

Judy'd favored their youngest – "the creative one," as she called him. And he'd busted the poor kid's balls. "Why can't you *create* something that pays your bills – like capital?" But Ben was no slouch on the uptake. They'd had a zinger eight or nine years back. The last big one. He'd asked that very question and had gotten the deserved answer.

"And end up like you?"

"Which is ...?"

"You tell me. I don't see anything but a shell."

"Hmm. Well, people collect shells, what the hell."

"Shells are shit, common as dirt," Ben retorted viciously then.

"Ben!" She who never intervened. His mother stared him down. And Ben stormed off.

He remembered feeling the dread that that might have been it, the final row. And he'd even been trying to avoid arguing. How had it begun this time? He'd mentioned Ben's homemade CD. That was it. He'd hated the music, had asked Ben to please turn it off – and then he'd made the impolitic comment that he better quit fooling around and get a real job.

"You're hopeless," Ben dismissed him.

"Me? You're thirty, for chrissakes. It's over. Put the goddamn guitar down."

"I love the guitar."

"Well, I love bourbon, but I'm not making a career of it."

"Really. Seems to me you have."

"Cheers," and he held his glass up to Ben. Ben did the same with his guitar.

There'd been something in that moment. They could have laughed. But they'd let it pass, instead resuming their argument hours later after the golden opportunity was long gone.

Now here he was living in his son's house, actually listening to him practice the guitar, the fight gone out of him. It was over alright. Ben was who he was. Always had been. And what's more, he was surprising his old man.

Ben and Lisa worked all the time – she at a diner, he bartending. Lisa took the kid to day care nearby during her shifts, so often as not it was just Warren and the old moldy house – and the dog, Sonny, who looked at Warren suspiciously. They stayed out of each other's way – Sonny in the backyard and Warren inside or on the porch. Or out here, walking.

He must be mad as a hatter to call Sacramento a dreamy place. But that's what it was for him. Each morning, down over the railroad tracks, past the empty lots and overgrown yards that crowded the prerefurbished Victorians. Sometimes he had to wait for the train. Freight trains. Imagine that. Old California. In the Bay Area, he'd seen only commuter trains, light rail, quaint streetcars, and cable cars for the past forty years. Then here they were again – freight trains – ploddingly rumbling along like forgotten bison, their heads down, belching steam. And they'd been here all along. The big yellow engines, the dusty sienna boxcars, forlorn empty flatcars, and the humble dignity of their metal wheels, sometimes squeaking, but never slowing, moving their load without complaint. Like mules really. Mechanized mules. He felt like reaching out and petting them. For God's sake. He felt like embracing them, he did. Ridiculous. He'd be crushed.

But then, in the middle of such a reverie of wonder and absurdity, the train would suddenly end and recede quickly, tragically, inevitably up the tracks. God, don't go. It always caught him in the throat. What could he do? Chase after it? He shook his head, amazed at how unhinged his emotions were becoming. He forced his hands deeper, more firmly, into his coat pockets.

Other strange things were to be found in Sacramento. Old California things he hadn't seen for years: A grand art-deco Firestone garage; a Catholic bookstore with a real nun at the counter; a Five and Dime. And then there was Shop O' Stamps, run by an old couple – old, as in late seventies. Nothing sparkly and ordered about it either – old dusty albums, green visors on their heads. Like something in Mississippi. Judy.

There were big parks too, spaced around. In Fremont Park, he saw a giant elm with a little metal sign nailed into its trunk: "Notice of removal." Dutch Elm disease. It was ravaging Midtown like a real estate developer with low-interest financing. He looked up into the tree, its enormous branches, which – if he read into them (and he let himself) – could be gesturing in exasperation, or hopelessly pleading, or dancing even. Judy could dance. Judy had always been his joie de vivre. Is that what a prostate was too? Silly thought. He remembered something he'd read about Diego Rivera having cancer of the penis. The doctors had told him they would need to amputate it. Mr. Rivera was appalled and sought out other practitioners, an experimental chemotherapy, resolving, "I would never abandon something that had brought me so much joy." Is that what he had done, just given it away, abandoned his own body? Or was it his longing for Judy that had made him empty the hold of the ship? Without Judy, he didn't need it anyway. What was he doing then, sending stuff off to the underworld, care of Judy? For safekeeping? Hell, he didn't have religion – what was he hoping for? Judy was like one of those old brick buildings they'd knocked down to make room for an OfficeMax, and he was like this tree, that stamp shop: slated for removal. And that was it. He'd never see Judy again.

He walked across the park to a bench to rest for awhile, but a homeless man interrupted his reverie. "How you doin', sir?"

"Fine." Not a very thoughtful rejoinder. Why had he said it? Simple enough: he wasn't going to engage some bum in conversation about his death process or the love of his life.

"You got a quarter?"

He fumed of a sudden and barked, "No." He wanted to say, *I don't even have a prostate, my wife's dead, one son's a deadbeat, and the other's a son-of-a-bitch. I got nothing. Don't ask me for a goddamn quarter.*

"How about a dime?"

"Leave me alone!" And he got up and walked away.

"God bless you!" the man called after him.

"Keep your blessings," he muttered.

There were so many homeless now. He thought of San Francisco, literally sinking under the weight of them. And here too, down along the American River, its shores lousy with encampments. He thought how that *should be* ironic, with a name like that, but it wasn't. The country had gone to hell.

He found himself back at the tree. The old wrecking ball of California had sniffed it out too. He'd heard something then: a chirp, like a squirrel. He stopped and looked up into the tree. The sound continued though he could see nothing. But he couldn't look away, and it became suddenly almost superstitiously important that he discover the source of this sound high up in the elm. Then he saw a shape, moving ever so slightly in a cavity way up in one of the top crotches of the great tree. *I'll be damned: an owl.* God, when had he last seen an owl? It means something doesn't it? He snorted. Death perhaps – for him. No news there. And for the owl? It means he'll soon be as homeless as that bum when they knock this tree down.

He shook his head and walked over toward the edge of the park where it bordered the street. Standing on the corner, waiting for the light to change, he felt how uncomfortable his coat was. He hated this coat, and decided right then to take it back. Why had he let Ben talk him into it? Well, Sacramento was cold, and for whatever reason he'd forgotten to pack a jacket. The move had been too hasty. How could he have ended up without a warm coat? When he'd called Scott to have a jacket sent up, Scott informed him everything was gone.

"We sold all of it, Dad; you don't need all that crap." That crap was a lifetime's worth of belongings.

"I need a warm coat, Son."

"We'll get you one, no problem. Anything you want. We'll go out to Macy's, or whatever they've got up there, and get you whatever kind you want."

"I'll see you Saturday," Warren said, holding back his anger. And he hung up, fuming. That was a Tuesday. He could wait until Saturday for a coat?

"Ben, I need a coat."

"I got coats, Dad."

"I need *my own* coat."

"Okay. Let's go get one."

But Ben didn't have access to his father's money like Scott did as power of attorney, so he couldn't take Warren out to "Macy's or whatever they have up there." They went to the surplus store on K Street and found him a practical warm *Dickies* coat for fifty dollars. Warren didn't like the place. He didn't shop in places like this. He'd worked hard, been successful; he felt like he was slumming, and it made him angry at his son. Even as Ben, with all sincerity, tried to help his Dad pick one out, he grew moody and grumpy. He stood there, watching his son – the goatee, the knit cap, the ugly tattoos all over his forearms. *I raised him to be an upstanding man,* he thought to himself, *and here he is, looking like a convict.* And shopping with them to boot.

"How about this one, Dad? Dickies are high quality; they last forever." Whoops. He wouldn't need it that long. Well, Ben couldn't take the comment back.

"It's fine, Ben. Just buy it."

"Okay," his son acquiesced demurely. Ben was being patient, he could tell.

On the drive home, he blurted it out: "I don't need your pity, Ben."

Ben looked at him surprised. "You're not pitiful. Whatever you are, you've never been pitiful. I'm the –" But he stopped himself before finishing the sentence that he knew he'd regret the minute it left his lips. He was trying so hard "not to fuck this up," as he'd termed it to Lisa a week ago at the Townhouse.

"The man's dying; I'm not gonna fight with him," he'd said to her with determination, looking straight ahead into the mirror opposite the bar as he'd downed a shot of Jägermeister.

"Well, maybe you need to have a real heart-to-heart talk with him, Ben. I mean, you can't just stay out of his way. That's not really dealing with it." Lisa looked at him, nudged him, raised her eyebrows.

"Lisa, shit, you can't have a heart-to-heart talk with

Warren McCrorey," he said with exasperation. "Besides, it's a bit late in the game. I think I'll stick with just giving him a wide berth and not causing him any undue grief in his last days." And he motioned to the bartender for another.

"Are you still trying to prove something to him, do you think?" Lisa persisted.

Ben sighed, closed one eye, slouched, and turned to look at her. She always knew the score. "Lisa, maybe I'm just doing it for my mom. Because she isn't here to do it. And Scott's an asshole."

"I'll drink to that." Lisa took the two shots from the bartender as they arrived and handed one to Ben. They clicked them together and downed them. Then they both laughed.

"Why don't you just pretend your dad is someone else? Or, like erase the last thirty years – just keep him in your mind like how he was when you were a kid. And don't think about Scott. Scott's not here, and even though he thinks he is, Scott's not even really involved anymore. He's already buried him."

Ben nodded. "I just don't want to fuck this up, and Scott's counting on me doing just that. That's how he's fucking involved, as a fucking bettor."

"And I'm a nurse." They both laughed again. "You won't fuck it up, Ben." She kissed his cheek then. "I know you won't. You're doing the right thing."

He nodded, sighed. "So, how are *you*?" And he'd asked it without adding the last part of the question – *with all this*.

"I think Warren's pretty cool actually."

"Is he saying much to you?"

"He doesn't like Sonny," she chuckled. "He's very sweet with Henry."

Ben smiled a sad smile.

Warren found Henry to be something that made him useful. He offered to watch him whenever he noticed Lisa was busy or overheard her on the phone about her work plans or what have you. She was in the habit of dropping Henry off at a friend's who did day care out of her home, but on occasion she'd leave him in Warren's care. He was by no means helpless, even though his doctor had informed Ben and Scott that the pain would get bad and the pain drugs would make him more or less disabled. That hadn't happened just yet, for whatever reason. The real pain hadn't started, though the cancer had moved to his bones and as such promised to give him a pretty good beating before the jig was up.

Lisa found it touching when she returned home to find Henry sitting on the floor playing with Warren's shoelaces as he dozed off in front of the TV. Touching, but also problematic. How much of this babysitting consisted of sleeping? Henry was generally a good baby – and at nine months not yet walking – but, still, it took next to no time for him to ingest all manner of things, and she was probably being negligent leaving him with Warren. But it wasn't just about Henry, and she knew that. Lisa had been standoffish at first, causing Warren to wonder whether Ben and she had argued about this arrangement. He didn't necessarily believe it was permanent anyway. Scott had miscalculated in the negotiations – a setback. Scott would set things right. He'd at least find out that Lisa wasn't a nurse. Ben wasn't a liar per se, but that had been a rather bold fib. In some odd way, he honored his son for it. He had benefited from Ben's determination. True, the place was a pigsty, but it wasn't a convalescent hospital or hospice.

"Hello, my dear man-child," Lisa'd say, picking her son up from the floor, "and what have we learned today?"

Warren would stir. "Sorry, Lisa; must have just dozed off."

She was already rounding the corner into the kitchen. "Want coffee?"

Was she hinting he should be drinking more of it while watching Henry? "No thanks."

"Henry, Henry, Henry, my sweet man-child," she'd coo to him, and Warren would hear the smack of her lips.

Warren thought it an odd nickname, but he'd grown attached to the little tyke, with his fat cheeks and knowing eyes. His lovely silences. An old soul he supposed, a "man-child," as she called him. And it occurred to him he really didn't even like his own grandchildren, who never sat still or shut up. Overstimulated. The world's gone to hell. But this little Henry. A little gem. Oh Jesus. He sucked it up. But suddenly he missed him terribly, and got up to go to them in the kitchen, at which he petted the child's downy soft head.

"He's a helluva sweet fella, Lisa."

She smiled. "You're not so bad yourself, Warren."

He smiled back at her, reluctantly, shyly. God, that must have been a first. When had he last smiled?

Speaking now to Henry, she added, "And he's got a funnier name than even you, Henry! How 'bout that?"

Henry just grinned. *Strange kid,* Warren thought. He never laughed or cried. He sort of pouted or grinned. That was the extent of it, and it was in some odd way tearing Warren's heart apart.

He wondered then: *Who was the kid's father?*

Maybe he was lucky not to have one. Or to have Ben instead.

He kept walking, block after block, past more condemned trees and ramshackle houses, all the way to the river, which he decided to avoid for fear of another confrontation with a homeless man. To think, in California you avoided nature because it was full of refugees. Nature, a refuge. Not for him. Not for them either. Not really.

He turned north, proceeding into downtown and its sorry pedestrian shopping mall. And there it was: the surplus store where he'd purchased the coat. He went in and found his way downstairs to the coat section, past the racks of thermal underwear and discount socks, where he asked the young woman about returning the jacket.

"I'll have to call the manager," she said tiredly.

Mrs. Sung arrived shortly afterward, looking firm and in control. "Can I help you?"

"Yes. I purchased this coat here a week ago." And he struggled out of it in order to hand it to her as he spoke. "And I just don't like the fit, and I'd like to return it."

"Do you have the receipt?" she asked, holding the coat out in front of her, eyeballing it for damage.

"Uh, yes, it's here in the pocket." He reached for it, but she pulled it away from him and found the receipt herself. Warren had kept it there for just this purpose.

She studied the receipt. "This is a week old. You've been wearing it?"

"Just a few times."

"Well, I'm sorry, sir, but we can't take it back." And she handed it back to him.

He looked at her dumbfounded, a man used to Nordstrom and Saks, where they'd take things back even months later – and without receipts. "I don't want it. I'd like to return it."

She interrupted him: "Where are the tags?"

"The tags?"

"Yes, sir, the tags. You don't think I'd take it back without the tags?" By this time he was aware she'd made up her mind not to take it back at all and was simply bludgeoning him with her superior position in the negotiations.

"I'm new here in town ..." He wished he hadn't said it as soon as he did. She was humiliating him and he was letting her do it, reduced to begging.

"And I'm running a business. You wore it, sir – I can't take it back. I won't be able to sell it."

He was taken aback, not by her reasoning, which was sound, but because he wasn't used to being treated this way by a retail manager. Did she think he was some kind of lowlife? Not a rhetorical question, he suddenly realized. He looked around at the other customers. This is where the river habitués shopped, where people like his son shopped. But he was different, wasn't he? Not to Mrs. Sung. Maybe not to anyone else either. He turned then to look at the pillar-length mirror next to them. His hair was messed from the wind, long straggly wisps of it hanging across his forehead and over his ears. What could he do, tell her he was an old man – and a dying one at that?

He considered suggesting an exchange, but his fury was growing, as was Mrs. Sung's impatience. She was looking at him as if he were a homeless man. He had his pride, and he snapped at her, sarcastically, "God bless you, ma'am."

"Have a nice day, sir." And she drifted away.

"Thanks for nothing," he muttered under his breath.

As he shuffled back toward the door, he spied the children's section, and he went over to look at the cheap little knockoff outfits for toddlers. He got a green one for Henry. The same green as his coat. He made sure to buy it from Mrs. Sung, who was clearly unnerved by the purchase. Give her something to think about.

He began his walk home, feeling tired and put upon. He'd walked too far today. And then he became confused. He didn't recognize the streets. Cars rushed by on a one-way thoroughfare; signals flashed green, yellow, red; signs shouted out invitations; the light rail swooshed by. He looked for a street sign: 16th and O. It was a grid – simple: letters and numbers. But he was disoriented. Which way did they go? Was P next or N? 15th or 14th? He was so tired. He couldn't wander around getting his bearings. He needed someone to tell him. God, he didn't even know what street he lived on. I live on some letter, with a cross street of some number. In the twenties I think. What kind of city … ? And his fury rose like vomit. Jesus Christ.

He felt hot, and suddenly profoundly fatigued. His anger morphed quickly into fear as he felt his legs give below him; felt the phantom of his prostate throb. He put his hands out, which slid off the trunk of a parked car, briefly grazed the bumper, and planted themselves on the pavement, though he hadn't the strength to hold his elbows rigid and thus break his fall. He landed hard on his side and lay there. Four blocks east, the train rumbled by, the long wooden red-and-white-striped crossing arm bouncing, its red lights flashing.

* * *

Lisa got the call from the nurse at the hospital.

"We have a Mr. Warren McCrorey here. Are you his daughter?"

"Uh, yes," she lied, anxious to find out what the call was about. "Is he okay? What's wrong? Is anyone there with him?"

"No, Miss McCrorey – is that your name?"

"It doesn't matter. Lisa will do."

"No one was with him when he was picked up lying in the street. He's a sick man, Miss McCrorey. He needs to be looked after," the nurse related in a slightly accusatory schoolmarmish tone.

"Of course. Is he okay?"

"Ma'am, he's a sick man with terminal cancer; he shouldn't be walking around at all. He appears to have had a stroke."

"I'll be right there."

She hung up and dialed Ben at the Zebra Lounge where he was bartending. "Hi, Ben? Ben, your dad's in the hospital ... I don't know. He was lying in the street. They said he's had a stroke. I'll meet you there. UC Davis Med Center." And she turned to Henry, who was sitting in his fullbody pajamas, playing mindlessly with several plastic yogurt tops. "Let's go, man-child." And she picked him up, grabbed her keys, and hopped in the old pickup to make her way across town.

"Call Scott! Call Scott!" Warren shouted at the nurse, who was attempting to calm him.

"Dad, Dad, it's okay. It's me, Ben." He'd run down the hall, leaving Lisa to walk alone with Henry in her arms.

"Dammit, Ben! What the hell is going on here?"

"You're okay, Poppa; you're okay."

Warren looked at him sternly then. Poppa? He hadn't heard that since Ben was five. "Goddamn it, Ben! That goddamn coat." But Ben was on one knee now, holding his father's hand firmly, and it calmed him. "Where's Scott?" he said, his breath slowing, but his brow still furrowed with anger.

Ben didn't answer him. He was glad Scott wasn't here and was anticipating the battle that would ensue when he arrived. He momentarily wished he and Scott were friends. How much easier it would be. As it was, he'd be the fuck-up again, having left his father to wander the streets.

The call was horrible, but Ben knew he had to contact his brother, if not out of familial responsibility, then because his father was asking him to.

"How could you? Jesus, Ben. Just walking around by himself every day? I knew this would happen. He would have been cared for if he'd been put in a home somewhere."

"Don't fucking start, Scott. Our father is ill and he's asking for you. That's all this call is about –" Ben related evenly, attempting to stay calm.

But Scott interrupted him: "Of course he's asking for me! You're killing him! And I'm coming up there, and I'm taking him back down here and getting him set up on the peninsula. For chrissakes, Ben, I could have done all this weeks ago – but, no, I gave you a chance. My mistake."

Ben held the phone two feet away from him and looked at it. He didn't hang it up, nor did he put it back to his ear. He simply left it on top of the payphone and walked away to find Lisa, who was sitting with Henry in the cafeteria, bucking him around on her knee, which he was clearly enjoying, flashing his characteristic grin.

She looked at Ben, her brows slightly raised. She didn't have to ask. He sat on the table next to where she sat in a chair and held her hand.

"Tomorrow's gonna be hard, Lisa." She squeezed his hand.

"You did nothing wrong, Ben. Scott's gonna do his usual pretend-he's-in-control thing. He's a joke. Really. In this kind of situation, guys like him are a disaster, and they don't even know it. Let's hope he gets a flat."

"What am I gonna do?"

"It's up to Warren really, isn't it?"

"No, Lisa. Scott has power of attorney."

"It's up to Warren," she emphasized again.

"How so?" And he looked at her, curious as to what she was getting at.

"Well, you're fucked in a way. *You were* in charge of his day-to-day care. Even though it's not your fault. I mean, even if he tells Scott it's not your fault, Scott will just dismiss it as the ravings of a broken-down, sick man. But it won't be, Ben. Not to you. Will it?"

Ben took a deep breath.

"Will it, Ben?"

"Lisa ... what are you trying to say?"

"This is your father's death, Ben. His. Not Scott's; not yours."

"What the fuck, Lisa."

"Just go sit with him, Ben. That's all you have to do. It's all you can do." And she sighed, adding, "The rest is just bullshit." She squeezed his hand again. And Ben got up and went back to his father's room.

There was a flurry of activity there, nurses moving about, checking his glucose and vital signs.

"Anything the matter?"

One of the nurses answered that his father's breathing and heart rate seemed to be erratic. "He's a sick man." And she shook her head. "He's got a lot going on here with the cancer and everything." Ben just looked at the ground.

"You're his son, yes?"

"Yeah."

She looked at him intently. "Let me ask you something. Is he a fighter? Do you think he wants to keep fighting?"

"Well, sure, he's a fighter like anybody, but ..."

"But what?"

"Well, to answer your question, I don't think he wants

to live a lot longer. He's been morose for months. When my mom died ..."

She just nodded her head, put her finger up, signaling she'd be right back, and rushed out, calling behind her, "Stay with him."

Ben felt suddenly concerned and surprised. Was his father dying? Right now? He stepped closer. Warren's eyes were heavy, momentarily opening, then closing again.

Warren looked at his son and he was glad to see him. He knew of a sudden he wasn't going to be able to hang on for Scott. No one had needed to tell him Scott wouldn't be up until the next morning, but he heard Ben say it anyway. There he was sitting in the chair next to him, leaning into his face, telling him Scott would be there in the morning. He tried to focus his eyes on Ben, realizing he was probably the last person he loved whom he would actually see.

Ben took his hand, and Warren squeezed with all his might, but he couldn't tell if anything came of it. He tried to turn his neck to look at Ben as his eyes filled. No longer able to speak or reach out, or even gesture, he cried.

He owed his son an apology. He had made something of himself. A good son, at his dad's side when it counted; at his dad's side when whatever his father was lay in a heap, broken, unmade by death.

Ben leaned in closer. He must have seen Warren's eyes filling. "Poppa, Poppa," he muttered softly, and his eyes filled up too, uttering that name he hadn't used for Warren since he was four or five, before the battles began. Full circle.

Warren tried to say "Ben," but nothing came.

Dreams. Another's well-being. Ben had kept faith. Who was he? He'd never asked himself that question. Why now – upon his death? Was that who Ben was? His death? Did he raise his death like a child and fight with him tooth and nail, call him names, hit him even? Was death an enemy you in fact loved? Someone you didn't get along with, who tore you down and made nothing of what you were and believed in. Who gave you *that*. Maybe the Buddhists were right, after all, that we had to learn to be nothing to die with grace. Ben had been telling him that all his life. A little late to make that conclusion. It's never too late is how the song goes. Was that Frank Sinatra or Tony Bennett, or Perry Como ...? I think it was all of them. Death could have been anyone. And if so, wasn't he lucky to have death as a son? Willful and stubborn, Judy's favorite. Was death family then? Judy. For God's sake. He wasn't thinking straight. This was madness.

But it didn't feel like madness.

He opened his eyes and Lisa was there next to Ben with the sweet little man-child, Henry, who gazed at Warren in that way of his – neither sad nor happy, simply watching.

He wondered then where the little outfit was that he'd bought for Henry. The last thing he'd bought in the world, what he'd left behind.

The coat, it's in the pocket of the coat. He tried to look for it, but he couldn't move. They'd find it, yes? He felt the child's hand. They must have put Henry's hand in his. So soft.

He let it take him; guide him. It was Ben's hand.

The Cervantino Baby

"No muchachas en mi casa, Beto," she wagged her finger. "No muchachas en tu cuarto."

"Muchach-*as*?" I enunciated, with emphasis on the "*a.*" "No problema, señora. No muchachas. Lo prometo."

She poked her finger in my sternum then to emphasize the point. "No muchachas, Beto, no."

What was I, a child? No – more like she had that elderly woman wisdom of knowing a cad when she saw one, even if she was wrong about what vowel to tack on the end of *her* word for trouble.

Señora Mendoza was my house mother, as they called them here in Guanajuato – *mi mamá*. I was attending classes at the Instituto Falcón to brush up on my atrophied Spanish before heading deeper into Mexico, and whatever adventures awaited me there. I'd signed on for a week at the school and then planned to take buses down to Querétaro, Mexico City, Puebla, Xalapa – for however long I could stretch out my money. I'd been assigned to the Mendoza family when I checked in at the school, and paid them 100 dollars for an almost completely private room. They lived in a tall house on the slopes behind the Universidad de Guanajuato's towering Spanish Colonial cathedral-like main building, and almost all their rooms were on the upper story, with just a washroom and one bedroom – mine – on the ground floor.

Like the tourist propaganda that had enticed me there – and why the place was so rife with language schools – Guanajuato was *truly* more of an old European hill town than anything in Europe. Settled by the Spanish in 1559 as a silver and gold mining center, it was full of beautiful old structures and charm to burn, with a rich history as one of the central players in the War of Independence – and since not much had happened since, it was beautifully preserved, almost frozen in time. Which meant I had the pleasure of walking out every morning onto the ten-foot-wide cobblestone Calzada de Guadalupe that snaked its way up and down the hill, all the houses rising in their varied colors along both sides, giving me a feeling of delightful dizziness.

I'd stroll down the hill and across the steps of the monolithic university building, its bells pealing the hour; and then down past the large basilica with its soaring belfries; and on to Calle Obregon, which took me into the plaza where businesses were opening up their doors, the gazebo in the middle of the square peacefully silent and solitary, watching it all, not inhabited yet by romantic lovers or the requisite mariachi players.

I'd usually see a cute boy or two, either opening up some store, hosing down the sidewalk, hurrying along somewhere on some errand, or, more likely, rushing to class. They usually smiled wide and made eye contact in the way of Mexican men, which I quickly learned was just how they greeted you and not an invitation to queer sex, as it would be in the States. Because when I looked back over my shoulder, they were never looking back. Still, it warmed my heart and roused my longings.

Pero, no muchachas en la casa Mendoza. I laughed out loud as I walked.

I'd keep that promise, and hold her to the feminine vowel when the shit hit the fan a week later. I'd also leave Isabel to clean up the mess. That wasn't fair, but *it was* partly her fault in a way. It was she who invited Isaias inside, after all, setting a dangerous precedent. To her credit, she did defend me when everything went south, but Mamá was in denial about a lot of things and would have none of it. And there's no more unreasonable woman than a moralistic Catholic who believes her daughter is a virgin when she's not.

Isabel had a story of her own besides, which she related to me one afternoon when I'd run into her in the plaza. I'd liked her immediately upon meeting her my second day in the Mendoza house and was thrilled to bump into her in town. She had a wide, infectious smile and sincere, kindly eyes. She was a schoolteacher and an athlete, a tad too feminist for her mother's tastes, but she played the devoted daughter to a tee. Señora Mendoza, mi mamá, was someone who was willing to be bullshitted, and my mistake was that I'd end up telling her the truth. But that was later.

First there was Isabel and her sad tale. She'd been "ruined," she said over lunch at the Restaurant Valadez, a popular sidewalk café on the plaza, by a Swede who'd studied at Instituto Falcón. *Ruined.* She was only twenty-one. I wanted to say, *You'll get over it. We're all ruined at twenty-one if we fall in love and get dumped.* But you can't say that to a twenty-one-year-old, so I just listened. Isabel was intelligent, but, goodness, she was dramatic too.

"I opened myself to him, like Jesus on the cross." And she threw her arms out. "When he turned his back on me, I couldn't protect myself." Her arms were still out, beginning to shake now from the effort. I understood – or thought I did. He'd crucified her and she couldn't pull free of the nails.

One tear rolled nobly down her cheek, which she didn't bother to brush away as she turned back to her salad. *What could I say?*

"I'm sorry, Isabel." And I held out my open hand on the table. She didn't take it; she just smiled and sighed.

"Do you have a girlfriend?" she feebly asked.

"No, no, I don't." As I'd just moved into her very Catholic

home and was in a foreign land, I didn't feel like telling her why just yet. She'd find out in time. *Oh, would she.* But I did feel a little bad in that she had just revealed a secret of sorts, and I'd held my cards firmly to my chest. But as I'd find out later, there was more to her story too.

She had friends at the institute, which is how she'd gotten her mother the gig renting rooms to students. It was good extra income for minimal effort. Mamá fed me breakfast and dinner, and while I ate, she talked at length about the corruption of Mexican politics, the madness of the world, and her sister who'd moved to Chicago and become a Protestant. I couldn't follow all of it with my rudimentary grasp of Spanish, but I got the gist. "Eres Catolico, Beto?"

"Si, Mamá."

She smiled, until I told her that now I was a Buddhist. She scolded me, told me it was wrong to dispense with the faith of my birth; that I could not do this in fact; that I was fooling myself and committing a grave sin; that I should go to Mass with her.

"I'm late for my evening class" was all I could muster as she sat back, eyeing me suspiciously and reiterating, as was her wont, finger wagging with admonition, "No muchachas en mi casa, Beto. No muchachas."

I smiled big. "Absolutamente no!"

I began to wonder just why it kept coming back around to that subject. *Were the girls of Guanajuato so loose?* Not from what I'd seen. It was Mexico after all, and the church kept most girls in major check, just like I'd seen in Catholic Italy or Eastern Orthodox Greece. But Guanajuato was an educated town – richer and more liberalized than much of Mexico – and that posed a threat to traditional folks like *mi mamá*. And then there was the Cervantino, which I wasn't even aware was beginning at the end of that week. And what came with the Cervantino were the dreaded Cervantino babies.

The Cervantino was a celebration of Cervantes and his work – primarily *Don Quixote* of course. The town swelled with students from all over Mexico as the theaters staged myriad plays – some so obliquely interpretive as to seem completely unrelated – recounting the misadventures of that man from La Mancha, his sidekick Sancho Panza, and the requisite slews of chivalric and caddish knights, comely barmaids, and damsels in high windows. Restaurants shifted their menus to Medieval Spanish fare and tapas, the trousers of the wait staff ballooning with gaudy stripes and knee-high stockings. There were parades, complete with huge puppetted performers on stilts mimicking windmills, the old Don, the sun and the moon; galloping horses; flamenco dancing; music in the plaza – mandolin solos interjected among the mariachi madness – and boys dressed as harlequins in too-long sleeves and big elfin shoes adorned with bells, flopping about like jesters.

I took a fancy to one of them, in fact. But that all came later. It was Wednesday, day three of my visit, with the Cervantino still a few days away and Isabel now giving me tragic looks, as if to remind me of her divulged secret, while Mamá had taken to eyeing me suspiciously one moment and then lovingly and ingratiatingly the next. She constantly offered food, comfort, and refreshment, entertaining me with family photos and tales of her girlhood in Jalisco, but she always ended every story with something admonitory about Mass and muchachas. I didn't always follow her as, like I say, my Spanish was spotty.

I didn't meet my padre until the third night. He'd been out of town on business – something to do with shoes ironically, as he rarely wore his, being mildly crippled and looking like he was experiencing a lot of back pain, the source of which I was unable to figure out or broach, mostly due to his kindness, his dignity in how he handled his condition, and the sighs of his wife and daughter. He was their Tiny Tim, only not so tiny, certainly not a child, sand obviously not named Tim. He was, as he proudly and boastfully stated, "Ernesto Quintero de Leon Mendoza y Vasquez."

I shook his hand heartily, introducing myself as "Beto Mendoza," and thanking him for adopting me, even if for but a week, as a member of his family. He beamed while Mamá nearly choked with emotion, patting my back as I stood before her husband. She guided me back to my chair, imploring, "Mas café, Beto?"

"No, gracias."

"No, no, Mamá, vamos a ir a una fiesta," Isabel chimed in half whining.

Mamá was crestfallen, no doubt imagining an evening of family bliss, not the usual middle-aged night alone with Ernesto and the TV. Isabel was all they had left, their four sons grown and moved off to cities with more opportunities: León, Morelia, Monterrey, Mexico. And now, even their newly minted son, in his maiden act, was heading out – and taking their last remaining child with him.

Mamá wanted to know whose party it was, and when Isabel related that it was Isaias's and Ezequiel's, she momentarily beamed before the disappointed frown returned to her face. Isabel rolled her eyes and guided me to the door, explaining to me as we walked the lamp-lit stone streets of lovely Guanajuato that Isaias and Ezequiel were twin brothers who had gone through school with her and had always been favorites of her mother's. Accomplished and dutiful, Isaias was a graduate student in the Archaeology Department where Isabel worked in administration, and Ezequiel was a fairly well-known and successful folklorico dancer. The party, she told me, was a reunion of sorts, inspired by Ezequiel's return home from touring through Central and South America with the Guadalajara Folklorico group he was a part of, and all their old friends would be there. I looked at Isabel quickly then, suspicious that she was taking me to meet some of her closest and oldest friends, worrying that she was setting herself up for yet another Swedish fall.

I stopped her on the street then, gently grabbing her elbow, and as graciously as I could, broached the subject. "Isabel, can I trust you with a secret?"

Her eyes lit up.

"Well, I hope you will keep this between us and not make it known to your mother. I'm gay … uh, … as in I like men. Me gustan los hombres?"

She reached out and hugged me immediately, expressing her happiness at the fact, and that it meant we could now *really truly* be friends. I was surprised, considering my earlier suspicions, reminding myself once again that coming out to most people was a cause for celebration and not as loaded down with the dreaded rejection and abandonment I so often feared.

Apparently, I'd made Isabel's day. She skipped along now, grabbing my hand, finally free to love me. She kept looking at me, then bursting out laughing, perhaps because she was already formulating a plan for that evening, the players of which I had not yet met, nor had I any clue about how charming they'd be.

We climbed the stairs and heard the music before we reached the door of the little house of the Moreño family and the beginning of what can only, for me, be called a rendezvous with a Grecian sort of fate.

There'd been no omens, of course, nor prophetic oracles back in the States predicting chaos in Mexico, but I recognized Ezequiel immediately, almost as if I knew him. He looked the spitting image of a young Che Guevara. And when his friends insisted he perform the Vera Cruz dance for us all – that's the one sans shirt (which he quickly dispensed with) – I blushed in awe, not just at the spectacle of his naked torso, but at his amazing acrobatic talent and finesse. Beside myself as he put the finishing touches on his performance – all eyes upon him – my eyes scanned the room desperately for Isabel, who, when I found her, was laughing hysterically – I think at my expense – and sitting next to Che's – I mean Ezequiel's – identical twin brother, Isaias, who was smiling at me seductively. I smiled back, stupefied at my good fortune, and then Isabel motioned me over. My mind was racing as fast as my heart, and – full of that sexual greed typical of men such as myself – I was already wondering whether both boys were queer before I'd even met Isaias, who'd just indicated in no uncertain terms that he was. *Wasn't there a lot of evidence that twins tended to have the same sexual orientation?* I thought to myself as I parted the bodies and made my way to Isabel.

Isaias put his hand out to shake mine in an epic gesture of physical contact that clearly communicated it was the beginning of something profoundly animal to come.

"Hola," he smiled brightly, as electricity pulsed through the palms of our hands. *The Guevara twins. Good God.*

"Hola," I stuttered back, my hand grown clammy with nerves. What I wanted to say was *Let's go!* – not knowing *where to* of course. Instead, I behaved myself and practiced my Spanish flirtatiously as Isabel midwifed our romance into full bloom, sharing with Isaias the few stories I'd shared with her, and prodding me to ask Isaias about his most recent trips to Mexico City, or about his illustrious sojourn last summer in Puerto Vallarta. He shyly looked down at his lap, and then – when Isabel ran off to the bathroom – demurely claimed that he was bisexual, and that Isabel's fantasies about his adventures were just that: the product of her own imagination and wishful thinking. I shrugged nonchalantly, letting him know that, whatever the case was, I was enjoying myself and had made no judgment about him based on Isabel's exuberant hearsay. But I sensed immediately his fear and trepidation.

Cervezas were proffered and dancing ensued, with Ezequiel – clearly the star – now and again taking over the dance floor à la *Saturday Night Fever* and treating us all to a stunning display of his acrobatic prowess. My God, I was crushed out on him and – being that he was in some odd public sense exhibiting his body and what it could do in grand fashion – consumed with lust, almost to the exclusion of the man sitting right next to me who looked almost exactly like him. But, of course – and unlike Isaias – Ezequiel seemed completely unavailable – he'd only briefly said hello to me when I'd first come in, and not in the fashion of his brother, either. Ezequiel wore the knit brow of the straightboy, and practiced the laconic clipped Spanish and the macho aloofness characteristic of the heterosexual male.

The hours passed, during which I spoke with an architect, an anthropologist, and a medical student – Guanajuato was clearly one of Mexico's old world upper-class havens – and saw not just one, but all my teachers, among whom was José, a gruff, bearded, Marxist-looking character who was a bit of a taskmaster about the finer points of the Spanish accent – rolled r's and tildas, as well as the "flow," as he called it, which meant his futile attempts to get American students not to overemphasize consonants and syllables, which, while common to English, made one's Spanish clunky and mechanical. He sat in a corner brooding, clinging to his gorgeous Spanish girlfriend, watching the revelers with arrogant disdain. Maria and Magda were more fun, dancing up a storm, chatting with all the students who were there, including myself and four or five others, making an obvious effort to impress the gringos Mexican style. And I *was* impressed.

When the party was down to five – Ezequiel and Isaias, an expatriate named Jill (clearly enthralled with Ezequiel – *how original*. Who wasn't?), Isabel, and myself – we decided to head down to El Beso for a nightcap. As we boisterously made our way down the hill, Ezequiel all the while jumping and slapping at store signs and light posts, his energy seemingly boundless, Isaias grabbed my elbow lightly and we slowed down, creating a distance of six or seven feet between us and the others.

"You can't be gay here," he said in heavily accented English. "Is dangerous. No touch me en la calle. Soy bisexual."

I almost laughed at that last line, but I also knew to heed and respect his warning. I'd been a dumb American in my enthusiasm for him and his brother – even perhaps in my confession to Isabel – and it was instructive to be reminded that we were in a small, conservative town in Mexico, and just as you could get mugged for looking like an American, you could also get beaten or killed for acting queer. I looked at Isaias and nodded with understanding, seeing in his eyes the danger I could be putting him in. He had to live here after all.

We ended up at El Beso near the plaza soon enough,

and it was full of middle-aged Mexicans. "Chilangos," Isabel whispered under her breath, voicing the derogatory name for Mexico City bourgeoisie who acted – when outside their cosmopolitan city – with all the grace of Germans in Greece. Drinks arrived, and I quietly watched Jill make a fool of herself with Ezequiel, who barely responded, sipping his beer and staring into the middle distance, while Isabel and Isaias chattered about university politics.

"What are you doing here in Guanajuato, Jill?" I finally ventured.

"I'm a writer. I'm writing a novel. I live in San Miguel actually. Lots of ex-pats there." She said it like it was a good thing, and I suppose it was if you were actually living in Mexico and not just passing through. For my part, if I didn't see an American for my three weeks in Mexico, I'd be delighted. I had the mirror, and that was enough.

"So I've heard," I answered, not adding that that was why I hadn't gone there.

Ezequiel stood up, and alpha male that he was, the rest of us did so as well. We jauntily spilled down the stairs and onto the street under El Beso's delightfully Spanish sign – funky, gloopy, Miró-like – another indicator of Guanajuato's identification with the continent. Ezequiel did a sort of bow to us all, leaving Jill hanging, and headed home back up the way we had come. Isabel and I were going in the opposite direction, so Isaias offered to walk us home. As Jill's hotel was on the way, and since she looked somewhat disoriented from Ezequiel's brush-off, she came with us for two blocks until we bid her goodnight at the Posada Palenque and climbed up the twisty-hilled streets past the university, bathed in its eerie green light, to 125 Calzada de Guadalupe.

Isabel gave Isaias a big kiss on the cheek and turned to put the key in the door, allowing Isaias to look over at me and communicate with his eyes that he wanted to *do it* now.

"Adios, Isaias," Isabel smiled, leading me in the door. But Isaias put his foot on the doorjamb when Isabel turned to close it and smiled mischievously at her. She opened the door wider, looked up the stairs, listened for a second, and then put her finger to her mouth and pulled Isaias in, pushing him behind me into my bedroom. Then up the stairs she clumped.

Un muchach-*o* en mi cuarto.

Things happened quickly. We laughed; we shushed each other as we stripped and wrestled together; we experienced the awe of our attraction for each other – the joy of how we made each other feel; the humor of how the bed creaked. Then came the quickening, and Isaias bucking and growling under his breath, "Que Rico," as we lost ourselves to each other.

Without missing a beat, he rushed to gather himself up, gave me a quick kiss and his phone number, and tiptoed out.

I awoke to the calls of mi mamá: "Desayuno, Beto! Café!"

This place was too good. My own private room, a mother who wakes me up and feeds me delicious food and great coffee, a stroll through one of the most charming towns in the world to an hour or two of school – and then, to top it off, I get to end the day with a beautiful naked man on top of me who knows what he's doing and can barely keep his passion in check.

"Buenas dias, Mamá," I greeted her with a kiss on the cheek. The exuberance of the laid.

She smiled in motherly bliss.

"Tienes cruda, Beto?" she teased.

"No cruda, Mamá. I'm a good boy."

"Un Catolico," she said with satisfaction.

"Hoy, soy un Catolico," I relented.

" ... y no muchachas en mi casa."

"No muchachas!" And I laughed heartily.

Isaias dropped in that night around dinnertime and Mamá asked him to stay for supper, which he did. Mamá praised him to me, which I began to think was his point in dropping by. Isabel acted coy, saying little, and then rushing off to some engagement halfway through dinner, while Papá just sat and listened with that beatific smile he always wore on his face, interrupted now and again by a little chuckle at the absurdity of his wife's flattery. I just nodded a lot and interjected innocently and frequently with "Como se dice?"s; "Mas despacio"s; and "Repite por favor"s .

"Both of you are like sons to me," she beamed in conclusion as she cleared our plates, and Isaias related that we were off to climb up to La Pípila, a hilltop statue commemorating the torch-bearing Indian miner who had set fire to the Spanish fortress and launched the War of Independence.

We both gave Mamá a hug. We'd made her happy – at least on the upper floor. Because before we left, Isaias hustled me into my room for a quick jackoff – even as Mamá was shouting down to us about whether we wanted *cocas* or *pan* for the long hike.

"No, gracias, Señora Mendoza," Isaias called back up to her while he furiously worked the passion from his loins.

Isaias smiled and kissed me deeply when we'd completed our little task, seeming less and less bisexual all the time.

I was a bit smitten actually, as he was a delightful fellow, handsome, sweet, full of a friendly kind of mischief – chasing little kids, scaring off pigeons, and handing me found objects: little flowers, centavos, discarded food wrappers that he'd make me read aloud to test my Spanish. But I couldn't quite shake that image of Ezequiel dancing like a Ukrainian. Truth was, I wanted them both.

We hiked up the series of steps to La Pípila in less than an hour, rewarded at the top by a grand view of the whole town – its churches and university, the little plaza and labyrinthine streets and tunnels, the colorful little boxy houses in purple and blue and orange, and the mountains all around and beyond – as the sky went yellow and pink and purple with the sunset.

Isaias dragged me into the bushes for another go, and then we went back down into town, where he showed me the fort where La Pípila had thrown the fiery torch and been killed, as well as the little iron cages hanging atop the walls where the four heads of the rebellion's ringleaders had been put out for display on spikes after they'd been beheaded when the insurrection failed. We ended with coffee and pan dulce down by the plaza, Isaias staring longingly into my eyes.

He had to work the next day, so I sought out one of the cliché tourist destinations from my *Lonely Planet* guide: El Museo de las Mómias. And that's where the trouble really began. The trouble being Ezequiel, because he was there, sort of walking aimlessly about, as if he were waiting for something. I was surprised frankly. He'd grown up in Guanajuato, and you didn't have to be a native to know that the mummies were the kind of thing you wouldn't frequent if you actually lived there. Basically, it was just glass case after glass case of the mummified remains of Guanajuato's residents of past centuries, who had unwittingly ended up mummified by accident due to the dry air and minerals in the soil where they'd been buried. There was a pregnant mummy, a baby mummy, a fat mummy, etc.

"I just like it here" was all he said, in his deep voice, by way of explanation.

He gave me the grand tour and seemed to know quite a bit about each of the dead displayed in the glass cases. "That's Alfonso – he was married to Elena over there." And he pointed with a jerk of his head.

Afterward we took a crowded bus back up to town together, and upon arriving at the big open-air Mercado Hidalgo, he suggested we have a beer at one of the cafés in the adjoining plaza. We had a few and chatted about folklorico and different kinds of music. As it turned out, he was a huge fan of Nirvana and grunge in general, and I had many such CDs in my room as I'd brought them along with my portable CD player.

As for what happened next, maybe it wasn't so much Isabel's fault as it was Kurt Cobain's. There'd been no indication that Ezequiel wanted anything but a copy of *In Utero*, but I'd be disingenuous to say it didn't cross my libidinous mind as we headed back to Calzada de Guadalupe to peruse my CDs – though when I'd engaged the fantasy, I'd laughed to myself at the prospect.

But it happened all the same, and as it unfolded, I knew I was not only stepping in a huge pile of karmic shit, but it dawned on me as well that Ezequiel was quite likely using the museum as his cruising ground for gringos – for guys who could never expose him. I was also thinking about how much I really liked Isaias, and how I would not want to do anything to jeopardize our little romance or hurt him. But Ezequiel's body was the kind that made you say, "Well, just this once," or "Who the fuck cares?" But my God, he was *his* twin brother – and he and Isaias really did look a lot alike, right down to the nitty-gritty details, if you get my drift, though Ezequiel was definitely more aggressive, selfish – even cruel. Things happened *with* Isaias; Ezequiel happened *to you.*

Mamá came home just as we were polishing each other off. I heard the door open, shushed Ezequiel, whose tough-guy face suddenly filled with the fear of God, and the two of us waited, suspended – in an odd position too – to hear her clump up the stairs. She didn't, and I knew then that my worst fears were just then manifesting. We heard her bags rustle, but no other sound. She was listening at the door.

"Beto?"

I said nothing. Ezequiel, panicked, looked at the window.

"Estas solo?"

"Si ... uh, no, ... mi amigo esta aqui." Ezequiel shook his head furiously. Mistake.

Why hadn't I just said I was with a friend in the beginning? Why the initial "yes" to her query of whether I was alone? Why the quick reversal to "no"?

She began screaming then, a lot of which I couldn't follow, but "Dios" was involved, as were "muchachas," "hombres," "mentirosas," and "promesas." Ezequiel took his cue and was out the window by the time she'd located the key to find me making the bed, the window wide open and wind blowing through the little frilly lace curtains. She turned on her heels, her face full of a quiet fury, and went back out the door and into the street, but Ezequiel was long gone.

When she returned, she barked, "Donde esta Isabel?!"

And it was in the voice of a person who would kill to find out.

"No sé," I shook my head, hoping she believed me. It didn't occur to me until right then that this room may have been occupied by one notorious Swede, if not a whole slew of horny gringos that Isabel had fancied. I hoped to God then that Mamá *didn't think* ... I mean I was a cad, but I would never be that caddish. Yet, hadn't I been? How was it different really? Whether with Mamá's daughter, Isabel, or Isaias's twin brother, Ezequiel, I'd transgressed in a family way.

My stomach sank, and I thought the best thing for me to do right then would be to pack up and get out of town. But then I thought of Isabel, and I wanted to clarify things for her sake, as well as to reassure Mamá that nothing horrid had happened. And I wanted to at least say goodbye and thanks for the memories to Isaias. These people had been good to me.

"There were no muchachas en mi cuarto, Mamá. Un muchacho, Señora, un muchach-*o*!"

Her face went white. "Dios mio!" And she shouted for me to get out.

From bad to worse. I packed up while she stood there. "Gracias, Mamá, gracias," I meekly offered, maneuvering by her with my bag.

"No soy tu mamá, Beto." And she crossed herself.

As I struggled out the door, Isabel appeared. Was that good or bad? Thank God she didn't look disheveled.

What's happening? her face seemed to say.

"Hola, Isabel."

By then Mamá was screaming to Isabel in very rapid Spanish behind me, and I simply walked away, down into town, where there were no rooms available because the Cervantino had begun.

Hordes of Mexican college kids were pouring into town, hiking up from the bus station, squeezed into the ubiquitous green VW cabs, or packed six deep in little Fiats. Others were busy preparing for the festivities, running up banners, painting each other's faces. At a loss as to what to do, or where to go, I just sat down on the basilica steps and watched, hoping something would come to me.

It didn't take long for Isabel to appear. Tears streaming down her face.

Ruined again.

I shook my head.

"Where's Isaias?" she gently asked.

Of course she thought I was with Isaias. "Did you tell your mom it was Isaias?" I replied, feeling like a horrid criminal covering his tracks.

"Of course not, but I told her you were gay and that she shouldn't have kicked you out for that. She's got to get with the modern world." And she shook her head righteously, but softened before saying, "Oh, but it's my fault for letting Isaias in the other night. I'm so sorry."

"Did you tell her that?" I thought of Watergate.

"Of course not; I don't want her to know it was Isaias."

I thought how crazy this was all getting. Isabel didn't want her mom to think it was Isaias; I didn't want Isabel to think it wasn't; and Isaias was out there somewhere, with just time separating him from the awful truth. And there I was, left to protect Ezequiel, who would get away with it all.

Just then two huge puppets of Don Quixote and Sancho Panza appeared. The parade had begun.

Isabel began weeping in earnest. I comforted her the best I could, but she was coming apart. "What a world," she moaned. "People are so cruel – and intolerant." Her ire rose now. "Do you know about the Cervantino babies?"

I looked at her and shook my head, indicating I had no clue.

She explained how the college kids came to Guanajuato from far and wide; how they drank and sang and paraded about; performed in plays and skits; danced to music; played guitars; filled the posadas to bursting – and fucked like rabbits. Nine months later, the students all long gone, the town watched an alarming epidemic of young girls waddle about, all hugely pregnant and due pretty much all on the same day.

"Cervantino babies," she reiterated. "A lady from Texas came down here and opened an abortion clinic. They drove her out of town. She came back the next year. They drove her out of town again."

Mexico.

I just listened, too worried about what was coming down with Isaias to get into a political discussion about abortion in a Catholic country.

But she had that ruined look on her face again.

"What is it, Isabel?"

"I had a Cervantino baby once." And she sniffled her tears.

I put my arm around her shoulder.

"Lars took me to the Texan lady. He paid for it, and he left right afterward."

More to the story.

"Isabel," I whispered, and held her close as she wept on my shoulder.

I half expected to see Isaias right then, but, fortunately, it was just a gaggle of harlequins.

"Isabel, I wasn't with Isaias," I confessed suddenly.

She looked at me, perplexed.

I shook my head.

"Who then?"

"Just don't tell him about any of this. Please."

She stopped crying then. "You met someone else?"

I looked at her, waiting for her to turn on me.

"I really need to just go. Will you walk me to the bus station?"

"But what about Isaias?" And then she did get mad. "You can't just leave!"

"I was gonna leave anyway eventually."

She looked at me then with fury. Her mother's daughter.

"Isabel," I pleaded.

She took my hand, and she walked me back to the university, and right into Isaias's office, where a dozen or so graduate students scurried about or slumped over papers in need of grading. Isaias played it straight to protect himself, but he understood what Isabel was saying: a misunderstanding about an American girl who was studying with Beto in his room, and how her mother had freaked out, thinking something was going on.

I looked at the ground. No one owed me this.

Isabel turned to me. "You can stay at the Moreños. Pay them the same thing you paid my mother."

Isaias smiled.

So I spent the next week in a bedroom in the Moreños' house, sleeping on a pad on the floor next to a bunkbed where slept Isaias and his twin brother, Ezequiel, who pretended nothing had ever happened, though he surreptitiously handed me the two borrowed Nirvana CDs when Isaias was in the shower, warning me, "Don't ever tell him."

Isaias came with me to Mexico City for a few days and we had a good time tromping through Chapultepec and hanging out in cafés in Colonia Roma and Coyoácan. We both decided we'd like to live in Frida Kahlo's house and particularly liked a painting there by Diego Rivera of a man on the seashore, under a huge bluff that made him look totally insignificant. Painted right after Frida had died, it was called, *Fridita, Mi Maravillosa.* We toasted each other that way from then on – a year later in Zihuatanejo; two years after that in Chetumal; and once a whole five years after in Mérida, when we'd long stopped seeing each other romantically (by then, Isaias had a lover and lived in the Yucatán's capital city, where he was a professor of archaeology at the university). Isaias had just told me about how Ezequiel had ruined his marriage when his wife caught him with a man, and that he was now drinking like a fish.

"Is he still dancing?"

"No, he gave it up."

I thought then of that first night's brilliant performance of the Vera Cruz folklorico; the shriveled faces at the Museo de las Mómias; I thought of the sad end of Kurt Cobain; harlequins; I thought of Isabel. And I thought of telling Isaias everything now that the cat was out of the bag on Ezequiel. I didn't have to protect *him* anymore. But then, I'd never kept the secret to protect him. I'd done it for Isaias, and Isabel, for mi mamá. And I realized right then that Ezequiel was my Cervantino baby.

A tear pooled in my eye just as the waiter came by with two more beers, which we lifted up, and in the only way I knew how to tell him, I looked at Isaias and, raising my voice, shouted, "Por Ezequiel, el Maravilloso!"

Skin and Bone

Eugene is a half-Lakota, skinny, punk-hippie of a fag with big green eyes, a bird's beak of a Plains Indian nose, crow-shining black hair, and a voice that's lower than deep water. And he's all about water. He's so skinny his face breaks up when he smiles, and if he were a dam, it would crack and fall and drown you and everyone else. Once he was actually hospitalized for his skinniness – a collapsed lung that the doctor said he got on account of being just too damn thin. His parents are dead and he looks lost, and like if he wasn't lost everybody would want to know what he thinks. But he is, so only I care. And he's only a messenger. And you're not supposed to kill the messenger.

I dreamed of him a thousand nights all the same, so much so that I don't know anymore what happened and what got dreamed. His visage takes me there to the dream place, where there is no time, no past and present, and all that confusing, painful, so-called order that files all the unfileable bliss and longing of our hearts into places it's too wild and child-gleeful racing and jumping to ever survive intact, or with any capacity to tell once again the truth of what was.

Dreaming Eugene in the Rapid City Trailways Bus Station where there are candy and cigarette machines, and closed-down, darkened ticket windows, a bored teenager at the snack bar tending the loud coffee percolator. Eugene's sitting alone in a red plastic booth in one corner, his knees up to his chin. Eugene was, is, will always be beautiful and kind-looking. I always want to hear his voice, the deep water of it, and he's all about water. Flowing, falling through my hands. Eugene was never mine; a fish I couldn't catch that kept chasing after my hook. It was as if Eugene owed me a dream and I owed him watching. We were mixed up.

I don't even know Eugene; never did. Eugene was necessary all the same in the way the sun is, and rain, and all things that touch us and remind us that we are here and it's rather intense, isn't it? I don't know why Eugene was all that to me because we were barely together and didn't belong together, but he was someone I knew from a long time ago – before my life, before his beauty. That's what I'd say in the dreams. *Where have you been? I've missed you so.* And he'd just smile like he remembered too but wasn't as excited about it as I was – like he was forever or something, and it was no big deal, this recognition.

"Oh, you again – how ya been?"

All I want to say is, *Not good, I've missed you, and would you mind if we fucked each other forever and ever?* His coy smile always follows. He's thinking about it. He'd do anything if you fed him love. And I fed him love, and so he did everything. But he'd go away. And I never knew if it was me, or his belly full, or something in him. And he didn't say. He never said.

He only spoke to me in my dreams. "Where ya goin' to?" he asks me in the Rapid City Bus Station. I want to say, *With you,* but I say, "Nowhere," instead, wanting to make him invite me. In my dreams, he always does. He stands up and looks at me long, and then he gathers up his backpack and walks outside, and he doesn't have to say it – I know he means *Follow me.* And so I do.

I always feel presumptuous in his presence even when he coaxes me like this. In all of him and everything we shared, there was something that was never wholly personal. Not like I wasn't always a person to him – he always was respectful that way, and kind. I just felt like I could have been anyone. Like he was a saint or something, minus religion and the good works. Whatever, it seemed as if it were somehow impossible to be personally, romantically loved by Eugene. I feel his heartbeat and that smile that threatens to shatter his face it's so awkward and eager – like he doesn't have the smile, the smile has him. He works for the smile. I don't know who he is and what it was and is between us.

I stand there now, next to him, touching his shoulder, exactly his height, both of us grinning across the few inches between our eyes.

An old Indian man arrives just then, in a dilapidated orange Dodge pickup. Eugene smiles and throws his hand in the air to wave, and when the old man pulls the wreck over, Eugene, the sun on his crow-black hair, hoists his gear up and into the back of the truck. And I do the same. The old man smiles, and that's pretty much all he does; never greets Eugene or anything; never gets out of the truck. Eugene opens the door with a loud creak and looks at me. Green eyes of gravity. I let his eyes tell me what to do and follow him into the passenger side of the truck.

We jerk forward out of the lot and onto the avenue that runs toward the freeway, past spindly-legged billboards and ugly plastic-looking, colorful architectural toys serving fast food. Rapid City is ugly and looks unloved. There are Indian winos everywhere and severe-looking white men in pickups, and very few trees. "It's a bad town," the old man says, grinning ear to ear.

Eugene doesn't even introduce me to the man, who I somehow know is his grandfather. Instead, he just smiles at me and at the old man both, every once in awhile saying, "Pappasan, Pappasan," like he simply likes the word or something. He only speaks in my dreams, and it breaks my heart, and I want to hold him like my child and feel proud that he's spoken. I want to make love to him and listen to him talk.

There is something between Eugene and the old man

that only makes that one word necessary. It is the communion of an old man and a young boy. I remember it with my own grandfather out in his garden. No conversation, just me walking around calling out his name and pointing at things. But Eugene doesn't even point. They both already know what's there.

The old man leaves the freeway, following a highway a short distance, and then recklessly banking onto a dirt road, laughing as he does so, all three of us falling into one another. Then we hit a big bump on the pot-holed, beat-up road, and the old man says out loud, without looking at me, "You've traveled all over this country and do you know what's underneath it?"

I just look at him, not quite understanding the question, as I flip through the rolodex of answers in my head. I think, *I don't know: dirt? rock? dead bodies?*

But he's just laughing, not expecting an answer. And then he continues: "I've never left South Dakota," he says. "Not once. The Sioux, they came out of the ground, right over there in the Black Hills. Paha Sapa. Where'd you come from?" And he laughs to himself, almost as if he is trying to stifle the teasing.

I know San Francisco is the wrong answer to his question. Even Ireland would be wrong. It isn't an answerable question, and I sense he doesn't expect a reply, evidenced by his laugh, so I say nothing, as we careen headlong now down the dirt road in the old pickup, past sagebrush and creosote under a vast blue sky. Then we're all three of us swigging from Pappasan's bottle of whiskey that fits perfectly in the coffee cup holder he's got attached to the dashboard.

Suddenly the dirt road ends and we're back on a highway again. Not long afterward, we're pulling off in front of a little shack under a big billboard with the faces of Indians on it. It says something like "DONT DRINK, courtesy State of South Dakota."

Eugene's grandparents live in this dilapidated hovel right off the highway. We all hop out, and Eugene and I lift our bags out of the truck bed. Pappasan marches up the steps and through the door as if he's forgotten all about us, and Eugene sits down on a crooked, creaking step that leads up to the listing porch running along the front of the shack and motions me to sit next to him. We sit smiling at each other for a long time while the old man does something inside I have a feeling is private and religious. Under the shadow of that enormous billboard, in that empty, desert-like, rocky land, it's warm, like 98.6, and I feel a sudden panic because there is no wind and it feels like I can't tell where I end and the place around me begins. It's like I've lost my skin and all the nerves in it that usually tell me in their routine electrical way, *You're you and you're here.*

With my skin gone, my bones start floating away off into the air, disconnecting from one another into a big, thin, white cloud. And I get frightened, trying to reimagine myself and by force of will pull my bones back into my body on the porch. I look at Eugene, hoping he won't notice my panic and that my bones are all over the place. I try to reach out and touch him. I want right then to grab him and hold him tight and get him to hold me, to give me a shape and a place, to make his arms and his eyes and his birdlike nose and strong mouth the boundaries to my world. He only grins with one side of his mouth and turns to look out at the landscape, as if knowing that's where I am now, and why should he give me a shape? He laughs and points out little parts of me – fingers and toes – floating off and away. I think I need to collect them up and put them back inside of me, as if I am a bag or sack where they belong. But I can't find where I am. "I need some skin, Eugene – quick!" I blurt to him. He stands up, rises up like Paul Bunyan, a thirty-foot man. He hugs me and my cloud of bones both, and then I'm back sitting next to him, wondering how he did it.

The sun is going down, and as the dusk sets in, lights come on over the billboard; bright streetlights out here in the middle of nowhere, illuminating the big, Indian face with the alcoholic nose looking down at us, watching the little house through the night. Eugene sees me looking up at the face and pats my thigh sympathetically, as if he senses my fear and means to reassure me that it's only that. Then he gets up and takes my hand and leads me inside. It's getting darker, the long shadows from the billboard reaching out like a giant dark hand to pick up the little shack from its rocky yard. I half fear that that shadowy hand will pick us up and fling us into space and annihilation, but whatever it is in Eugene's calm eyes suggests that the hand holds us, covers us, and protects us.

Inside the house, it's quiet, the air warm and heavy. Pappasan is already snoring in bed, a bottle of whiskey on the nightstand next to him.

Eugene then takes off all his clothes, and I get to see again how beautiful he is. How orange and thin, the bone and the skin of him, the crow-black shining hair on his head, under his arms, and at his waist. And he nods toward me to do the same, all the while holding a finger to his closed lips so I'll be quiet. He is as beautiful and comfortable as always naked, but I am sort of nervous to be naked with him with his grandfather right there, and I suddenly want to go somewhere else; to grab him and run into the desert and make him in the weeds. But this is Eugene's dream, or that part of me that's him, and I have no choice but to defer.

Eugene comes to me and undoes my belt and then he undresses me completely and leads me into the bed with him and Pappasan. I feel nervous, uncomfortable, and excited all at once. Eugene reaches over and puts his arms around me, pulls me to him, and we begin to kiss and push our waists together. I'm tense and flustered with Pappasan there, so I just let Eugene do whatever he wants to do. He grabs my cock and pulls it up and down and I follow his lead. The skin and the bone of it. What's underneath the skin? Dirt? Dead bodies? I climbed out of my mother; that's where I came from. He touches me and outlines my body, inch by inch, and then he pulls it all back out of me until I am nowhere or spreading like the darkness and my blood out across all those Badlands, and his eyes lock on mine, and we both look like that billboard to each other, lit up in the blackness.

We sleep through the night in that bed with his old Pappasan. That isn't his name; I somehow know that. But you can't call him by his real name unless you know him. I sense he has some kind of medicine power, some sorcerer or magic power that commands respect from those who come looking for the man you can't name. They whisper – like a dream within a dream I meet them – "I'm looking for Pappasan." Sometimes they talk about Big Mountain down the road, his sacred place of power. They talk about Rocky Flat and the ridge and the water places out there. "Down the highway, just past that big billboard," they say.

"That sign keeps changing," Pappasan chuckled when he saw me looking at it as we'd pulled up that afternoon. "First it was beer, then cars, cigarettes – now it's alcohol again. But this time they *don't* want you to buy it! Whiteman never was able to make up his mind."

I ask one of the visitors why they call an Indian man Pappasan. "Isn't that an Asian name?"

The man I ask – he looks like a schoolteacher – laughs: "He got it out there in the South Pacific during the war and he's been Pappasan ever since." But didn't he say he'd never left?

I remember old Pappasan saying things now and again as I intermittently awoke. But I can't remember most of them now. Somehow it didn't matter. I do remember him saying – a voice from out of nowhere, disembodied – "It don't matter with wise things anyway. They're like food – even when you don't pay 'em any mind or remember 'em at all, they are feeding you still in the dark part of you that doesn't speak or think."

When I wake up in the morning, no one is in the house. I go out on the porch and look down the highway both ways and then over at the billboard's shadow that's now long and climbing up the butte on the opposite side of the road. The picture has changed again. Now it's Eugene's face and it's all about HIV and safe sex. After awhile I see a truck in the distance and watch it approach. The truck pulls over, revealing a softly smiling man's face who claims he's Eugene's uncle. He says he had heard Eugene was back. Then he asks me if I want a ride, and I say sure.

I fall asleep in the cab, and when I wake up I'm somewhere entirely different. It turns out to be some small town in Nebraska. I'm in another bus station and it doesn't feel like a dream anymore. Eugene's uncle must have left me here. I don't know. I don't mind. I sort of miss Eugene, but this is how it goes, this sort of Möbius strip dream/reality thing with him.

I know I can't go back. I imagine my own face on the billboard now, with an eager look in my eyes – and below my face "BEWARE" in big red block letters. This time the ad would be for the American Indian Movement and would say, "They took our land, our culture, our buffalo, our future, our language – don't let them take our religion and Eugene, too."

And then I remember something from out of the night that Eugene had shown me. It was a piece of black velvet affixed to a board with Styrofoam figures hanging off it on pins. But I can't remember when he showed it to me. Perhaps I'd awakened with him and he'd shown me things, walked me around the house, silver bright with a full moon. Perhaps he too, like Pappasan, got inside my dreams that I dreamed in the dream. I remember it was very special to him, this piece of fabric. The Styrofoam figures were like clear or whitish cheese puffs, silver-transparent, or grayish-white, like water or steam. He said each represented the bones, the skeletons of what they'd been. What they'd been represented by a bowl of orange cheese puffs on the table next to him. But these weren't the usual cylindrical cheese puffs I'd seen before. They were made up into little figurines, the same as the silver-white ones on the black velvet board: animals, fish, insects.

"These are all the same things as the others before they become bones," he said, digging his hands into the orange cheese puffs: The sea urchin fullbodied, the human figure not yet a skeleton, the bear and the sow bug.

Then Eugene was climbing out of the floor, pushing up the floorboards, laughing with that smile, as if to say, "See what Grandpa's ideas get me into." He climbed fully out and went to the window. It must have been the dawn darkness of five o'clock. Pappasan was gone, that early morning gray light, the sagebrush, the empty road, the big billboard that on that morning was advertising a casino, black aces and red kings, a moon shadow stretched to breaking aimed straight down the highway. I looked at him and said, "You are so beautiful. I don't know what to do about it." I kissed him passionately and he kissed me back the same way.

"That's what you do," he said. He pushed me onto the bed and fucked me while I watched the cards shuffling on the billboard beyond, red and black and white and hearts and diamonds; clubs, the ace of spades.

And I remember words from out of the night, or the dream, or the morning, or nowhere out there in the Badlands, of old Pappasan mumbling, "We see the bones. We are the bone people. You see only the skin. You are the skin people. That isn't bad," he murmured, "just different. We all have problems from the choices we made or the fates we married. When you know the bones, you know where you came from, but not where you are. And the skin – well it's the opposite: You know where you are, but you don't know where you came from. We both got a lot of trouble, you and I ... me, I see the bones." And then he laughed his giggly laugh, and out the window the billboard went blank.

TREBOR HEALEY

Recipient of The James Duggins Lambda Literary Award for Mid-Career Novelists, Trebor Healey also received the Violet Quill award for his first novel, *Through It Came Bright Colors*, and the Publishing Triangle's Ferro-Grumley Award in Fiction for both *A Horse Named Sorrow* and *Through It Came Bright Colors*. In addition, he has penned the speculative fiction novel, *Faun*, and a homoerotic poetry collection, *Sweet Son of Pan*, along with three collections of stories – *A Perfect Scar & Other Stories*, *Eros & Dust* and *Falling*. He co-edited (with Marci Blackman) *Beyond Definition: New Writing from Gay and Lesbian San Francisco*, and co-edited (with Amie Evans) *Queer & Catholic*.

www.treborhealey.com

About ReQueered Tales

In the heady days of the late 1960s, when young people in many western countries were in the streets protesting for a new, more inclusive world, some of us were in libraries, coffee shops, communes, retreats, bedrooms and dens plotting something even more startling: literature – highbrow and pulp – for an explicitly gay audience. Specifically, we were craving to see our gay lives – in the closet, in the open, in bars, in dire straits and in love – reflected in mystery stories, sci-fi and mainstream fiction. Hercule Poirot, that engaging effete Belgian creation of Agatha Christie might have been gay ... Sherlock Holmes, to all intents and purposes, was one woman shy of gay ... but where were the genuine gay sleuths, where the reader need not read between the lines?

Beginning with Victor J Banis's "Man from C.A.M.P." pulps in the mid-60s – riotous romps spoofing the craze for James Bond spies – readers were suddenly being offered George Baxt's Pharoah Love, a black gay New York City detective, and a real turning point in Joseph Hansen's gay California insurance investigator, Dave Brandstetter, whose world weary Raymond Chandleresque adventures sold strongly and have never been out of print.

Over the next three decades, gay storytelling grew strongly in niche and mainstream publishing ventures. Even with the huge public crisis – as AIDS descended on the gay community beginning in the early 1980s – gay fiction flourished. Stonewall Inn, Alyson Publications, and others nurtured authors and readers ... until mainstream success seemed to come to a halt. While Lambda Literary Foundation had started to recognize work in annual awards about 1990, mainstream publishers began to have cold feet. And then, with the rise of e-books in the new millennium which enabled a new self-publishing industry ... there was both an avalanche of new talent coming to market and burying of print authors who did not cross the divide.

The result?

Perhaps forty years of gay fiction – and notably gay and lesbian mystery, detective and suspense fiction – has been teetering on the brink of obscurity. Orphaned works, orphaned authors, many living and some having passed away – with no one to make the case for their creations to be returned to print (and e-print!). General fiction and non-fiction works embracing gay lives, widely celebrated upon original release, also languished as mainstream publishers shifted their focus.

Until now. That is the mission of ReQueered Tales: to keep in circulation this treasure trove of fantastic fiction. In an era of ebooks, everything of value ought to be accessible. For a new generation of readers, these mystery tales, and works of general fiction, are full of insights into the gay world of the 1960s, '70s, '80s and '90s. For those of us who lived through the period, they are a delightful reminder of our youth and reflect some of our own struggles in growing up gay in those heady times.

We are honored, here at ReQueered Tales, to be custodians shepherding back into circulation some of the best gay and lesbian fiction writing and hope to bring many volumes to the public, in modestly priced, accessible editions, worldwide, over the coming years.

So please join us on this adventure of discovery and rediscovery of the rich talents of writers of recent years as the PIs, cops and amateur sleuths battle forces of evil with fierceness, humor and sometimes a pinch of love.

The ReQueered Tales Team

Justene Adamec • Alexander Inglis • Matt Lubbers-Moore

More from ReQueered Tales

Through It Came Bright Colors
Trebor Healey

Neill Cullane is a closeted, conflicted 21-year-old who lives in two worlds: a San Francisco suburb where he's the middle-son of three young men, and, a short drive away in his beat-up VW bug, a seedy portion of the city's downtown. At home, he's the dutiful son of Frank and Grace, and devoted older brother to Peter – who is battling a cruel, disfiguring cancer – but in the city a chance encounter drags him into the orbit of Vince, a troubled, gregarious, very out gay transient. Moth to a flame, Neill is swept up and away by this secret lover, a beautiful junkie/philosopher/thief whose burning desire for truth lights a path Neill is destined to travel. Through Vince, Neill learns about honesty and love and finds the courage to confront his family in the face of tragedy and loss.

Trebor Healey's multi-layered, lyrical prose illuminates a unique, intimate look at a young man's struggle to live openly and honestly, to love and to be loved, free from shame and guilt. It's a compelling family saga of rare emotional, spiritual, and poetic depth.

"I read passages of this novel out loud again and again, absorbing the truth beneath its lyrical language. Trebor Healey understands the beauty and cruelty that spill forth when men dare to express love to one another. He holds up a magnifying glass to the human heart, and his gaze is unblinking." — K. M. Soehnlein

"Trebor Healey delivers coming out as apocalypse – tender, destructive, punk. He tore down a worn-out block of queer lit and built it back up. Sweet, sad, gritty, and real." — Michelle Tea

Winner of the Ferro-Grumley Award for Best Novel in 2003, this new edition includes a foreword by Felice Picano (*Like People in History*).

Boys Like Us
Peter McGehee

Boys Like Us Trilogy, Book 1 – Peter McGehee's debut novel is a rompish, bed-hopping affair – a modern comedy of manners – in which our twentysomething protagonist, Zero MacNoo performs all the rituals – sexual, familial, and grievous – required of urban gay males in the early 1990s. It is a remarkable comedy about life, love, and friendship in the age of AIDS.

Zero, an Arkansas expat who has swapped out Little Rock for the cool cotemporary tones of Toronto gay life, is perplexed by the curveballs of fate. His best friend has been diagnosed with AIDS; Zero is frantic to organize a circle of support. And when Arkansas also calls, it's to support his mother's second marriage and confrontations with the zany array of crazed Southerners he calls family ensue.

"... a gem of a novel. *Boys Like Us* is funny, sexy, tender, and touching – often in the same sentence." — Larry Duplechan

"*Boys Like Us* is an affable, enjoyable story ... McGehee has the ability, through an ingratiating style and witty observations, to transform Zero's everyday life into something we care about."
— Michael Bronski

"Accomplishes what may seem impossible: a humorous romp in the face of widespread death."
— *Library Journal*

Funny, bittersweet, outrageous, and moving, Zero's adventures make up the first part of *Boys Like Us* trilogy. This new edition is accompanied by introductions from Dr Raymond-Jean Frontain and long-time collaborator Fiji Robinson.

Fidelities: A Book of Stories
Richard Hall

The *Los Angeles Times* says "Richard Hall's prose displays a rare polish, and his accounts of ordinary and exceptional lives unfold in graceful cadences." *Fidelities* is a stunning collection of stories that explores the varieties of gay experience – love stories, both passionate and compassionate; tales of suspense; narratives on the theme of AIDS; even a ghost story. Among the most adept and technically accomplished writers of his generation, Hall's third and last collection of short stories is an eloquent work of immense power.

The author of the novels *The Butterscotch Prince* and *Family Fictions*, Hall's short stories give a sense of having been distilled and polished over time till they glow with depth and wisdom. "Diamonds Are Forever" highlights a gay man and his married sister who are incapable of seeing the shared traits that make it so difficult for them to accept each other; the story's carefully paced wrangling over an heirloom is masterful. "Avery Milbanke Day" features a 70-year-old writer – his seven novels about "the literature of hesitation" long neglected – decides to stay with his old dying lover and nurse him through a final crisis instead of attending a public celebration of his novels and himself. In "Country People" the author presents a gentle, eerie metaphor for the search for a sense of history, reflecting on previous generations of gay men and lesbians.

> "A rich, poignant collection ... The ruminations in *Fidelities* are remarkably palpable, utterly believable. Enlivened by precise flourishes of description, they touch directly on the reader's empathy button, and hold." — *San Francisco Chronicle*

> "Hall's stories evoke comparison with Henry James or Maupassant, Hemingway and Fitzgerald ... A luminous collection ... Hall has found in gay life stories to amuse, entertain, and move." — *Lambda Book Report*

Hall's final publication before his death at age 66 from AIDS-related causes, this 30th year anniversary edition celebrates his art at its peak. This new edition includes a foreword by Alexander Inglis.

Slashed to Ribbons
in Defense of Love
Felice Picano

Felice Picano's first collection of gay short stories spans the period 1975-1982 as published by the pioneering Gay Presses of New York. Read again forty years later, they are a delicious time-capsule of gay life mostly before AIDS and set in iconic gay meccas such as New York and Fire Island. In "Spinning", we get inside the head of a DJ busy spinning for the customers, tricking in his mind and deftly conjuring up the disco subculture which has since faded away. In "The Interrupted Recital", we eavesdrop into the classical music world where ego clashes lead to disastrous outcomes.

There are marvelous character portraits as in "Teddy", about a handsome Vietnam vet back home for a quick furlough. Or the evocation of Christmas in multiple New York households in "Xmas in the Apple". Longer works such as "Hunter", set in a writer's colony, are pure horror fiction. The longest piece, the novella "And Baby Makes Three", spreads its wings recreating Fire Island of the 1970s and features Picano's trademark surprises and miscues which make the tale memorable long after the last page is turned.

First published to acclaim in 1982, this new edition features a foreword by Eric Andrews-Katz (*The Jesus Injection*).

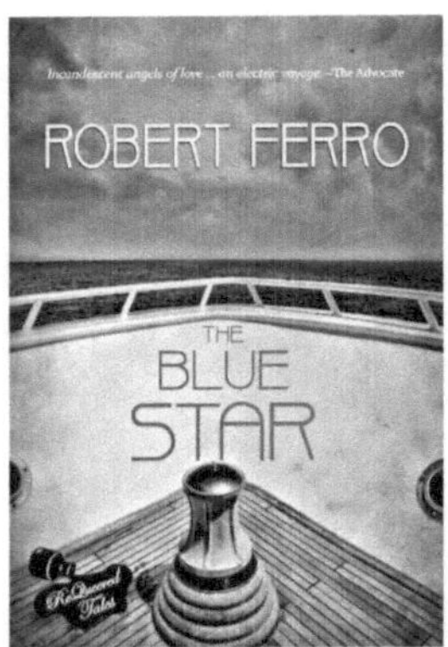

The Blue Star
Robert Ferro

Two heroes, reflective Peter and Byronic Chase, indulge their youthful appetites in Florence. Over the next 20 years their paths diverge and reconverge. Chase marries into the Italian aristocracy and Peter pursues his passion for Lorenzo, a beautiful young Florentine. The past impinges on the present as the story of Chase's ancestor, Orvil Starkweather, is revealed -- the secrets of his life sounding a counterpoint to Chase's. New York City's Central Park and the imposing figure of designer Frederick Law Olmsted provide a mysterious connection to Chase's life. The story of the two men unfolds in Florence and New York exposing the unimagined and startling connection with the past, and taking them finally on a fateful cruise up the Nile aboard the luxury yacht.

"Incandescent angels of love ... an eclectic voyage. Authentic fiction ... surprising, sad, funny, wise ... communicating gay experience knowingly and sensitively ... a treasure!" — *The Advocate*

"Enthralling ... euphoric imagination ... we can never forget the bliss we are allowed to share." — Richard Howard

"A lush chronicle of the heart's education ... Ferro revels in life's ups and downs in a prose rife with pleasures rich as those described." — *Village Voice*

Originally published in 1985, this new edition contains a foreword by Andrew Holleran (*Dancer from the Dance*).

Life Drawing
Michael Grumley

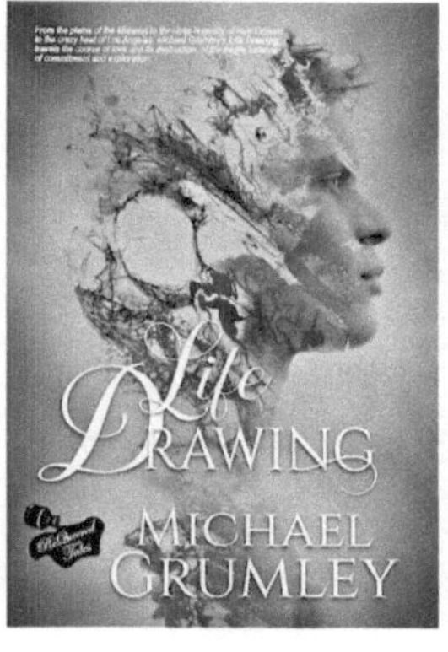

Born in Iowa to the sounds of Bob and Bing Crosby and the Dorsey brothers, Mickey grows up to the comforting images of his living room TV and the reassuring ruts of his parents' life. During the restless summer of his senior year in high school, drifting away from the girlfriend he could never quite love, Mickey spends a night with another boy, and his world will never be the same.

On a barge floating down the Mississippi, he falls in love with James, a black card player from New Orleans, and in time the two of them settle, bristling with sexual intensity, in the French Quarter – until a brief affair destroys James's trust and sends Mickey to the drugs and sordid life of Los Angeles.

"A simple, classic, engaging, and beautifully written tale of a boy who ran away from home, a man who didn't make it in the movies, an artist who found himself earlier than most and did it all west of the Mississippi, in places which, while very American, few Americans have ever been." — Andrew Holleran

"*Life Drawing* affirms the rich complexity of passion in the story of a small-town boy's difficult journey to manhood. Michael Grumley's crisp, direct language brings to life the demanding wonder of sexuality and the delicate tightrope of love between black men and white men." — Melvin Dixon

Originally published in 1991, it was Grumley's only novel, completed in the month's leading to his death from AIDS as he was cared for his lover Robert Ferro. This new edition contains the original foreword by Edmund White (*A Saint from Texas*) and afterword by George Stambolian (*Gay Men's Anthologies Men on Men*), close friends of the couple.

Short Stories 1988-1991
Stan Leventhal

Collected together for the first time in one volume, Short Stories 1988 – 1991, are the twenty-nine stories Stan Leventhal included in *a tiny herd of elephants* and *Candy Holidays.*

The first collection are stories about male relationships and span many literary styles including romance, fantasy, western and erotica. Some are funny, others are serious, but all invariably "playful". There are clear auto-biographical elements, as in much of the author's work. Several stories are about writers and the writing process (as life intrudes); "Schoolmarm" is set in the old west when a substitute school teacher meets his cowboy; "The Crystal Storm" offers us a lonely Warrior King, whose eyes "flash like jewels on fire", as he interrogates a handsome visitor, "unarmed and definitely not hostile". The longer pieces flesh out characters in clandestine meetings with lovers that end in a gift, or a group of tight-knit friends growing into adults at college ... there's even a vampire tale.

"Stan was a literary activist who always gave to, built and endorsed literature and writers. I can see still see Stan in his apartment window on Christopher Street, next door to the Stonewall Inn, overlooking Sheridan Square as he typed away." — Michele Karlsberg, LGBTQ publicist and friend

The second diverse, entertaining set of tales also cover several genres. In "Candy Holidays", two lovers break up, live apart, and then come back together again, the narrative catching glimpses, of them at Halloween, Christmas, Valentine's Day and Easter. "Razorback" is a dark futuristic tale about surviving in a burnt-out city in which all order has withered and chaos reigns. In "Oasis Motel" a young man on a business trip in Los Angeles finally breaks through the sexual barrier that has contained him all his life. "Seder" is the story of a gay Jewish man's attempt to reconcile his spirituality with his sexuality.

Both collections reflect issues confronting the lives of queer people in America in the late twentieth century. This new omnibus edition features a foreword by Sarah Schulman (*Let the Record Show*), close friend of Leventhal and author of numerous works of fiction and social history.

Something Inside
Conversations with Gay Fiction Writers
Philip Gambone

In the late-20th century, gay literature had earned a place at the British and American literary tables, spawning its own constellation of important writers and winning a dedicated audience. This collection of probing interviews represents an attempt to offer a group portrait of the most important gay fiction writers.

The extraordinary power of the interviews, originally set down from 1987 to 1997, brings to life the passionate intellect of several voices now stilled among them Joseph Hansen, Allen Barnett, John Preston and Paul Monette. Others such as Scott Heim, Brad Gooch, Lev Raphael, Alan Hollinghurst and Michael Lowanthal were just tasting fame, even notoriety and have gone on to richly deserved acclaim. Published near the height of mainstream accolades for gay fiction as a category, Edmund White, David Plante, Andrew Holleran, Michael Cunningham and Christopher Bram had already enjoyed wide readership and two decades of scrutiny and broad readership.

Many of the pieces are accompanied by portraits from Robert Giard who set out, with urgency during the mid-1980s AIDS crisis, to capture gay artists in their prime; these images make a unique and profound contribution to this collection.

> "A rich collective portrait of some of the most important and interesting gay writers of the last three decades."
> — *Montreal Mirror*

Philip Gambone, a wise and insightful questioner, draws out incredible detail, emotion and personality in a context which still makes for compelling reading thirty years on. The author includes a 2022 update welcoming new readers to this indispensable resource.

☙

**If you enjoyed this book,
please help spread the word
by posting a short,
constructive review at
your favorite social media site
or book retailer.**

**We thank you, greatly,
for your support.**

And don't be shy! Contact us!

*For more information about current and future releases,
please contact us:*

E-mail: *requeeredtales@gmail.com*
Facebook (Like us!): www.facebook.com/ReQueeredTales
Twitter: @ReQueered
Instagram: www.instagram.com/requeered
Web: www.ReQueeredTales.com
Blog: www.ReQueeredTales.com/blog
Mailing list (Subscribe for latest news): https://bit.ly/RQTJoin